ALL
the
WATER
in the
WORLD

Also by Eiren Caffall

The Mourner's Bestiary

ALL
the
WATER
in the
WORLD

A Novel

EIREN CAFFALL

ST. MARTIN'S PRESS
NEW YORK

First published in the United States by St. Martin's Press, an imprint of St. Martin's Publishing Group

ALL THE WATER IN THE WORLD. Copyright © 2024 by Eiren Caffall. All rights reserved. Printed in the United States of America. For information, address St. Martin's Publishing Group, 120 Broadway, New York, NY 10271.

www.stmartins.com

Design by Meryl Sussman Levavi

Library of Congress Cataloging-in-Publication Data

Names: Caffall, Eiren, author.
Title: All the water in the world : a novel / Eiren Caffall.
Description: First edition. | New York : St. Martin's Press, 2025.
Identifiers: LCCN 2024034292 | ISBN 9781250353528
    (hardcover) | ISBN 9781250353535 (ebook)
Subjects: LCGFT: Apocalyptic fiction. | Novels.
Classification: LCC PS3603.A3774 A78 2025 | DDC 813/.6—
    dc23/eng/20240729
LC record available at https://lccn.loc.gov/2024034292

Our books may be purchased in bulk for promotional, educational, or business use. Please contact your local bookseller or the Macmillan Corporate and Premium Sales Department at 1-800-221-7945, extension 5442, or by email at MacmillanSpecialMarkets@macmillan.com.

First Edition: 2025

1 3 5 7 9 10 8 6 4 2

For Dex

ALL
the
WATER
in the
WORLD

I

THE MONSTER IN THE WATER

<u>The Monster in the Water:</u> This is the hypercane, the biggest kind of hurricane there could be. It is maybe not something that has ever happened on earth. It is maybe something that never will. It is a theoretical idea, that's what Jess said. It is a possible outcome that Jess studied, where nonlinear weather changes could supercharge atmospheric conditions and produce superdense eye walls and fast-moving storms. Hypercanes could pull energy from the warmer water and spawn tornadoes and locally intense downdrafts. The rain could be sideways or include hail. It could have a very fast rate of precipitation per hour. It could have the most destructive winds possible, ranging up to 200 mph. I have never seen a hypercane, and maybe they are not real and will never be real, like a monster in the water that never comes.

—From the Water Logbook

1
WHAT WE SAVE

I can feel water and I can feel heavy weather on the way. Mother said, "You're like a dowser, Nonie, like those people who can feel water under the ground and help farmers find it, only you do it with water everywhere." What she said is so. I can understand water—floods and rivers over their banks, storms and clouds and placid days when the droplets sit in the air like they are thinking quietly of joining the earth.

But the storm that took Amen, that storm I didn't feel. It was too big. It was the one that broke the floodwalls. That was the last night of the Old City and the museum and Amen and everything that trapped us, when the wide Hudson opened its mouth wider and became the sea and the sea came to us and we took off north, no matter how scared Bix was, no matter how hard it was to leave Mother behind. It was the storm that started something new.

We still lived in the place we called Amen, what had been the American Museum of Natural History. Time made us shorten that name. We said "A-M-N-H," for the whole place—the ancient rooms we tended, the collections we protected—then "Amen," when it only meant the village we made on the roof of the museum library, the name a prayer to keep us safe. And we were safe up there a long time, Bix and me and Father and Keller, and Mother—before we lost her—and the rest of us working to save the collections and be there, just be there, saving each other too. I was young then, thirteen, Bix sixteen. I was a blur of closed heart and quiet voice, scared of the dark and of losing home, cozied in a place Mother made for us on the roof, where time and space were as fixed as they could be in The World As It Is.

Father said we would run north to Mother's land, Tyringham, our taiga, our last safe place, if we lost Amen. We made the go packs and canoe, learned to hunt, worried about the dogs and the Lost, about guns, about how people outside Amen fractured into groups by color, about everything between Amen and Tyringham. We worried about losing Amen.

In the Museum Logbook we kept a list of all that might be lost, everything in the museum. The adults made notations on anthropology, archaeology, geology, paleontology, ichthyology, hydrology, geography, entomology, the museum records no one could read anymore on computers. They made notes from memory or books in the library, from listing the contents of cases and storage drawers and displays. And there was my list, my shadow list. In margins and on back pages, I added drawings and notes on water and how I understood it, the clouds, the shine on a puddle, the animals after they drank, the rainbow over the city, the way to feel the pressure drop for a squall, or the build of a hurricane. I added them to help me remember, and for other people to find one day, if all they found was the book.

The Museum Logbook was to keep understanding alive, the most important work there was for Amen, a race against rot and mold and time to save things, even the memory of things. My Water Logbook was only for the future. I was young then and didn't know why I was making it. Now I know it was to make the new way of knowing that might put it all right again, the new thing I'm standing at the edge of, here where there is drinkable water and where people are in the rooms of the house writing and cooking, and I'm about to leave again, but only for good reasons, remembering what was left behind in that storm.

My Water Logbook didn't help me see that storm. I didn't know what it would bring—the journey and the people who helped and the ones who harmed. That storm, that last storm of Amen, was a hypercane, like Jess predicted, the Monster in the Water. It moved faster than thought and faster than sense. It swept in to take everything, and I didn't see it. I was a girl on a roof, and I couldn't tell everyone, "The end is here."

2
HYPERCANE

Everyone else was asleep on the roof, in tents and structures up there, sweating out the November heat. It was so still; all the air was sucked out of breathing. I couldn't sleep. I didn't know why. Something wasn't right, but I couldn't feel what. I took the plastic bag out from under my pillow and looked at the photograph inside it, smoothed the bag's wrinkles out and looked at Mother's face, not smiling at the camera, but pointed toward a microscope, her profile blurry in the darkness.

Then the air was pulled out of my lungs, the world inhaling before a scream, and a wind hit the longhouse hard. Bix's body tumbled into mine, face-to-face and staring. I felt Bix breathing, felt her fear, wanted to reach to her, like she was small, and I was small, and we were in the twin bed in the old apartment and Mother was still alive and would lie down with us and brush our hair back and kiss our foreheads and say, "Good morning, my sea butterflies."

Lightning flashed. "Nonie! Bix!" Father's voice.

"Allan!" Keller was reaching for gear. The wind scattered all our things.

Bix slipped into big-sister bossing, she almost screamed into my mouth, "Go, Nonie!"

I found shoes and go pack. In my pack I had the Logbook, wrapped in oiled canvas and safe from rain, tucked under my rain shell for extra protection. I felt for it. It was there. I'd kept it with me for months. There was strange weather. There was so much to make note of. It felt safer to have it with me always after Mother died, no chance to lose it in a storm. I shoved the baggie with Mother's picture in next to it. I felt for my water bottle, the ammonite.

A sound like a giant taking a bite out of the top of a forest echoed overhead, and the roof above me was gone. Shock drained into my blood.

"Run!" Father yelled. I put the pack on my back and ran. Bix and Keller and I reached the longhouse door as the wall poles buckled. We pushed outside. I turned to look as the house crumpled, going down like one of Keller's shot deer, knees failing under it.

"Run!" Keller shouted.

It only took a second for the place we'd lived for eight years to fall to the hypercane. The storm didn't care at all. I stood and stared.

"Nonie!" Father called, running for the stairwell, Bix and Keller behind him.

I stood still. I couldn't remember what to do. I knew I needed to follow, but I watched the storm build behind them. I moved one foot in their direction. I made the seconds small and fast. This was how it was in a night storm. We got up. We got safe. In a bad storm we ran for the museum library below us, the windowless stacks, safe as a thick-walled bunker, dark, mold-smelling and caked in lonely days and nights spent waiting out storms.

I stumbled, followed Father and Keller and Bix through storm-pitched pieces of Amen coming apart, faces of people I loved flashing past, the pressure sinking so fast my teeth itched. Around the broken frame of our house, tarps and poles of other structures collapsed in the gale, people crawled from under on their bellies. Wind moved through Amen, a curious animal, ate up what it found until there wasn't a thing left to eat. My ears popped. The pressure fell, wind braided and doubled with a funnel cloud forming over the Park, coming our way.

I saw Jess and Beaumont at their hut, she was pulling out a pack, he carried a jug of water, a lantern, his bow. She was carrying baby Evangeline in a sling around her body, stooped over her so the rain wouldn't hit the baby's face, compass around her neck. She looked up and saw me. I screamed at her, "The Monster in the Water?!"

"Yes, Nonie!" she yelled back over the storm. "Get to the stacks. I'm right behind you!"

"OK!" The baby worried me. There was so much wind.

"Remember the shark," she yelled, hoisting the pack onto her shoulder. I remembered what she'd told me. When I was scared and started to disappear into silence and blankness, I could think about how you can hypnotize sharks by rubbing your finger down their snout. It calms them so they don't panic. When I started to panic and go back to quiet, to hiding, Jess said I could rub the skin between my thumb and forefinger with the fingers of my other hand and I would feel calm, too, and maybe not need to disappear at all. "Go, Nonie! I'll be right there," Jess yelled over the wind.

I found speed then, my feet obeying where my mind did not. A downpour of water came, almost too dense for moving, a heart of lightning, random hail, a voice of the wind that shut out thought, and then I was running to catch Bix's advancing back, chasing her like a ghost through the unknown air.

3
LENINGRAD

Mother was never afraid of the water like Bix was. She was like me, she loved it. She studied sea butterflies—pteropods—at Amen. Mother worked at the museum in The World As It Was. She was the one with keys. She brought us there when the city fell down. We went to the safest place we knew, big old doors and big old locks and lots of other people with keys who walked there through the water one night and stayed on because no one was coming to save anybody.

I was in love with Amen already. When we were small, before things changed, on Sunday afternoons Mother went in to get more hours in the lab and Father walked Bix and me around the dark, still rooms while people we didn't know looked at the bones and the birds and the beasts. We would lie under the great blue whale, and I would pretend I was under the ocean. It was a place that said time broke everything before and repaired it new. Sometimes new was better and sometimes new was worse. But if there was a change, it would change again. As the broken world turned outside the walls, I longed for the quiet rooms that taught me that.

Mother didn't like the subway entrance, brought Bix and me in from the street, up the big stairs and to the big doors, right past the statue of Teddy Roosevelt. She catalogued pteropods in a basement lab. The sea butterflies told her everything she needed to know about what was happening to the world, the change of chemistry in the ocean, the things we were doing to break it, the things we might do to make it whole again. It was the only work that mattered, she said, sometimes when she forgot to be humble, and in the joy of walking into the museum. In her voice, there was something else, too—greed, hope. The picture in my plastic baggie used to hang on the fridge in our Tenth Street apartment, her head bent over a microscope, looking at a specimen, mouse-brown hair tied back in a ponytail, long beak nose pointing at the instrument like an arrow. There was another picture of the lab, too. Mother with her arms around another worker when they got a grant, champagne bottle on the table in front of them. That picture was lost in the flood. The World As It Is doesn't let you keep things, but her body kept that arrow gesture in her bones, her whole life bent toward research, never wavering, even when she couldn't work like that. She had keys to the kingdom. She won them herself. She gave the museum to Bix and me.

By the night of the storm that took it, Amen only had a few people left, all too scared or stuck to take the walk north, sleeping on the roof in lean-tos and made-up structures. Used to be only tents there, then the rule was if you stayed, you built solid. The roof was the only way to survive the rotting city, the people who might break a window and get into Amen until they saw there was nothing that would feed them. We were high on the roof, safe from people with guns or dogs, the old building rotting and dangerous below. Shelters kept the rain off, fought the heat. We had a garden in the Park. When we went, we carried the two guns we had left, the ammo we saved, the ones who knew how carried bows we made or scavenged. We grew food. We had bees. We went out. We came back. When we were lucky, the empty city echoed around us, dog packs off hunting deer. The longer we were in Amen, the luckier we got, the quieter it was, a whole city moved off to find good water.

We were like the people in Leningrad, Father said, in the

War, the Second one, when the Hermitage, a museum bigger than ours even, was left for dead in a dying city but the curators stayed. There wasn't much left, but in Leningrad in the siege in the War the curators stayed and ate restorer paste to stay alive and wrapped the dead and laid them in the basement until the thaw and chipped the ice off the paintings while the siege went on outside. All that mattered was that the art remained. Even if they could have run away across Lake Ladoga and into the edges of the taiga forest and hidden with what they knew, they wouldn't have left. They belonged to the art and the art belonged to them and it was a sacred duty. But so was the vision of what it would be one day when the siege was over and the windows replaced and the broken walls repaired and the museum alive again for everyone, for the world that mattered, the one they wanted.

That was us. Only the siege was storms. We stayed because we had to, because Bix was too terrified of the water to go, but we also stayed because it was the work, Mother's and Father's work, the reason they met, the work of keeping what was left until the world was ready again.

4
THE END OF THE ROOF

Keller reached the stairwell first. He grabbed the metal pipe wedged in the stairwell door handles. He wrenched it free. I left the door wide behind me, ran after Bix, deeper into the dark.

I was halfway down the stairs, rain blowing in through the open door, trying not to fall as I ran. I heard a woman's voice, turned to see Jess and baby Evangeline and Sergio and Louis framed by the doorway, lit by a burst of lightning. I was deep in a well, sheltered, turned awkwardly to look at them, and they were up in the storm.

Outside was a growl of wind louder than anything I ever heard, reaching down to the echo chamber of the stairs. Behind the growl, a blow shook the building, a pressure change took my breath, a funnel cloud reared up, it was so huge that I could see it through the doorway behind Sergio and Louis and Jess and Evangeline. The hand of the cloud reached down and grabbed the doorway, the bricks and concrete where we slept, the stairwell above me, the people standing there, as if they were dust, and threw them all out into the sky.

5
WHO WE WERE

Bix was contradictory—bold and terrified, full of action and stuck. She liked to disappear in her own way, from the water after she got scared, into dark corners, into Mother's vinyl record of Bix Beiderbecke on Tenth Street. It was jazz, had a cover with a picture—the horn player in a bow tie. Bix loved the solos, the lilt, the ease. The music had something of the way things had been long before we were born, optimism. It matched her. "Before the crash," Bix said, when electric was new and Old City was smaller and brighter, like a fresh-cut jewel, and cars made their way into the music and everything. Bix made sure she kept a piece of that time in her mouth with her name. She wanted it in all our mouths, made sure no one called her Beatrice. Made sure no one called me Norah. Like Father, she was impulsive.

Father liked a lantern and a hand tool, things to build or fix or sort or organize, people to help, a project, a way forward. His skin a wall of freckles so dense they formed a new color on him, his hands knuckled, rough, his red-brown hair wavy, trailing past his ears, his beard thin and ready for the knife. Like him, Bix had accelerated curiosity. Bix looked into every dark corner and every single space and never even wanted a lantern. She followed Father around instead, and the flint knapper, Oliver, who had been trained to do it for his anthropology fieldwork and used it again at Amen and taught Sergio. She learned to make edges and fix knives and shoot arrows, to make a good fire and find deer in the Park. She would be all the music and the boldness and be called "Bix." I wouldn't be myself. She'd make me into the word "no," as if, calling me "NO-nie," she could say "No" every day. I wanted a girl name for her, even though she'd never wear girls' clothes. Not a dress. Not a chance. At Amen, she cut her hair with a pair of scissors she kept from rusting wrapped in an oiled washcloth in her pack. Her hair was red-brown, curled like Father's, blunt cuts twisted into wavelets when it was damp. She had Father's pale skin, wide mouth, freckles. Her eyes were Mother's blue, like mine, a golden ring around the irises.

I liked the only mystery Bix hated—the ocean. I wondered why she never took that mystery from Mother, like I did. I had Mother's straight brown hair, her nose like one on a Roman marble head, and half of Father's freckles dust-covered my nose, drawing attention to it. Everyone said I didn't smile Father's and Bix's big grins. They showed their teeth, almost to yell something they wanted to do. Like Mother, I was quiet. I started talking again a year after we came to Amen, but I didn't talk like everybody—I said full sentences mixed up with silence and science and the formal books Mother read us at night, Verne and Stevenson, little professor. There was a right way to say things and I didn't know how to do it wrong. Bix and Mother and Father all said my brain wasn't wired like other people's. I could sit with Mother in the lab for hours. I could organize all the plastic sea-creature toys in my room, so they lined the windowsills. I could remember all the animals in the museum, even without the Logbook. I didn't understand how Bix felt sometimes, or Father or Mother. I had to watch their faces and think about what they meant when they spoke. I had to do that with everyone. Keller and I could talk about animals. We made up a game about animals. It made me settled and calm when we played, asking my brain to shush and concentrate and remember. Mother knew to play the game when I was scared. Bix and Father never did. The museum was perfect for me, dark and quiet, organized and private, like the world inside my head that no one ever saw.

Keller and Angel and Mano could have left Old City without us, but they stayed. Keller was an entomologist, he had keys too. His wife Angel was a librarian in Washington Heights where they lived, and then she was our teacher. Even though Mano was Angel's nephew, they looked like mother and child, same thick black hair, same dark eyes, same laugh like wheezing. Mano was Keller's son—no question about it, no foster about it, Keller said—even if he didn't watch him being born. For me, Mano was Manolito, playmate, sibling. For Bix, something else. Keller was a wall of person, solid and laughing and bigger than anything around him. His wide shoulders had a stoop. His brown skin always looked warm and quiet. He'd had a tummy to carry around because in The World As It Was, Angel fed him too much mofongo. Mano would tease him about it. Keller kept his beard and hair trimmed. "I did locs in college, Nonie," he said, laughing, "and Angel likes my hair short. I never can argue anything with Angel."

6
WE HELD ON

The ripping away blasted my ears flat, pitched me down the stairs onto a pile of Father, Keller, and Bix mixed with chunks of roof and brick. The hand of the funnel reached in, pulled my legs up into the cloud. Bix grabbed my arm. In the tangle, she held a railing still secured to the broken wall. I screamed under silence, my hearing dead from the blast to the roof, "Bix!" One of my shoes loosened as the storm pulled me, my legs pointing to the twisted gray.

Then the roar of the wind moved. The funnel let go. I slammed back onto the stairs, Bix's fingernails left moons of blood on my skin, my knee hurt. I tasted blood. My ears rang. Bix pulled me to stand, then turned and started to run. I stumbled after Bix down the stairs. I looked back at the hole where the roof once was, saw another funnel hit, sending a wash of rubble over us. In place of Amen there was only the black of all the clouds. In that blackness I heard a scream behind the ringing in my ears and did not know it was my voice until I felt the raindrops in my mouth. The World As It Is didn't work if you screamed. A pummel of hail poured down. Then the hail stopped. Rain waterfalled in, collapsing on my head like a giant's overturned bucket. Fear curled into my spine in a blind swiftness.

"Nonie!" It was Father. "Nonie, take my hand." He grabbed my hand with his. I had the shakes. The screaming gave fear a tiny hole into my heart to fill up my body until I couldn't move. But if Father held my hand I could walk. Father was always there, and everything was safer with him. I looked down to see he held one of Bix's hands. Keller held

Bix's other one so as to make us roped together, all four. Keller looked up at Father, rainwater hitting his face, his skin hard to see in the shadows of the broken stairwell. Keller led, trailing the length of us, kicking away pieces of wall from what was left of the stairs. Father and Bix and I snapped behind him like the end of a downed power line in a storm. Our chain: Keller and Bix and Father and me, Keller and Bix and Father and me, Keller and Bix and Father and me. All holding hands, all heading down and away. We ran together. We didn't stop. We held on.

7
THE WORLD AS IT WAS

torms always came. They took things. They took things before I was born, Mother and Father told me that: bits of the coastline, glaciers, reefs, whole islands, cities— San Juan, Miami, the Azores, Shenzhen, Mumbai, the Philippines, Bangkok, Abidjan, Nagoya, New Zealand.

They took water from the inland and gave it to the sea, crops failed, forests caught fire, tall mountain ranges burned with the trees along their ridgelines. People moved to places where the food was. Countries filled and emptied until the people themselves were the floods and the droughts. Mother and Father watched it happen on their laptops, reading articles, looking at pictures of loss side by side on the couch on Tenth Street, the electric off and on.

Mother told me it was slow at first, the way the world changed. You could forget about it. People talked like you could fix it. A storm would pass, and they'd put things back together. Or one day there was no gas, and you learned to live without your car. "You learned to live without bananas, without airplanes," that's how Mother said it. She said it like losing taught you lessons you needed, until you were happy to have a day with fresh water in your apartment and a bath.

It was slow enough you might have babies, like Mother and Father. Them wondering if that was smart. Bix first, born in a hospital with power and lights, before martial law. Me three years later, born at home in the dark.

Things fell in slow motion. Rolling blackouts, waves of refugees heading north and west, army everywhere, gas rationed, food scarce, the president in a huge ship offshore.

In Old City they built floodgates that kept the sea outside, blocked the ocean getting up the river, made the city an island we lived inside, a bowl that flooded up from the sewers when the storms came. In the Old City, weather was a gamble. It was hot nearly all year. Dry when you needed water. Flooding so it couldn't be managed. Cold snaps would come and plunge you into ice, then melt and flood again. All the time everyone hoping it might turn around, until they knew it wouldn't, until the world warmed up so fast you couldn't catch your breath. Every year the storms were bigger—moving the ocean up into the streets. But there was electric sometimes, there were people in the city, none of us ever imagined Amen. There were jobs and grocery stores. We had a ration card, we drove places, and you could just take a car out on the road like that, like it was nothing.

8
THE WORLD AS IT IS

In the dark my ears buzzed. We ran toward the stacks. Water collected at our feet. Another downdraft hit. The wall next to us shattered. We ducked the bricks. Darkness and wet gravel engulfed us. Lightning came in through the hole. Father's face stood out in the flash, mouth wide, dull yelling. He looked back at us from the damage, skin pale, wet strands of hair on his forehead. "They're gone!" Father screamed at Keller over the noise, the words through cotton. "The stacks are gone!" I looked to where they would be, there was only rubble in their place. We had no safe place, no water, no food. I wiped the rain from my eyes; my shaking hand came away covered with grit.

Used to be, when you left the stairwell, there was a door, and then through that door a hallway that led to conference rooms and one that led to the stacks, deep and away from the light. It was a research library. Someone used to sit at the desk in the main reading room, take book requests, and go behind the strong, thick door to find the books where they were safe and climate controlled. We'd made the stacks a warren of supply storage, extra water bottles, food and lanterns, ammo, fresh arrows, things to read, and places to sleep. But now, it looked as if the whole space had become another roof. Books were everywhere, rain was everywhere, bits of wall and brick and metal were everywhere.

"Out of the library, get into the museum!" Keller ran through the crumbling stairs to the library reading room, through a hole that had been a wall. The chaos took the memory of the room from me. That reading room was our school, those tables were where we worked. Now there was nothing. I followed blind, remembered only Jess's face, baby Evangeline's black hair. The library fell to the funnel clouds, microbursts, getting in through the holes of the ones before. This storm was like nothing else. The doors were locked to the Lost. Every night at lockdown the sentry for the night locked it all up, put up barricades and chains so we could be the only ones in the library in case, in case someone Lost came, someone without people.

Keller got to the barricades he'd piled up before we'd gone to sleep that night, pulled barriers away, hauled tables back, fumbled for keys in his wet jeans pocket, unlocked a sturdy metal chain from around the door handles. All of us drenched.

"Astor Turret," Keller said, quiet as he took off the chain on the door.

We were on the fourth floor, Astor Turret was, too, had a good view out to the city, big windows. I looked down at my hands, they were still shaking, there was blood on one from a cut. I didn't know how it got there, rainwater washed the blood away, but it pulsed back with my heartbeat. I looked at Bix, hood pulled up over her short hair, the fabric plastered to her, soaked pack on her back. She looked at me, her face a shadow in the dark, fear of water back behind her eyes, stalking her. Watching her eyes, I could see the story flashing on the shining whites, the story she told herself about how water meant drowning, and if she went near it, she was gone. Bix could flip between broken and sure. There were two ways I could lose her: she'd disappear in the face of water, her eyes blanked out, or she'd wander fearless into darkened corners, a magnet pull in the unknown.

Keller freed the chain and pushed wide the library doors and ran through them. He put the keys in his pocket, habit;

he'd never need them again. Wind shook the building. The pressure plummeted. The pound of thunder came through the fog of my ringing ears. I willed myself not to cry. Crying was useless since Mother.

9
NAUTILUS

When I was four, we still lived in the apartment on Tenth Street like people used to. One night, a hurricane edge rolled through. I was too little to remember that storm, Bix says. But she's wrong, it stays a strong shadow with me, the first storm that showed how storms would be when I was big. That was the storm when Mother taught me to find the water, to see it slant, like she did, to know it and not be afraid of the shape.

I felt the coming in my body. I could not name that feeling then. But I knew it was something wrong, something big and off, like maybe how a wildebeest would feel if it couldn't see a lion coming through the grass.

She was reading me to sleep when the wind started. I curled tighter to her, and she tried to settle me in the dark and warm of the covers, tucking them up against my throat. A gust rattled the window glass and startled us both. She slipped out of the sheets, rose to look out, became a shape against the window. A noise, crashing glass somewhere, sounded so loud; it shocked her. She came back quick, wrapped her arms around me, nightgown soft between us. She listened; I looked up at her. She closed her eyes, slowed her breath, kissed me, put one hand on the top of my back, like feeling for my heartbeat.

She could feel me freeze and listen to the big voice of the storm outside. She said, "Breathe, baby." I breathed. The rain was hard on the glass. "Breathe, baby." She turned and slipped between the sheets, held me, hummed in my ear so soft, her heartbeat so soft. Everything was hard. Everyone was leaving. Everything was changing. But she was turning back the fear. She was the soft core of the world. Her skin like nothing, like no skin, like clouds. I smelled her fear sweat, the end of the day on her, the water in her, the calm. "It'll stop, though," she said, "it always stops," believing it now, building a warm yellow light, and us inside it. "Let's pretend we're underwater. Let's talk about all the fishes we can think of."

"The nautilus?" When there was electric enough for the laptop, Mother played us movies of reefs, rays, tiny ptero-pods she studied, dumbo octopus, nautilus, siphon moving it back through the ocean, swirled like the core of the lolli-pop I had one Christmas.

"The nautilus," she said, "and the cuttlefish, and the anem-one, and the puffer fish, and the parrotfish, and the jellyfish."

The lantern in the bedroom let me see her sharp nose, pointing at me now. "And the *Archelon*? And the *Helico-prion*? And the sea butterfly? And the monkfish." I jumbled all the eras of the ocean together and she laughed in the lantern light, the wind rattled the windows. I curled closer to Mother, afraid—understanding how fear could be sharp. I reached for her hand.

"Everybody. They're all out the window, and we're in the bathysphere, and there is nothing but water everywhere, so there's nothing to be afraid of, because we are safe and warm in here." She hummed again and I could see the fish outside, and us inside the iron walls of the submarine, mov-ing in a world of water that was safe, so safe.

10
THE SOUND OF WATER

Keller ran through the doors to the library reading room. He pushed deeper into the fourth floor of the museum, and we followed. The blank corridor from the library was a zero, no windows, flayed carpet, anonymous walls without feature. At the end of that hallway was the Hall of Vertebrate Origins, where Bix and Mano and I used to play. Eight years since the floods took the rooms of the museum down to crumbling.

The Hall of Vertebrate Origins had windows up high, but it was hard to see in, the tall space full of raw echoes. Many of the exhibits were packed up in The World As It Was, and there was obvious emptiness everywhere. There were creaking chains in the wind. The walls were tall and the floor was marble, like much of that part of the building. My feet were wet and so they squeaked and slipped in the dark. Above me, the coelacanth model, an ancient, huge fish, hung rickety. Next to it, a *Carcharodon*'s jaw on the floor, full of its ancient shark teeth.

That room led to the Hall of Advanced Mammals. I could hear our footsteps now, my ears ringing less, the rain distant behind the bulk of the huge building. Round lamps swung in the wind from a broken window. It was so dark, when the wind blew, drops hit my face. My feet knew the route, one I walked nearly every day, the spot where the titanosaur had been, its bones carted off to deep storage, the metal frame left, a sharp skeleton of what AMNH was. I knew where to step to miss the spikes it left in the floor. In the early days in Amen, I played here, looping yarn over the spikes to make a spiderweb while Mother and Father and Sergio took apart the Irish elk and mammoth bones and packed and labeled and sorted to save them.

There was a flash of lightning. The room ahead was clear for an instant—the Hall of Primitive Mammals, next to Astor Turret. This room had been empty a long time, the fossils gone, the ground sloth moved before we came, only the glyptodont left, a hunching dark shell in the corner, too heavy to move. It was a gateway, a storage room for tools and scavenged packing material.

I walked forward into the dark, collided with Bix. She'd stopped at the entrance to the Turret, too scared to go in. The sound of the water was instantly enormous, and, facing that room and all its glass, she was completely frozen. I looked at her, so still. Father came and looked her over, searching for injuries from the stairwell, the funnel, the debris. He didn't see any, only her blankness in the face of the storm.

"Bixie? The water isn't here. We're OK, we're safe in this room, OK? Hold my hand." He took her hand and looked over at me. He put a hand on my shoulder. "Nonie? What hurts?" I pointed to my knee, my ears, my tongue. "That was a big one," he said. He reached to my knee and felt for the scrapes. The bruise hurt. "You can walk?" I nodded. "You can run?" I nodded. "Good." He opened his mouth to show me to open mine. I could still taste blood from where I bit my tongue. "You can talk?" I nodded, and he leaned in and whispered near my ear. "You can hear?" I held my hand up parallel to the ground, made the so-so gesture. "That will get better soon. That was loud." He searched my face for anything else that was wrong, looked at the cut on my hand, then leaned down and kissed my head. Still holding Bix's hand, he stood back up and looked at Astor Turret, and I did too, watching Keller as he walked into its darkness.

Astor Turret was untouched by the storm. Huge windows lined the curved walls. We were three floors above the ground and the street. Most days those windows were a wide-open eye onto a world of sun and big trees, curling vines. Below them was the graveyard we'd made, Mother down there under the earth. We could sit there and soak in the sun without worry, Father or Keller working nearby, copying facts into the Logbook. Bix and I would sit there and feel close to Mother and to the Old City as it sank into itself, a comforting jungle of stone and brick where New York City was before. Astor Turret let us look on it, and we could almost flick our memories back and forth. There was The World As It Was, the one when we were so small, newly come to AMNH. Flick. There was The World As It Is, behind the glass, a deer below us, grazing, a grave marked by a chunk of old wall.

In the dark of the storm, the intact windows looked out of place. Their glass unbroken, the rain leaned against them. Then the lightning flashed, and I could see rain bands that looked like waves, and the water rising in the city outside, rising so fast, up to those windows so high above the ground, rain like the whole ocean pouring down their slick surfaces; the noise of its pounding rivaled the wind. Bix stood still and Father let go of her hand. "Stay here," he said to her, and he and I walked forward to Keller.

We stood at the window and took it in, the ocean coming to us. It had never done this. Not in all the storms and floods. The city was gone at last.

"What is it?" Bix asked from where she was frozen.

"Surge," Father said, the terror of being trapped sharp in his voice.

Keller looked at Father. "Floodgates?" he asked. "What else could make it flood so fast?"

"Has to be," said Father, shaking his head. "They finally collapsed."

Keller nodded. "Guess they weren't the thousand-year gates the Army Corps promised." The shock made his smile come out crooked. "They lasted longer than I thought they would."

Father shook his head again, deciding something. Then he looked hard at Keller.

"We need the boat," he said.

11
HOW BIX GOT SCARED

The night we came to Amen was the night I knew I needed to keep a Logbook of my own. That storm took our apartment on Tenth Street and our life there and was when Bix learned to hate and fear the water as if it were coming for her alone, like she was its property and its lost debris.

We didn't try to sleep through storms by then. They were too unpredictable. Mother and I and Bix sat on the Tenth Street couch. The storm rattled the windows first and then the dusk came, and then the dark came. We sat there, Father making sandwiches to put in our go packs. The packs were by the door. The portable kayak was by the door. The ten essentials in the bags. Our coats next to us on the armchair. Then the electric went. The light was dull. I looked up at Mother and her eyes were blank, the glass eyes of the stuffed rabbit in the polar diorama.

"It's coming," I said.

"What's coming?" she asked.

"More storm," I said.

The world inhaled and then the windows blew into the room. There was sound and a shimmer of something and a light rain of something solid and the sound of Bix whimpering and then a long scream. Father ran from the kitchen and went to the windows, looking back over at us. "You OK?"

But Bix was screaming from the sound, from the way it flattened our ears back to have the weather be so big so fast. Mother brushed bits of glass out of my hair. "Bix, Bix, Bix," she whispered.

Father was at the sill. "Storm tide," he said over his shoulder. I'd never heard him terrified.

Mother nodded at him while he scrambled for his coat and pack. She looked out to the sky, dark from the clouds, put on her pack and mine. "Come here, Bix." Bix stood up and Mother helped her on with coat and pack. Father picked me up, took the folded kayak in his other hand, looked back at the room. Rain came in at the window. I thought of the books getting wet. We'd never see the place again. I didn't know.

Father took me out the door and I listened to Mother and Bix running behind. We ran down the inky stairwell, through the lobby, glass everywhere, out the door, down the steps to the street, out into the world of wind-whipped garbage and rain. There, water already reached to Father's knees, waves came in a pattern, the wind pushed them, objects in the tide hit buildings. Then I saw over Father's shoulder, up the street canyon, a high wave on top of the waves already there, a leapfrog wave, taller, faster, the way they get in a tide surge.

Mother and Bix came out the door of Tenth Street straight into the flood, they ran to us, didn't see the building wave behind them. It moved so fast that they were caught and lost under the roll of it—Bix's hand sucked from Mother's hand as both submerged.

Mother screamed "Bix!" as she went under and pulled herself out, surfaced like a shot, screaming and soaked, clawing out toward us. I could feel the wave catch Father, make him start to buckle and brace in the pull of it. He let go of the folded kayak and it sped away on the tide, another weapon of the water. He scrambled, saw a stoop, walked up the steps, put me down, wrapped my arms around the railing, yelled at me, "Hold on to this railing, don't you move from here, Nonie! Don't budge!"

He left me crying, ran back to them, dove into the water, pulled Bix out, put her on his hip, grabbed Mother's hand, ran back to me. On the wet stone of the stoop, he pushed the flood out of Bix's lungs, Mother sobbing and crying. The look in Bix's eyes when she came to was death whispering at her back. We crouched on the stoop. Mother gathered Bix into her lap, and we watched the tide below us throwing around bicycles and flower buckets. Father held me and curled into Mother and Bix, all of us in a wet, embracing pile together. He breathed slow so my breathing slowed, then looked at me with relief in his eyes. He put his hand on Mother's hair, smoothing it down, kissed her forehead.

"AMNH," Mother said, looking up at Father over Bix's head, her eyes all fear.

"But Clare. What about the plan with Clare?" Father said. "'When things go bad, we'll meet on Ninety-Third, we'll all get to the farm.' That's what we all said."

"Not tonight." Mother looked at Father, and he nodded, and kissed her, looking so astonished to have all of us alive that he never said a thing more.

12
WATER LOVE

We needed the boat. I could hear Father's words in my head, knew he was right. Water came down from the sky against the glass. Water rose from the streets. Not like any storm surge or rogue wave from my Water Logbook. This flood rose like rainwater fills a barrel: steady. Water came up to the first floor of the museum, up the apartment buildings across West Seventy-Seventh, rising to the second floor, then halfway up, like it wouldn't ever stop. The ocean poured through the city, and everything was caught in it— boards and plastic pipe, a Styrofoam cooler and office paper, a traffic cone and tree limbs, bottles.

Lightning flashed and showed a pair of dogs, wild and struggling in the waves. I sucked in my breath—I hated dogs since Mano—but then a vortex dragged them down into the blackness and they were gone.

I closed my eyes. I could feel Keller's hand on my shoulder.

"Nonie," he said. I opened my eyes. He looked at me. There was fear in his eyes, a mirror of mine, remembering Mano. Then he closed his eyes, opened them, and said, "Nonie, it is my turn, right?"

"Your turn," I repeated; the words didn't make sense in my head.

"Animal in Mind. It's my turn, right?"

I thought of the rules of the game. The first person thought of an animal, modern or prehistoric. They gave clues about it, until the second person could guess the species. Yesterday, when we last played, we were walking in the sunshine on the way home to Amen, coming back from the garden in the Ramble in the Park, walking where the sea now stood, Father somewhere in the lead checking for the Lost and for dogs with the rifle on his shoulder. I remembered that the rifle was in the stacks and the stacks were gone. Walking in the middle of the line coming home from the Park, I felt safe. It was my turn yesterday, *Ounalashkastylus tomidai*. Something like a seal and polar bear and sloth and hippo, vacuuming up the seafloor in Alaska. Extinct. Keller didn't know it. Even with all my hints. When I told him what it was, he said, "That's a fake animal. Evolution wasn't taking its medication that day." And we laughed. Sometimes you can't explain how things are.

"Yes. Your turn." I looked back out at the water, but he took my chin and moved my face back to look at his.

"I have an animal in mind," he said, smiling at me as if there were no flood, only us. That was how you started the game: *I have an animal in mind.* He let go of my chin and took my hand. "And it is something that loves to swim. It cracks open urchins and sleeps on its back."

"You aren't trying," I said. "I know already, too easy." My eyes drifted back to the window.

Keller took my chin again, turned it away from the window. "Too easy?"

I looked at him. "Sea otter. Too easy."

"We have some things going on right now—I thought I'd give you a softball."

"California sea otter. *Enhydra lutris nereis.* They eat the urchins so that the urchins don't eat the kelp in the kelp forests. Because they grasp the kelp when they sleep to keep from floating away."

"That's how they hold on to each other, they wrap each other up in kelp," Keller said, his face serious, but then lighting up like he was going to make a joke like he did, like he always did, even when things were bad. "Kelp, I need somebody," he said.

He looked at the blood on my face, brushed it off, brushed off water dripping from my hair, picked up my cut hand, like Father did.

"Are any of the kayaks left?" Father asked Keller. "Oliver took that canoe Louis found last year when he went north. So now it's just the portables in the stacks. And I didn't think those walls would go and take the kayaks with them."

"Those walls took everything. But we hid that boat, right?" Keller looked away from me to Father. "There's that one in the Halls. The birchbark. The emergency one. Unless someone took it?"

I knew what Keller was talking about. There was a birchbark canoe in the Hall of Eastern Woodlands. That Hall was behind extra locked doors, closed before the floods to public sight. The people whose people had made the things kept there were getting them back, and it took a long time. People like Father working to pack and send and alert and protect as the things went home. But the boat was lost, stuck like we were in the world as it came down, suddenly too big to ship and pack and truck to where it belonged. We had a rule—we didn't alter collection items for our own use unless we had no choice. We could take a loom to make more blankets, but if we could scavenge modern tools from the ravaged hardware stores ten blocks away, we left the stone axes where they were.

The canoe was in a glass case. I saw it when we were losing Mother and she couldn't travel. Bix was too scared even to hear the word "boat," but I loved it. When we saw it, Father understood that it could be a secret boat, one the Lost would leave alone if we left it where it was. We could pretend it was fragile, too old and brittle to be of use. Even if the Lost found it so deep in the museum, it would look dusty and ancient. If our kayaks were stolen, we'd have it.

Keller and Mano and Father learned how to make pine pitch from a book in the library, harvested pine sap from the Park, boiled it on the roof and painted the canoe, but didn't make it look too good. They did it as close as possible to how it would have been done by the people that made the boat. "We have to honor the owners, the Haudenosaunee," Father said. Then they put it back in that part of the museum where the Lost never went.

I thought about the canoe all the time. Bix and I only learned to paddle in the Turtle Pond in a collapsible kayak. Bix fought the lessons. Mother taught me how to love the water. As terrifying as that storm was out the window, some water love lit up in my chest thinking about the canoe. I had more of that than any of them. I had to give Father and Keller and Bix the water love Mother gave me, put them into the bathysphere with me, kick our fossil selves loose from the place we were stuck. No matter what we wanted, or what we felt, we had to leave Amen. It had been life and safety and work and home. Now it was just another place under the waves. Father was right—the only things that mattered were the four of us and the Logbook. We could always make another Amen after we left this one.

"I remember," I said. "I remember where we keep that boat."

13
BEGINNING AMEN

The night we came to Amen, we swam from that stoop and through the retreating water and onto dry land. We walked past the bodies washed up in the mouth of subways, the bloated woman on the sidewalk. Father carried Bix, and her already too big to be carried. Mother carried me. Father says we fell asleep halfway to AMNH. Mother had her keys to the museum. They were in her pocket, always, in case. Mother let us in, electric out and security with it, and we hid in the dark of the New York State Environment rooms, them awake next to us until morning, when we found the library and the others. Keller had keys from before, too, he and Angel came, and Mano, Sergio and Louis, more people. Keys were the best things anyone saved. Big old locks would slam in place, make a satisfying noise.

Mother said that you don't know what will trap you until it does. At night, emergency blankets from our go packs over us, extra clothes from the gift shop keeping us warm, Father told Mother that Clare was waiting, and we had to go. Mother begged him to wait. The city trapped us as it fell. In the first days there was the buzz of terror. Old City filled partway with water, then it filled all the way with chaos. The water receded, back behind the floodgates, pumped out before the pumps broke, but the chaos didn't recede. I wouldn't part from Mother, let every word go and wouldn't speak, didn't want to have words if they didn't keep me safe. Bix lay on the floor, humming with her eyes closed, shutting out the memory of water. Mother looked like she was being hunted. They waited too long. Finally, it was well past any time when Clare would have waited. We stayed anchored to the Upper West like it was the last place.

The city made noise as it died. No one went out. I could hear gunshots if we got close to windows. I could see fires at night in the buildings, smoke on the air. There were soldiers. Soldiers didn't pay attention to the museum. No one trusted soldiers at Amen. We didn't come out. We didn't leave the collections. We didn't leave each other. Then there weren't any more soldiers. Everywhere was flooded or burning. There was too much work to save any one place. Or that's what Father said. There were fewer people after that, maybe evacuated. We hid in the stacks. Rick found a pile of cans from the cafeteria pantry. When that ran out, Father and Keller and Rick and Sergio went to scavenge in the dark, found a rifle in the street which they kept as if there were ammo. Careful Father, pocket full of first aid supplies, wasn't right with a rifle on his back.

That's how it was until the Mosquito Borne came, taking mostly everybody, probably all over the country. The army gone inland. Hospitals empty. Antibiotics stolen or ruined. It was a warm winter, so no bugs died, and the fever came and didn't stop. "Some kind of dengue?" Keller said when it started. "Supercharged by the weather, by the heat." After the first wave, there was a rare frost, and Father and Keller went out with an axe to split the ground, bury our dead and start a fire on the whitened grass to burn the Lost they found on the museum steps. Then a quiet came down, an empty city where packs of dogs or Lost people made the quiet something other than safety.

Inside the museum wasn't safe at night. Sometimes people got in. The subway stop in the basement was the mouth of the underground ocean, tunnels breeding bugs, a never-ending causeway to the oily sea. Roofwise we were shut

behind so many doors we'd not be found, free of mold and
crumbling walls, mosquito-filled rooms and windows breaking in a storm. We were in the air where we could see and
hear weather coming a long way off, where we could get to
the stacks, where sickness had less hold.

The night we came to Amen, I started my Water Logbook in my head, before I could write it in the margins of
the Museum Logbook, before that existed. Amen asked you
to make your own way to stay alive. I flipped through the
storms, trying to find a system. This was how you learned
something. Keller made lists, sorting insects into categories,
adding to field notes from before and expanding on what
changed, what was new. He could do it without thinking because he'd been doing it all his life. I kept adding to my list
because there were so many new kinds of storms, so many
new kinds of water after we came to Amen: a hurricane that
took all the trees in our garden, a tornado that dropped a
ring of dead deer in the Park, a nor'easter that sent sideways
rain, a flood that came up from the subways and sewers and
kept us inside for three days, a wind that dumped all the
water caches and flooded the roof.

I could feel water then, even from the beginning, like
you can feel sweat on your skin. When a rain came and it
was clear that the subways were filling and the basement of
Amen would be flooded, I could sense it like the prickle of
sweat coming up on the back of my neck. I could feel when
it was full of evil things, chemicals leaching, or the stink of
corpses, or rats who were quick enough to swim with the
rising tide. I could feel when the water coming was good.
Sweet rain showers would roll through, twice a day sometimes, as they made their way over Jersey. I'd tell Mother
and we'd go to the roof above the library, what would become our Amen. We'd stand in the bright downpours and

dance, an old pickle tub at our feet catching fresh water to drink and scrubbing at itchy skin while the rain pooled on the stones that lined the roof, slicking them down, the sunlight coming in from under the clouds, caught so everything was alive.

At first, I felt naked up there on the roof, in the weather all the time, the water in the air so loud I couldn't sleep. In the tent we used before Father built the longhouse, I would curl with my head under Mother's chin and press into Mother's throat to feel the air come in and out of her, to hear her mumble, "Nonie, you're choking me." I'd feel the vibration in my skull, my foot touching Bix's foot under the dirty sleeping bags, and I'd calm down and sleep shallow until dawn.

There were rules about water. Everything we drank came from the sky. The look of any other water was pure evil: the shine on the top, the slick smell of it, salt and oil, full of dislodged garbage and leaching chemicals and waste. Touching it was not allowed. "Lord knows what's in there," Bix would say, "enough to give you ten kinds of pneumonia." She was right, but she didn't see water like I could, how it was more, broken and altered, but beyond us.

Our daytime work was down the stairs and past the locked doors. We broke open cases to stop the rot, wrapped bones and hid them, listing in the Logbook where they could be found, brushed damp off totem poles, kept books from molding. Everyone found work when the world came apart, even if that work was only scavenging food enough. The work of Amen was saving things. If I were older, like Bix, and I remembered more of the way things were before, I might have minded the work. Bix did it, but she minded. I didn't mind because Mother told me it mattered, and Keller told me it mattered, and Father showed me every day it mattered. I heard everything they said and didn't say—*work will save you*.

On the roof, over months, Father built the longhouse for Mother. She was dying and they didn't tell us. She was dying and we couldn't leave, even if Bix was able. Water came up in Mother's body, from her kidneys, drowning her. It wasn't like the Mosquito Borne, wasn't from the storms or any other thing, only from a bad gene. "A bit of code that's all wrong," Mother said one night in the longhouse, explaining it, "that tells my kidneys to stop working, keep all the water for me, not let any of it go." Bix looked at me over the covers, like she knew something, but wouldn't say.

Later, under the whale, she told me, "Mother's dying." But I wouldn't hear it.

Mother was like the weather—good on some days, then not. Bix told me, "If there were hospitals, they could have given her a new kidney like replacing a generator part." Mother lived with her drowning body a long time, poison like the poison in the water inside her too. We were the same as fossils: floated down in the streambed, come to rest, blanketed up by silt, hidden from predators and weather, bones replaced by mineral.

"The World As It Is doesn't work if you don't have people," Father told me, "and you have to be kind. People who don't know that get Lost. Lost people don't know that what it means to be a human is to care about other humans. They forgot that a better world is coming."

"That's why we made Amen?" I asked him.

"That's why we made Amen."

"And that's why we keep the collections?"

"We keep them because we have a duty to the future."

When I first saw the canoe, I was working with Father in the Hall of Eastern Woodlands. Father found broken glass in his flashlight beam. "Someone's been here," he said. A Lost person took the bows and arrows listed on the cards; the fasteners pulled free marked the shadow of their place.

On the opposite wall was a diorama, its case intact, of a Haudenosaunee village before contact, the people of the longhouse skinning pumpkins under a tree, woodsmoke ringing the village. It was hard to look at that village, so like Amen, so unlike it. It was waiting for the flood, just like we were. People like me were the flood, pushed the Haudenosaunee out of their land, drowned them, sent illness, took their things and stuck them in cases. Father looked at me. "Nonie?"

"Yeah?"

"What's up, kiddo?"

"I don't know," I said. "That looks nice," I pointed at the diorama, "that home."

He put his hand on my head, pushed my hair back. "I wish I could give you that." He looked into the diorama like he was memorizing it. "If I could, I'd find a place like that, to make something new. But until then, we can be sad about Tenth Street, right? We don't have to like what happened. And we don't have to pretend it is OK?" I shook my head, and he smiled with sad eyes. He turned away and I followed his lantern light shining on an unbroken case housing a huge birchbark canoe. "Look at that. It probably won't float."

"Will we need a boat?"

"I don't know."

I looked back at the village in shadow. "Is that what it's like up north?"

"Up north?"

"With Clare. In Tyringham. Mother said that Clare went north, and that we should go if you say so, and that there was a farm. Her farm, their farm."

"It was your grandfather's farm. If it's still there."

"She said we should go if you say."

"I don't know, Nonie. Bix is scared. And there's more work to do."

"Leningrad."

"Leningrad."

"But what if the Nazis took it? What if the curators had to leave the Hermitage?"

"Your mother and I thought that they'd go to the taiga, or the edges of it. In the winter, they could walk out over the ice on Lake Ladoga. Leave the city. They could disappear into the taiga, wait out the Nazis until they could rebuild the world."

"So, the farm is the taiga?"

"Maybe. If there is still a farm." He picked up the Logbook and looked at the canoe. "Let me get this into the Logbook and we can get back."

Amen was all we had to get back to. It was enough if we had Mother, but if we ever lost her, Amen wouldn't be enough. I knew that the day I saw the boat.

14
EASTERN WOODLANDS

"You're thinking of our secret canoe in Eastern Woodlands," Father said.

I nodded. "I can get us there."

Keller looked out the window, the flood rising to the second floors of the buildings. "Are you sure the thing will float?"

"Mano did a good job on the pine pitch. We didn't test it. Maybe it will? But I'm sure we won't," Father said.

Keller laughed, shaky. "True. OK, Nonie. Get us to it."

I turned even before he said my name, ran past Bixie so to skip the pull of her, frozen where she stood. Astor Turret was the fourth floor, the Hall of Eastern Woodlands the third, I was running to the water, to the danger, taking the paths of the building's dark wet maze by instinct. I heard Keller's steps echoing behind me through the ornithischian dinosaurs, broken glass barriers, metal ramps. Somewhere behind him was the sound of Father's voice, coaxing Bix down the stairs. Sound of the flood came up the marble below us. On the third floor I ran into the Hall of African Mammals. The room was two stories tall, with the upper floor all balconies, a connected square overlooking the central diorama on the floor below. I ran along the galleries, dark dioramas of African animals behind glass next to me. Down below there was a herd of taxidermied elephants walking in a central display, no glass to enclose them, so tall their trunks reached for the upper railings. Mano liked to play there. I looked over the side; there was enough light to see the elephants' legs submerged. In all the floods, water never came so far up.

"Keller!" I pointed to the elephants.

"I see it! Keep going!"

I ran down galleries, into rooms of birds, rooms of mammals, rooms of primates, the sound of water everywhere.

The Hall of Eastern Woodlands was pitch-black but dry. In one of the corners would be the boat. I stopped running. I tried to remember how all the cases were. The boat was at the back, in the corner.

"Keller? Light?"

I could hear his running feet come up short, his hand rustle in a pocket for a tiny flashlight. "No lantern," he said.

"Down here." We walked to the back corner, passing cases I remembered. We passed looms, dioramas, blankets. "There!"

Keller's light picked out the corner of the birchbark canoe.

"No way to know if she's seaworthy. We don't have much choice, do we?" Keller's voice smiled in the dark. Even in the chaos he was like that.

"Nope."

Father and Bix caught up and we stood there, eyes set for the gloom, straining. The whiteness of the birchbark made the boat shine, the bleached sides made it hover, a dark ghost against the darker shadows. It looked underwater already.

Bix stared at the boat. The shadows around us, which would have sucked all her curious notice, all her fearful bravery, didn't hold her at all. Bix in a flood was not like Bix. She stepped to the glass, put her hands on it. "That won't float!" She turned back to Father, pleading.

"We've got to take it, Bix," Father said, "in case."

Keller exhaled, knowing we had to tell Bix things to keep her moving, but hating it. "No other option, Bix." Impatient.

"What if the water gets up to the Turret?" His voice was starting to rise, clipped with how fast he thought we should be going. He pointed to the far corner of the room. "We have to break the glass." We never broke the glass unless there was no other choice. Our keys were lost in the stacks. Breaking the glass meant Amen was over more than anything else. "Get your sister back, Nonie." I took Bix's hand and led her away from the case, away from the coming shatter.

Father found a piece of pipe on the floor. "Close your eyes." He smashed hard, and the glass shattered. He worked every day against a broken case, against lost history. Shards bounced off my legs. Father and Keller kicked out the last of the glass and stepped into the case, pulled the canoe carefully from its ties.

Keller took the pipe from Father, smashed a case next to it that held three carved wooden paddles of different designs. "Nonie, take these." He walked to me, poured them into my arms; they tumbled out and I gathered them, stooping.

"OK, Allan, flip it." They turned the canoe over, rested the gunwales on their shoulders.

Then there was a big noise, sound of thunder, suck of wind through this deep room, and a crashing sound like the one when the roof went, but far off. I looked at Bix, Father, and Keller under the boat. The sound of water came into that place, and the floor was running with water.

"Nonie," Father's voice was muffled under the boat, "get us back."

I gave Bix one paddle, put the other two in the crook of my elbow, took Bix's hand and pulled her. We moved blind and clattering through dark halls, along the balcony of African animals, past the elephants. Only the tip of a single trunk visible above the flood. The stairs were wet, above us the walls or windows breached, rain pouring in to meet the

sea, the slippery marble hard to manage, the sound of breaking glass.

Father and Keller stumbled behind Bix and me; with the
canoe on their shoulders they could only see their feet, the
water moving up. From how fast it took the elephants, it felt
like the ocean would grab them as they followed us, slowed
by the weight of the boat.

At the top of the stairs, I retraced the way back to Astor
Turret. As we came to it, I saw that all the windows were shattered. A wall was gone, a hole from floor to ceiling, the storm
pouring in, water pouring in. Water was coming up the stairs
behind us and it came past my shoes. I could feel it soak my
socks, my ankles. I stood, holding Bix's hand, looking at the
emptiness where the windows were, where the wall was. Bix
dropped her paddle. I set mine down. They floated toward
the stairs. Behind us, Keller and Father splashed in, took the
canoe off their shoulders. Father gasped.

"Well," said Keller, "we dodged that blow."

"No kidding," said Father.

The canoe tilted, floated in the water, bumped into the
wall, washes of new rain moving it. Keller looked at it.
"Look! It floats." He grabbed the paddles and threw them in
the bottom of the boat.

Father looked at him, smiling. "See, we got good luck
after all."

Lightning hit and through the empty windows, I could
see the flood at the lip of the windowsills. The water was full
of wreckage—tree limbs, wooden pallets, a length of gutter,
a plastic barrel from the roof, a dead deer. Storm clouds
were low and moving very fast; the rain washed the building
of the fault of standing still.

"It gets any higher and we have to launch," Keller said,
looking at the sea, not thinking about Bix.

"Launch?" Bix whined, shook her head. Since Mano died, she was stubborn with Keller.

"Yes, launch," Keller said, softer. "And hope we make it right out of this city." Bix flinched. Keller wasn't tender with Bix since Mano died. Me, he forgave. I was the youngest one on the day of the dogs in the Park. Bix was older. Keller didn't mean to think she failed, but he did think it. "It's time, Bix," he said to her, trying to find a kind tone.

"There's no place left to go in this building." Father walked close to Bix, took hold of her shoulders. He never noticed what held Keller back from Bix. "It'll be underwater. We're leaving."

Bix cringed, started to cry, shaking her head back and forth, sinking. But Father held her, looked at her, let her see his fear. It was stark, the fear in him, made me want to be afraid too. The waves were high, the boat was small, we had nothing to eat. But the fear in Father made Bix lean into him. He bent under her weight, rocked back on his heels and balanced. He hadn't cried since Mother. His searching eyes hit on me, and he whispered at me over her head, "Take her, Nonie, I can't get her in that boat without you." I nodded, tried to calm my hands. He was right. Bix would listen to me about water when she wouldn't listen to anybody else.

"OK," I said.

He pulled Bix up, wrapped arms around her and whispered to her.

Keller came next to me, looked over at the two of them. "Hey, little warrior." He leaned sideways, rested his temple against the top of my head.

He never had Mano in his eyes when he saw me. It seemed like he was still seeing the year we met, the year I spent serious and silent. He talked to me like anybody, even when I wouldn't talk back. He kept doing it, taught me how he listed what he knew when things were bad, taught me insects, the evolution of arthropods. When I spoke at last, he didn't treat it like anything had changed. It was easy with us. I never had to be forgiven.

His hair was wet with droplets shimmering and caught in his curls. I closed my eyes in the calm coming from him. He was a big force of deep gray cloud, covered everything in quiet and made it possible to think. Father had the feel of lightning coming off his skull, jumping and lit. Keller straightened, lifted his skull from mine. "Don't worry." He looked out the broken windows. "That flood scares the hell out of me, too."

15
PLACE YOUR FOREHEAD
ON THE GRAVESTONE

All the time we were in Amen we were stuck and sleeping, as if we could stay there forever. We were underwater already, only the floodgates kept the big ocean out of the city and let us think we weren't. Mother told me not to fear the water. The water is only doing what it must. It is old and it is smart, and it has been changing forever, and we can no more fight it than we can fight the sky. We are it, and so there is no reason to be afraid.

Coming home tired from the garden once, Mother said, "Take off these boots, butterflies," and Bix and I pulled off her worn-out mud boots. Her leg swollen, her skin a yellow cast I thought was a tan. But even drowning like that, she looked like something strong and bright had happened to her. Bix went to help cook. I took off my shoes and climbed up to Mother on the longhouse shelf she shared with Father. She was cold. I pulled the sleeping bag over us. She closed her eyes. "Nonie," she asked me, "did I ever tell you about the RV *Sally Ride*?"

"No." I curled in Mother's armpit, feeling her sweat from the day.

"It was the ship I went on a long time ago, when I was in grad school, before Woods Hole. The government put people on the ocean. They made a fleet of ships to study what was happening to the ocean and told them to stay out there. I knew some people that went. I didn't go because Bix was on the way."

"They're sailing out there?" I thought of the picture of the woman in the bathysphere I found in a book, her face framed in the hatch of the sub, looking out like she just discovered joy.

"I like to think that they are. Maybe they made it when all of this came apart." She was quiet, eyes closed, the hope of something deep in her. Faith like an ocean, faith in the ocean.

"Me too. I like to think so, too." And I let faith into me as if the ocean were the whole healing secret to The World As It Is.

"If things ever get back on track, if we ever pull it out of the fire, Nonie, I bet you'll be a scientist, a studier of the bits of things that end up telling a kind of awful and beautiful truth. You can feel the truth of small things in your bones, like you can feel all the weight of water. And it will take someone like you to heal it up." She opened her eyes and looked at me, and I knew she was willing the ocean to fill my veins with a tide of hope.

If I had known what was coming, I'd have left the roof in the dark before the storm and run to the cemetery and crawled onto Mother's grave and been with her one last time before the wind and the rain left her stuck at the bottom of the new sea. I'd have pressed my forehead against the rock we used as her marker and felt the coolness of it. If she were alive, I'd have asked her everything about Clare and the farm in Tyringham, our taiga, and how to get north. And, like always, she would have said, "All shall be well, and all shall be well, and all manner of thing shall be well." And I would have believed her.

16
LEAVING AMEN

Father handed Bix over to me, a toddler I had to keep from falling off the edge of a roof. She grabbed my wrist. Fear poured off her, contagious, it made a picture flash into my head of Evangeline and Jess, snatched by the wind. Bix could tip me over, the ballast of her deadness. I took her hand in mine; I remembered what Jess said about the shark. I remembered that if Bix was anything, she was contradiction—terrified and fearless, deadened and primed to spring. I had to count on her coming back, if not in that moment, then soon. I rubbed the back of her hand with my thumb, concentrated. I could feel my body, the cut on my hand, the bruise on my knee. I wanted to lie down right there, sink into the flood as into a cot and sleep.

I thought of Bix's Tenth Street bed, feather comforter, soft yellow pillows, yellow sheets and cotton blanket, a painting over it. A friend of Mother's made it when Bix was born: a cat lying on its side in a dory tied to a sycamore with peeling bark, above it a night sky full of stars. In Bix's bed we'd listen to Mother sing, "'Oft, in dreams I wander / To that cot again / I feel her arms hugging me / As when she held me then / Too-ra loo-ra loo-ral.'" Standing in the flooded room, I hummed the song before I knew it, rubbed Bix's hand. That was a boat Bix could love, the boat above the bed while Mother sang. That was the one we were going to, whether Bix knew it: Mother's boat. Whether any of them knew it, the canoe was Mother's boat.

Keller and Father waded past us, moving the boat to the broken wall of the next room. I pulled Bix to follow the canoe, humming. "'Hush now don't you cry,'" I sang. She looked at me, locked eyes. "I'm here. We'll be OK. I got you," I said, like she said to me that time under the whale, then looked back toward the hole in the wall. Her body softened next to me. I could lead her where I wanted. The water rose past my knees. It was fast and foul. I didn't let it touch my cuts. I had an entry in the Water Logbook about water like this. Corrupted and stinking—*infection water*—the kind that makes you sick if you let it in your body. Father and Keller steadied the canoe for us. There were no seats. Bix sat in the middle of the hull. I sat in front of her. Keller looked back to Father, climbed into the bow. Father pushed us to the open gash in the building; the water was high enough that we didn't touch the rubble. I stopped humming, put my head down. The canoe held.

The current felt alive under the hull. Keller took up a paddle. I laid mine across my lap. Father pushed us out of Amen. We slid through the blasted hole in the wall. Father stepped off the last edge of the building and jumped into the stern. It was dark, storm clouds north, rain easing, waves a choppy vortex. The boat hit a crest, dipped into the trough of a wave. We bumped a wash of floating garbage bins and dead rats, water splashing over the sides. I looked over my shoulder at Amen, past Bix, her eyes a blank, past Father's shut face. The water's eddies and currents dragged us back toward the mass of the building, the vortex of the hole drawing the ocean inside. Father and Keller fought the waves in silence. The hole we'd come through was the mouth of a cave, one we kept escaping. We hit the flat side of a wave. At the front of the canoe Keller was trying to keep us upright. Over his shoulder I saw a shape rolling on the surface of the water. It looked like debris, then I made out an arm. It was a body. "Father?" I yelled. "Someone in the water!" I saw the other arm, a bare foot, the back of a head, the face down.

"A body?" Keller stopped fighting the waves. He and Father turned to look, shifted the boat dully in the current. Keller was close enough to touch it, he drew it closer with his paddle, turned it over. Sergio's face stared up, green eyes under level brows, black hair full of gray falling to cover them, big, curved Aztec nose. His barrel chest, round shoulders all there under the wet Brooklyn Cyclones sweatshirt, half his skull missing; the wound bisecting his forehead left his eyes intact. I screamed. Keller reached to try to draw him up to the boat.

"Let him go," Father said in panic as we tipped under Sergio's weight. "He'll sink us!"

"We're going to tip," Bix screamed, scrambling back along the canoe's ribs, feet pounding against the bottom of the boat hard enough that she might crack it, running away from the waves.

"We have to bury him!" I yelled. Keller was dropping Sergio back.

"Where, Nonie?" Father yelled, struggling to keep the boat steady. "Where are we going to bury him? Bix, calm down! Let him go, Keller!"

Keller snapped, "I'm already doing it!" He pushed him away with his paddle. Sergio tossed, open-eyed; the next wave turned him so that his face was under. Bix put her head down into her lap, but I watched him, pitching, his head aloft, then his legs, one sneaker still on.

"Nobody's left," I said to the water.

"No, Nonie," Father said. "Nobody's left but us."

I was queasy from the roll of the boat, exhausted from balancing my muscles, from running, from crying. I wanted to throw up, sleep, go back inside, back to the roof. I wanted Sergio to be alive. I wanted Amen to be alive. Leaving Amen was walking away from the side of a grave. The person wasn't there, only the body under the soil. Bodies of people we love die, we leave them. Something of them remains in us, something we have to keep like we would a fossil, a story no one remembers, a Logbook. I knew that a place is just a body, no longer alive without the people that ensoul it, but it still hurt to go. There were four of us that the loss of Amen didn't take. I had to think about our bodies. I had to concentrate on us to stay awake, to not throw up, to stop shaking, not worry about Mother's grave left behind below the waves. I had to listen to Mother's voice in my head, "Breathe, baby." I had to love us. I had to love what was in the boat. I had to love the breath filling Father and Bix and Keller and me as we left Amen.

II
THE RISEN SEA AROUND US

<u>The Risen Sea Around Us:</u> This is what the sea is now, all the seas, all over the world. I don't remember what it was like before the sea rose. Jess says she thinks that it has come up sixty meters. I think that she probably is right. She says that weather modeling showed that's how high it would get if the glaciers were mostly gone. And since we can't track them from here, and we can't go to the seawall to see how things are, I am going to write here that her modeling was correct. That matches the places that we know were drowned before we lost touch, so we can use the map to see how many places still might not be underwater. The risen sea has less salinity than the sea before. It is lighter and slower, because there are fewer of the big gyres that used to push the water around the globe as the water rose and fell because of its specific weight. I can smell the sea sometimes from the roof and it smells like salt and like ozone, but I have never seen the risen sea.

—From the Water Logbook

17
FARTHER ALONG

In the canoe, outside of Amen, I listed what I knew: clothes soaked, kneeling in water on the raw ribs of the boat, pack wet on my back, no food I could remember, bruised knee stiff, wet cloth of my hoodie stuck to me, dawn around us, waves higher than the gunwales, Bix shivering, Father and Keller getting us away from Amen.

Bix's voice was muffled, her head in her lap. "Is there somewhere we can go to wait?"

"Wait for what?" Keller asked.

"For the water to go down."

"That's not going to happen this time." Father dug into a high wave. "The Upper West is like every other coastline. Any person left alive will be looking for a boat, and if we stop anywhere in this city, we're dead."

"Mother told us to go north," I said quietly. Below us there were treetops reaching up from the flood—skeletal hands in the rolling water. The wind stripped the last leaves from them. Those were the trees near our cemetery. Mother and Angel and Mano were down there. So were the babies, the women who'd died having them, the Mosquito Borne dead, Sean who jumped off the roof. I couldn't see the grave markers. "Mother told us." I reached back to hold Bix's hand. "It's OK. We're together." She looked up at me and, for a second, I saw she remembered, us under the whale—she made a promise I was now promising back.

Everyone was silent a long time. This was a quiet of ending, the tops of the buildings hovering over the flood like giants in the sky. The silence was there inside and outside the wave sounds, inside and outside the small sweeps of rain that ran fast with the clouds as the storm dissipated and the light of dawn came up in the distance.

"Seems like the boat is holding. We should go north over the Park," Father said.

Keller said, "Good. Fewer buildings there, fewer eddies."

"Fewer bodies. There'll be snags, though, and we have to be on the Hudson before dark."

"I know." Keller sounded tired. Father talked like he was leading all the time. Mostly people let him. Keller did and didn't.

"Nonie, you'll have to look out for snags," Keller said, out of breath. "Can you do that?"

"What are snags?"

"Under the water there might be trees, light poles. If the canoe hits one, she could tear. We'd sink." My skin prickled, thinking of how far down the water went, slicks of oil on the wave crests. I nodded. "So, you have to be extra eyes, OK?"

"Yes." My voice was tiny. I would be the eyes seeing the worst things.

When dawn broke at Amen there was always a haze like a cell structure. Water bonded with the sky, made a thin tissue hanging all across the world, made the air full of the future heat that would come to grind you down. But, that morning, the dawn was empty, every drop of moisture was in the new sea, the sky full of clouds shifting in the fast wind. The new sea coursed with lost things. Debris swirled and rose in the water—headphones, water bottles, flotillas of paper, broken birds, photographs. In the mud of the Park after a storm, photographs surfaced, bleached and peeling, evidence of lives in The World As It Was, lives that included trips in planes, cakes with candles, people in fresh clothing with white teeth and no idea what was coming, a child on a three-wheeled bicycle, a newborn screaming with a red face faded pink, a man holding it, on the edge of laughter, eyes slapped wide, joy pouring out of his smiling mouth. A wave pushed a pile of paper toward me, perched on it a photograph of a woman reading a book to a child on her lap, brown skin and dark eyebrows, her long nose like Mother's. These were snags Keller didn't warn me to look for. A raft of objects floated past, empty water jug, plastic fan blade, yellow hairbrush, hubcap. "Can we go closer?" I pointed.

"Why, Nonie?" asked Father.

"A water jug, for collecting rain." We collected everywhere, even in a downpour at Amen, people took their coats off, caught the water, twisted the nylon into funnels, filled water bottles.

"Nonie, we can't touch anything in that water. And it isn't raining."

"We'd wash it off." I turned to look back at him.

"Nonie, water is usually bad when it's from a flood, right?" Father was about to say his rule: *Never drink anything but rain.* "This is worse—the old sewers, Fresh Kills, Indian Point, oil storage, garbage, medical waste, chemical drums—it's all in there. Don't touch it, you've got cuts, and we can't sterilize."

I was looking back at Father, but I noticed Bix behind me, looking at the water in the bottom of the boat, three inches and rising from dripping paddles, waves breaching. We were touching water all the time; it was in the boat with us. "We're sitting in it," Bix said.

"Can't be helped," Father said. The raft of debris floated closer, and Bix grabbed a dented metal pot with a black plastic handle perched upside down in the middle, drew it into the boat. "Bix!" Father yelled. She scooped out the water at the bottom of the canoe. "Oh. OK." He softened. "Good idea, honey."

A swarm of insects sailed unmoored over the water. They became a windswept cloud moving around us. Keller stopped paddling to watch. "Bees," he said, "the swarm made it out."

"They lost home," I said.

"They did," said Keller.

"Where will they go?"

"Land. Like us."

I watched to see where the bees went, farther along.

18
NOSTALGIA

The route was slow. You could walk north a long way, fast. I thought the boat would be faster still. But paddling over the Park was exhausting, glacial. We had to snake around the treetops. A few hours in, we felt something like a current pushing back for the whole of the morning. Father and Keller working to sweat while we moved hardly at all. I saw snags, trees and bodies and parts of buildings and lampposts. Slowly, the blocks of the drowned city ticked by. From our place hovering over the Park, there were distant western cliffs, to the east the answering wall of towers hazy and gray. By noon we had barely moved. By early afternoon, the wind changed. The water changed. Under us was a push north from the water, making it easier on Father and Keller. The heat came up through a sky that was clear of any sign of the hypercane.

Keller put down his paddle, took off his jacket, thought about sitting on it, remembered the dirty water in the hull, balled it up next to his thigh against the birchbark. Father stopped paddling, too. We let the water drift us. The wind settled. The water settled. The waves rolled us. Bix bailed new water out. We took turns peeing in the bailing pot, tossed it over the side, heads turned, pretending there was privacy. My clothes dried and I got hot. We were still awhile like that.

"Nonie, can you see if my hat is in the pack? And a bandana? We should cover up," Father said. I found the ball cap in the bottom, AMNH embroidered on it, faded to barely readable. I found the blue bandana for his neck, he tucked it under the cap, made a curtain. "Any zinc left?" I found the jar full of zinc oxide we'd scavenged, cut with beeswax and deer grease for sunscreen. It only worked a little. We passed the jar around. I pushed my hood back, wrapped a bandana over my scalp, let my ponytail out, left my nose to freckle. Keller found his straw hat, veteran of rainforests. Bix sank in her hood, hot, blinkered. She hid her body, always had, chest bound down with cloth, sweatshirt over her curves, baggy across her ribs, down over the hips, Father's T-shirt from college under that, NORTHWESTERN across her chest in purple. I had small curves then, didn't like to tell anybody. I wanted to stop time where Mother left me, a girl at her hip. For Bix, it was something else.

I was thirsty, licked my lips and found them cracking. "Bixie, in your pack, anything to eat?" I asked her. The heat, no drinking water, made me dizzy. The boat pitched in the odd current. "Take your pack off. Let me look through it."

"Check mine, too, Nonie," Father said. "It's with Keller's."

The packs were damp from the bottom of the canoe. I went through the pockets. Father made sure every pack had the ten essentials in it—shelters, socks, fire starter, sunscreen, first aid, city map, flashlight, knife, food, water. Those changed over time. Some got lost or broken and we couldn't replace them. We ran out. The first aid kits changed, got used up. Everyone had basics, but we added things. In my pack I had the Logbook, my pictures of Mother in the baggie, a rain jacket, a T-shirt, second socks, a map Father gave me of the Park, a stone with a tiny crinoid, a lollipop Rick scavenged a year ago, my knife, honey Jess stored in a sealed test tube. Keller's had matches, boxers, a roll of bandage, a tin cup, a baggie of seeds, the latest of his notebooks, a pen he took from the Amen gift shop that wrote wet or upside down, second socks, a wool hat, a compass, a brass watch. In

Father's there was a T-shirt with AMNH on it, two bandanas besides the ones we had on, a sweatshirt, second socks, a rag, a compass, the jar of zinc, a black birch twig he kept to chew for back pain. Bix's had the most complete ten essentials, also a trowel from the garden, rain jacket, her hair scissors, clean rags for her period, an old gum wrapper she kept to smell, poison-ivy tonic from witch hazel she found in the Park, second socks, goldenseal salve, a folded paper I knew was a drawing of Mano's. Underneath was a piece of pemmican wrapped up in a waxed cloth, a water bottle with a little in it.

"Bix!" I looked back at her, held up the food so she'd see.

I broke the pemmican up and handed it out; it was salty and rank, full of venison smoke. The taste of the berries in it made me teary with pleasure but I hid it. It made my body soften, no longer a cage of worry wrapped around an empty stomach. I felt my tiredness, aching knee, scabbed cuts, cramped legs, pants wet from the canoe leak. I drank, the water stale but good on my throat. We shared it around.

I could see the edge of the Park a long way off in the haze, how the open water came up against the canyons of buildings to the north of us. "We have to get to the river," Father said. "It won't be safe over there, too close to the buildings, to people. If we keep going north after the Park, we're in the street grid for ninety blocks. We need to get to the river and it's only, what, five blocks from here if we go west?"

"We'll be in buildings from the Park to the Hudson," Keller said.

"I know, but if we don't go west, we get stuck in the city longer. Until dark, probably."

"And it'll be dark early. November. So we gotta hurry. We could go through Morningside Heights. The buildings are lower."

"Think we can take Ninety-Third? We're close."

"Why? Why Ninety-Third?"

"Nostalgia, I guess. And I think it'll be faster."

"Nostalgia?" Keller asked. Father always said, *See what is, not what you want.* He could be closed up when someone was lonely for the way things used to be. Nostalgia was a thing that could trap you. When he broke the rule, fear prickled my skin, same as when Bix walked into dark corners. But he had lived in many versions of Old City. He was born in the Upper West, his father a painter with success that made them money. His parents sent him to a school with uniforms; he hated it, but graduated with grace enough to pass as rich. When he wanted to, he could smile and have people agree. Keller had tight shoulders, worry slipping into his muscles. "You need to see something?"

"I need to see home one more time."

"It isn't home anymore."

"No. And I know, we could go by Washington Heights for you."

"I don't ever want to see that place again. Last time I was there was hard," Keller said.

"I could say it's faster to take Ninety-Third," Father said.

"But you'd be lying." Tension left Keller's shoulders. He smiled at Father.

Father shrugged and smiled too. "End of the world and I still want to see the old house."

"Probably a bad idea."

"Probably a bad idea."

"OK, Safety Pup." Keller turned back. "We'll take your route. We'll go to Ninety-Third."

"OK," Father said, then, "Thanks?"

"We'll see," Keller laughed. "Maybe you shouldn't thank me yet. Can you find the turn?"

"I think so."

"Tell me when you do."

We paddled a long way in the featureless water. I looked for landmarks from the map Father made me. I looked for trees I'd known from walks with Jess. I looked for the place we'd lost Mano. It was all flooded and nothing remained. Father slowed the boat, made noisy patterns with his paddle, turning us west toward the cliffs. "I think that's it," he said.

"Ninety-Third?" Keller asked. "Already?"

"Yeah. I recognize those buildings on the corner. This is Ninety-Third."

We banked to the buildings and closed the distance, moving west toward the setting sun, the canyons coming closer, ominous. We slipped slowly into the canyon and a tiny wash of shade. The coolness was welcome, but the buildings were too close. The waves changed in the canyon, they softened, the going was faster. Keller looked over his shoulder, random noises made him startle, expecting to see the Lost. Sound traveled up against the walls, people might hear us. On Ninety-Third there were towers and maybe strangers on all sides, in broken-windowed apartments, sitting on rooftops, waiting.

The buildings of Ninety-Third were soft, the window glass shivered, useless teeth slipping out of an old skull. The stray flag of a bedsheet hung out a window, wetly flapping in the quiet. On a high floor a lamp sat behind unbroken glass, waiting to be lit. A row of brownstones stood flooded, their flat-topped roofs sprouting a forest of trees and vines, moss caking all the brick. We stayed in the center of Ninety-Third. There were snags close to the buildings.

"What block was it on?" Keller asked.

"Ninety-Third and Amsterdam. This is Columbus, it's the next block."

Afternoon sun made submerged shadows. I looked south down Columbus. The light played under the water, showed far down, not to the street, not to the bottom, but enough to see what the water hid. In the center of the street the sunlight showed a wall of wreckage underwater, a storm-made barricade of broken buildings and their parts. I knew a storm could do that, sweep across a city like a tentacle and form a wall where the surge stopped. Miami went under to Hurricane Rina, and that storm made a wall. It took apart South Beach, pushed by ocean and wind. There were pictures of it, the standing barricade the storm made from the swept-clean city, full of bodies and stoves and lumber and tires. Bix showed them to me in an old magazine in an Amen office.

The wall under Columbus Avenue had garbage, printers, bus shelters, window screens, carpet, awnings. It stretched from one side of the street to the other. It had scraped loose broken pieces, streetlights and lampposts, bathtubs and drainpipes and bricks, bicycles and delivery vans, stacked them up as tall as the flood. Deep under I could see the top of a city bus, door flung wide, shifting back and forth in the waves, silent, taking point on the wall like a battering ram.

"Look!" I yelled, and everyone turned to see.

"What did that?" Bix asked, staring.

"The surge," Keller said, staring into the deep. "The floodgates going, all that water coming in so fast. Like Miami, like Galveston in 1900."

Bodies were trapped in the tangle; I could see arms and legs. A man's face was caught in the X of two I-beams, thin with a long beard and eyes shut, sleeping in the water.

And then the moment was gone. A cloud blocked the light, the water was green and blank, the shadows lost, only the lone snag of a bent pipe poking up.

"Don't stop," said Father. Those faces could have been anyone from Amen.

We crossed the intersection, then floated down the block, past a row of houses, roofs above the water, bird's nests and creeper vines. "There it is," Father said, back-paddling, stilling the boat in front. He took his paddle out of the water and put it on his knees, closed his eyes, freckles dusting his eyelids, the first rest he and Keller had since the sun came up. Keller scanned the canyon. This building was a snag.

"This where Aunt Clare lived?" Bix asked.

"Yeah. That's where your mother and I were going the night Tenth Street went under. We had that apartment in the family for two generations, it's where I was born." He rubbed a hand over his eyelids. "Rent-controlled—they couldn't raise the price. Your mother and I were living on Tenth Street when my mom died—Grandma Kat, not Grandma Ida. Your mother was pregnant with you, Bix, and we weren't going to move, so we asked Clare to keep the apartment in the family. She kept it until the night that Tenth Street went. We didn't make it up here to meet her. That was the night we came to Amen."

Keller's voice turned gentle. "Light's fading."

"I know. We should go," Father said. But he took his paddle off his lap and put it into the water and rowed backward to keep us hovering there.

"We're in the worst place. Anybody could see us," Keller allowed with regret. I could see he was starting to be anxious. Keller watched everything, was slow to choose his course, paid practiced attention to danger. Father had a bubble of confidence that made people feel safe, but Keller didn't believe in the bubble; that kept them together.

Father said, "OK, you're right, Keller," his body softened,

his eyes sad. He stopped back-paddling and pulled deep into the water to start us moving forward.

No one talked as we neared the river, there at the end of the canyon of crumbling towers.

"My turn, right, Keller?" I asked.

"Yeah. Your turn."

"I have an animal in mind, and that animal is modern, an insect . . ."

"Thank you! An insect!" Keller laughed.

". . . it is very old and very big," I said, picturing the weird, enormous bug. "And it was thought to be extinct by 1920, but then in the sixties climbers were on Ball's Pyramid, and they found some of the insect's poop and later went back and found a colony of twenty-four of them."

Keller started to chuckle. "Now you gave *me* a softball. Is it fair if the animal is one that I taught you? I showed you their weird picture! The tree lobster, the Lord Howe Island stick insect, the resurrected bug."

"*Dryococelus australis.*"

Keller was quiet for a while. "I hope they made it."

I wondered if we'd see the floodgates, unless they went in the storm—the gates all up the Hudson and the East River from the mouth of the Verrazzano. Maybe they were waiting like dominoes for years, crumbling under the weight of the ocean. Father told us about them when storms kept us in the stacks, so we'd understand what kept the ocean out.

"Before you were born, hurricanes came up the coast in the fall, but they missed the city. Still, no one knew what to do with the water. All the coastal cities tried to plan, all over the world, as the water rose, and the currents died and the storms changed. Miami went, and Boston built seawalls, and Washington, until the government got on the boats. The Army Corps of Engineers transferred up from Miami and

New Orleans. New York was special, so they made floodgates, starting where the sea meets the rivers, and they built
on each side of the island, and they kept New York dry, like
the Hudson is almost normal. The storms still get in, and the
surges come through the sewers, and Tenth Street isn't ever
going to dry out—water goes where it wants. But as long as
there are floodgates, the ocean can't get us here."

Below me in the murky water were wide gaps, roads underneath marking the edges of the city as it faded. The light was
shifting, the November sunset coming, the ocean everywhere,
no floodgates in sight, no borders, no edges, the buildings in
Jersey poking out of the water, like they had in the Upper
West, everything gone under the Atlantic.

"That's the Hudson?" Bix's voice was full of vertigo.

"It was," said Keller.

19
A RESURRECTION OF BEES

Keller told me his mother was devout, pale brown skin and thin as a rail, the same way Angel looked, but not Puerto Rican. His father he never talked about except to say he was a minister, and he was dark, and his sons were dark, and they all stayed in the city where they were born, but not Keller. For generations in Joliet, Illinois, all his family bent toward the pulpit. He was the first who wasn't clergy; he was a scandal. From when he was old enough to be outside alone, he spent Sunday mornings in the overheated, dry, dead fields, looking at the ground for new beetles until someone found him and hauled him back to sing at service. Howard University turned him into a biologist, grad school at Cornell an entomologist. He'd been everywhere before the planes stopped, looking down. He'd been in Borneo and Peru, racing to understand what was happening, like Mother, making lists, catching creatures before they evaporated or moved.

In his pack he always carried the notebook with the list for that year. When he finished a notebook, he added it to the Amen library, summarized it in a Logbook entry. He trained Mano to help, letting him draw bugs next to their names in the list. Mano lit up when he drew. Keller saw what you loved, led you around all sides of it until you owned it. One night, sitting on the roof of Amen, tending the fire we kept going in a scavenged washing machine drum, I asked Keller why he chose bugs and not God. He laughed, shook his head, brushed ash from his hands, scratched the beard growing in on his soft jawline. "I have everything of the infinite in insects, Nonie. Do you know how many there are?"

"No. How many?"

"Nine hundred thousand kinds named, little warrior, maybe thirty million unidentified. In The World As It Was, we thought there were maybe ten quintillion individual insects alive on the planet. With this weather, even factoring in the extinctions, I'm sure there are lots more than that." He laughed. "Largest biomass there is on the earth." He had pride in his voice. He worked on something The World As It Is couldn't kill.

"That's a lot. A big lot."

"Yup, that's a lot." Then he hummed an old hymn, "Farther Along."

We went to our garden in the Park Ramble only when it was daylight. We hunted in the Park—deer and, when things were lean and hard, dogs descended from the ones people used to keep, coyote, rabbits and squirrel. We walked east from the cemetery to get there, through storm-broken groves of dead and live trees tangled with vines. The ground of the Park smelled swampy, nervy, mossy. Things sat wet in the Upper West, and they sat a long time. Nothing froze. The Park whirred with bugs, like the Carboniferous, when the coal of the world was laid down in fossils, the earth had giant insects, extra oxygen, no humans. Three hundred million years ago, beings like us, mammals with thin lungs and no exoskeletons, would drown in the richness of the world. When I walked there, the animals in my imagination followed me, like a parade under the trees. I saw the trace fossils of before: ancient bulbs surprising you with tulips, follies like castles, benches to watch from, sculptures, fountains gone still, running paths cracked with frost breaks. It was a practical ruin, an in-between, with deadfalls we used for firewood, our garden, and Keller's beehives camouflaged in a broken thicket.

Keller said, "Honey is an excellent thing to keep in a first aid kit, Nonie."

"Bees will keep us safe," I said.

"That's right, they will," Keller said. "As long as there are pollinators, a place can be rebuilt. Bees are resurrection."

Father made our shelter, the longhouse, he and Keller both. The morning after the first night we slept in the longhouse, I saw them shaving outside. They were next to the fire where they heated water from Rick's rain barrels in a dented pot. They were different from each other, Father short next to Keller, skinny. They shared one razor, traded a bar of Yardley English Lavender soap Rick scavenged from an almost empty Duane Reade, shared the mirror. Keller looked out past the heat haze and the piles of tools and plastic and wood and gear, tubs of water, nylon tents and drying clothes, called out into the sunshine, "Baltimore checkerspot! Never seen that this far north." He reached for his notebook, wrote down the name of the butterfly.

Father grinned, which showed the hole from the molar Sergio pulled with pliers. "You ever planning to stop with that list of insects?"

"Only thing my Ph.D. is good for, Safety Pup."

"Look at us—thinkers forced to be makers against our will."

"Only thing your degree got you was a house that white people shouldn't build."

"That's what Deirdre is always telling me."

Mother teased Father. "Appropriator," she called him, told him he'd copied the Haudenosaunee with his longhouse. He worked at the Met, a curator of early American architecture. He was a city child playing pioneer, knife in his pack, the knowledge of making fire from flint, went to college in the Midwest like Lincoln on the prairie. He understood what was wrong with building Indigenous things. "It's hard though, they built things that work. Hard not to borrow." He'd worked before the crash trying to give back what museums took from the people who owned the land, the artifacts. "Imperialism at its finest," he said about the longhouse, "or its worst. White people can't stop stealing good ideas, even when the empire's gone."

Keller called Father "Safety Pup." He told me there was a cartoon dog on cartons of milk when he was in school, the safety pup there to teach kids about danger, that was Father's nature. Sometimes Jess called Father "Boy Scout." At night, Keller and Jess sat at the fire with the whiskey Jess kept in a metal box, the bottle cushioned with towels to keep it from smashing in a storm. They talked about what it had been like to see people play music in a bar. They wished the guitar hadn't gotten broken, and they talked about how, when Sean died, they lost the best voice on the roof, and how he liked whiskey. They talked about how long it was going to last, this bottle, because they'd been nursing it awhile, and it was lucky Deirdre didn't drink anymore, and Angel wouldn't since Mano. It was late enough, and they forgot to be quiet. I could hear them talk about Mano and then talk about dogs and then talk about how The World As It Was came apart.

"I knew it was coming," Jess said, "I was in class when they taught us the modeling, I saw the feedback out there, in the data. I knew that nonlinearity was a possibility. Hell, it was happening, I saw it happening. But I couldn't picture it, you know? I couldn't picture how we'd lose the seasons, how it would be tropical heat in November, but still have blizzards that melted into heat waves. I couldn't picture the way the storms come and then come back. Not the polar cold fronts in the south. Not the new hurricanes, the hot winters, the king tides, the typhoons going east then west then east again. It should have been easy to see. It was in the data."

"It was easy to see," said Keller. "Look at San Juan. Look at Miami." He got silent for a minute. "But maybe hard to accept. Look at Allan."

Jess laughed. "Boy Scout." She laughed again.

"Safety Pup," said Keller.

"He wasn't in climate," she said.

"No, he was in chimneys."

Keller teased Father about what he studied: houses, towns, buildings from when America was all chimneys, no radiators, no generators, no electric. Father talked about how, if we didn't live on the roof, we'd have to choose a place with a chimney. I overheard Keller tell him once, "You picked the right thing to study."

"Happy accident," Father said back. "I pretended it wouldn't get here. I thought I could sell my car, walk more. People like Jess were working on it. I was sure they'd figure it out."

Keller and Father came to Amen as city boys, Midwest and Eastern. Jess grew up in Alaska. When the city died, she used all those skills again. She found deer marks in Central Park—the scrape of antlers on bark, their markings in the undergrowth, their scat. Coyote scat was easy to find, rabbit and dog, too. We shot animals from Amen's broken windows. They liked to browse in the cemetery. Deer was best for pemmican, but you could use coyote, or dog. I liked making pemmican, another stolen good thing. I liked eating it. We took dried meat, ground it to powder, blended it with berries, animal fat, and honey, mixed it in a plastic pickle tub Jenny Perkins cribbed from the cafeteria, shaped it into sticks, set it out on racks along the roof next to the rain

barrels. Someone watched out for crows for two days while
it dried.

I didn't like to hunt. I understood skinning, taking the
bodies apart to see the bones. Making the body dead was
harder. When I was eight, I was taught the bow. When I was
ten, the shotgun. Bix was taught these things first. I hunted
with her and with Father, or her and Keller, or all of us. We
practiced on the roof, had a target. I'd watch Mano and Bix
try to hit it. We learned to aim on the roof, then took one turn
with the gun in the Park. On the roof, Sergio sat with us. He
learned to flint-knap from Oliver; he hated arrowheads missing the target, landing on parts of the roof we couldn't reach.

"Jesus, Nonie," Sergio said, "with aim like that we'll run
out of the arrowheads we made in a week!" Keller liked him,
liked that he was the exterminator at Amen, that they shared
bugs, liked that Sergio and his son, Louis, who was grown,
had been there before any of us, holding their keys, working.
They knew the whole building, where the rats got in. They
knew what bugs could make you sick. "Worst insect on the
planet," Sergio said, "mosquitoes killed more people than
war." Louis didn't talk; he was shy.

Maybe I'd have been a good shot if I kept working. When
we were allowed to take bows to the Park, Bix stood next to
Father and Keller and dropped a deer across a meadow in
two tries. We walked to the body of the animal, and it was
so quiet, bleeding on its side. I could see the fear in the
deep brown ponds of its eyes, intelligent and full of feeling,
nothing like the diorama deer.

"It's not dead," Bix said to Father.

"We'll have to help it go," Father said, and took out his
knife. Bix looked at him, knew he'd do it for her, and made
a choice to do it herself. She held out her hand and he gave

her the knife, then stood by her and showed her how to cut its throat while he stroked the deer's muzzle. I hid my face in Keller's shoulder after the stroke and waited for the sound of the life leaving it. When it was quiet, they taught us to dress it. Walking home we spotted the rest of the herd. Father and Keller put the deer down and Keller stood at my ear, steadied my elbow, told me, "You're good." I missed. From then on, I always missed.

They tried to get us ready, on the off chance of something bad. But the storm made it so that we only had the safety of what was in our packs, not the bows and guns in the stacks, not the extra food and water. Around us were people on the move, making do with what they could find or beg. We never thought we'd be without food, without shelter, without bows. We thought we'd choose the manner of our going. But The World As It Is doesn't let you prepare.

20
UNDER THE SPIDER SPAN

The river was deep. So deep and so wide it was a sea. There was space and quiet. I felt my stomach flipping. The sky clouded up again. When the sun went down there was an indigo sky. Squinting, I could pick out the span of a wide structure crossing the river.

"A bridge?" I asked.

"Yeah," Father said. "That's the George Washington Bridge."

"I know that one!" Mother had fieldwork when I was little, we'd driven over the George Washington, our last time in a car, on a ration card, after the blackouts. I remembered pieces: us driving over the water, so very high, while sunlight came in every window and we moved fast, going west, Bix singing, "George Washington Bridge, George Washington, Washington Bridge," over and over and over until Mother said, "Beatrice, please stop, honey, that was one too many times to be fun." We waded into the corners of a swamp, I found a frog, held it in my hands and watched it breathe, in and out, throat pulsing against my thumb.

"Are we going under?" I asked. "Under the bridge?"

"I guess we are," said Father.

Bridges were something else in The World As It Is, magic ways out, ways to cross over floods without touching the ruined water, choices and movement, danger. People could wait under a bridge, like spiders in a web. And you would be the fly.

The bridge came close.

"Why are we going so fast?" Bix asked, the loom of the bridge showing our speed.

"We have the Hudson tide behind us," said Father.

Bix, her voice flat: "Rivers don't have tides."

"This isn't a river," said Keller, "I mean, it isn't anymore, but it wasn't before either. Not down here, anyway. Down here, so close to the Atlantic, it's a tidal basin, technically, a fjord. The tide pushes a crazy long way north up the Hudson. I don't know how long we've got until it turns, but when it shifts it'll try to drag us back south out to sea. We'll need to get off the water when it turns."

"Can we get out over there?" Bix pointed to an island of rocks rising to our west.

"Those are the Palisades," said Father. "There might be people there."

Bix asked, "So we keep going?"

"At least under the bridge," said Keller. "We'll have to see when the tide shifts, see where we are."

"Why not walk out on the bridge? There are roads."

"We'll have to use roads to get to the farm. The Hudson won't take us all the way. But the tide moves faster than we can walk, and the boat'll keep us safe. No one can get close to us in the middle of the river without us seeing them." Father's voice was soft; I could hear all the miles between us and Tyringham.

We reached the bridge when the indigo sky turned black. The river was only ten feet under the bridge deck. I saw remains of a settlement on the dark roadbed: tents, a sleeping bag, tarps, torn, scattered, broken. No sign of a single person living, but a dead foot poking out from a tarp at a broken angle, torn clothes fluttering through the fencing.

We slipped under the girders, into the darker dark, into the cave the bridge was, echoes sounding, the drips off the paddles in the quiet, the metal grid over us, the flaking paint and rust, wound with vines. No one spoke under there.

Then we were out from under, and the sky was our ceiling.

In front of us, the emptiness felt like freedom. This was what the people on the RV *Sally Ride* must feel, I thought, that the water made them free. But water was just mystery. Anything could be there. The Hudson stretched north. The dark silver water held the stars reflected. Land rose to the west above the flood. To the east, the last city buildings bobbed.

Sitting on a hill above the Hudson, beyond the city, in a nest of dark trees, was the bulk of a building, a castle, and, in the windows, there were lights.

I sucked air through my teeth. "What's that?" I pointed ahead.

"I don't know." Father's stunned voice was flat. "Keller? Is that the Cloisters?"

"Could be." Keller was full of wonder. "It's in the right spot."

"The Cloisters?" Bix's voice was groggy and thick. "Sergio talked about that."

Sergio and Louis, out on a scavenge, met Lost people, unarmed, tired, needing shelter. "They said they knew we didn't take strangers," he told Father. "They heard a rumor that the Cloisters was open. They were headed there. I gave them water. Got them a little farther."

The river was quiet, the building looked alive. "The lights," Bix said.

"I know," said Father.

"It's like *Babar's Castle*," said Bix.

"What?" I asked.

"A book we had," said Bix, "on Tenth Street. Mother used to read it to us. There's a castle at the end, a drawing of one. It's on a hill at twilight, and there are lights in the window."

"Maybe they have food," said Father. Then the lights

winked out, the darkness of the river was darker, dying leaves shivered on the distant trees.

I looked back. Bix was curled like a wood louse at the dark bottom of a sea. She sat on the wooden stays of the canoe with her legs up to her chest, arms crossed and resting on her knees, staring where the lights had been. I couldn't see her expression, only the wet shine of her eyes. Then something shifted under us, and the water turned under the boat. It was as strong as a hard wind, a hand, a surge, a tide; the Hudson tugged us south as if it had a leash, back to where we'd come.

"Tide's shifting," Keller called. "Time to get off the river."

They doubled their strokes against the hard pull of the tide, and we moved to the black shadow of the Cloisters' tall tower, peaked roof, and high walls.

21
THE SHORE

We got closer to the Cloisters and there was a park under the water, a forest of drowned trees. I couldn't see snags in the dark. Our hull scraped branches until we heard the shush of grass and weeds against the canoe and hit land.

Keller stepped carefully into the shallow water, then turned and pulled the canoe higher so we could step out into grass. The canoe shifted as he did, and I lurched awkward out of the boat, trying not to put my shoes in the wet, onto a narrow band of hill. Bixie nearly fell out in her eagerness for solid ground. Father came after. Keller took the gunwale and dragged the boat farther up the bank behind him.

We heard a strange cry on the quiet air. I looked at Keller.

"I think that's a goat," he said.

"Sounds like a baby."

Father stood by Bix. "That was weird," he said.

"Right!" said Keller, miming eagerness by rubbing his hands together comically, then "Where's the door?" with a wave deeper than worry under the humor.

"Ha!" Father shifted. "Look at that. That whole west wall flooded. I haven't been here in a long time, even though we were part of the same museum. Medieval stuff, twelfth through fifteenth centuries, not my department, stuff from before machines and printing presses and factories."

"They went even further back than your chimneys," said Keller.

"Yeah," said Father. "You want to leave the boat here?"

"Yup. And I want to have it ready in case they don't want to see us."

"What do you mean? Sergio said they took travelers."

"You? Nonie and Bix? Sure. But they might not let me in."

Father forgot, forgot that the refugee waves made people afraid, forgot that people only traveled sorted by color now. Keller never forgot. Maybe Father only pretended, so that he could force the world to think like he did, remember how it was before, everyone complex and shifting like the people at Amen, like all the people we knew, color and gender and everything moving like rain on a river. After the city died, we saw it everywhere, how people re-sorted themselves, maybe thinking that would keep them safe. After a while there was never a group of the Lost that looked like us at Amen.

Father looked at Keller. "Maybe, but you don't know that."

"Maybe I should stay with the boat, let you scope it out."

"No," Father said, "we should try. All of us together. I don't think we should separate."

"I'm not going up to that gate until I know they aren't going to shoot me," Keller said. "Sergio never said whether the Lost he talked to were Black or white, Allan. You don't know."

My stomach turned, fear for Keller, hunger from the day, thirst, all of it mixed up.

"I don't think they'll shoot you," Father said. "But let's hide the boat."

22

THE DAY THEY SHIPPED THE BONES

"Tell me again about what it was like," I asked Mother on the roof looking at the stars.

"We had lots of help. Because the other museums were closed, and because of what happened at the Met, it was easy to get curators to come and help. Everyone knew it had to be done. There wasn't any way around it. There were so many floods, all over, the coastal cities had been putting it off for too long."

"How did you do it?"

"It wasn't easy. It was hard to get packing material by then. There weren't any big boxes. There were bans on people getting things that could be used by the military for evacuations, or for protecting federal sites. People hoarded boxes for years before, looked all over for them. The curator of paleontology got arrested for keeping materials. I don't know if he's still in jail. Sometimes the National Guard would confiscate it all because they needed to pack up forward bases or the mayor's office or whatever."

"Nobody was looking after the bones."

"I wouldn't say that. A lot of us got to know each other for years, packing up the art museums, from conferences. When they asked for help with their collections, we came. Then they did the same."

"Did it take a long time?"

"Not really. When it was time, we worked really fast." She watched the stars wheel above the roof, the whole city below us, some dots of light in the towers, in the Park, someone with a fire or a lantern, someone with a stockpile or a shelter, someone passing through from somewhere worse to some-where better. We were fixed while the stars whirled above and below.

"I stood in the loading dock, such an ugly spot, with the deputy curator of paleontology on the last day we could get a truck, which we didn't know was the last day. The truck was packed with the last big things, the really important things, going inland to a vault. She cried and cried. Like she was saying goodbye to family she'd never see again."

"Did she ever see them again?"

"I have no idea."

"What if there are other places like Amen?" I asked.

"There are a lot of places like Amen. The Field Museum in Chicago, the British Museum, I mean, so many I couldn't list them all. Some are going to be broken into and ruined, or caught on fire, like the Met. But lots will be like us. Better, even, because we have the subways and all that water. There will be lots of places that are so dry that there's nothing to worry about at all, and all people will think about is keeping the looters out."

"Do they need Logbooks?"

"I think everyone needs Logbooks. Because if we all have them, then we can put them all together and keep the in-formation somewhere central. That's what they did in mon-asteries in the Middle Ages, they kept all the books, and they made copies, and that's how there were any philosophy or math or natural history records from Rome and Greece. We have them because people copied them. And they kept them away from looters and Visigoths. That's what you do in the darkness."

"That's what you do in the darkness."

"And you never know in the darkness who is holding the light. We don't know what's happening in Chicago, you know. They have fresh water out there, and maybe the cities that aren't flooded are close to OK. Maybe someone is coming to help, an expedition being organized right now. And maybe that's happening in other places in the world. There could be places that still have electric or government or communication. We don't know because no one came back here once they left. Museums were among the first places that had computer networks to connect us, so there was one central place to go to see what everyone had. I like to think that somewhere there is someone who figured it all out, and that when the Logbook makes its way to them it will be like a check-in, you know, like they can compare what we saved from the water, and where we put it, to the last known inventory that was in the computers, and then if anyone comes back here to excavate or go underwater to save things, you know, like in the far future, they'll know where we put it all, and what we couldn't protect. And it will save them some work. Because we hold a really important part of the story now. In World War II there was a team of French Resistance fighters and curators that wrapped up the most important paintings and statues and carted them off to the country so the Nazis couldn't loot them. The secret records of it were smuggled around so that no Germans found out about it. In England, they moved the entire collection of the most important rare bird skins from London into a tiny building in the country so that it wouldn't be bombed. I thought about that a lot before the Met fire."

"Father worked there?"

"Yeah."

"What if we lost all the Logbooks? And all of Keller's notebooks and everything?"

"You know they're in the stacks, in the storm shelter. That's the safest place we've got."

"But it is all the work. What good is being Leningrad if we don't have all the work?"

"The good is that we remember it. And the good is that it is all recorded somewhere. And the good is that we have that one central book, the one you're always writing in. If we had to go someday, take off and leave Amen, we could grab that one and go."

I decided that what Mother told me, the way that curator looked when the last of the bones went away, that meant we had to do something. I had to do something. That night, I took the central Logbook with my Water Logbook in it like a shadow story, and I found oilcloth that was newly waxed and waterproofed, and I wrapped the book up and put it into my pack, underneath the baggie with the pictures and my rain shell, and waited, in case we didn't get to be Leningrad forever.

23
THE GATE

When they were done hiding the boat, Father led along the edge of the wall. "The entrance is to the back of the building," he said, "facing away from the Hudson. I think that main door is probably underwater, but maybe there are other ways in."

The grass stiff under our feet, I tripped over branches I couldn't see. My knee ached from where I'd fallen in the hypercane; I was slow and dizzy. Bix's step was surer every inch away from the water. The grass crossed a path of cobblestones that disappeared behind us into the flood. We followed it to a stairwell, a road, finally an arched gate out from under the trees where the light was better. There was a wooden door in the wall next to it, and through the metal gate was a roofless, cobblestone courtyard littered with broken trees and chunks of stone. In the courtyard was a boat flipped on its gunwales, a pile of scattered hay, a few matted goats, a heap of forms rolled and covered in cloth—human bodies stacked together.

Father walked closer; Keller caught his arm.

"What?" Father asked.

"I'm going to stay back." Keller's voice was low.

"We'll ask." He turned to Keller, whisper-talking. "If there's anyone left."

"*You* should ask."

"You don't know they'll be white. Maybe the Cloisters is full of Black people, and *you're* the right person to knock on the door."

I could hear a cross laugh in Keller's quiet voice. "I'm

pretty sure that the people who set up shop in a castle are going to be white. Museums: last refuge of the ruling class."

"You know, everybody loves a fortress with extra security."

"Right, and thick goddamned walls and gates."

"And stone floors where you can build a fire. And chimneys."

Keller laughed. "What I wouldn't give for a nice brownstone, or a mall."

"Or a high-rise where you have to walk up forty floors?"

"Or a mansion with windows you can open and an iron gate. Honestly, Allan, who keeps keys to museums, anyway?"

"White people? Or maybe not. You don't know. You had keys. Maybe it's like Amen. Maybe it's mixed?"

"Nevertheless. I'm standing back."

Father nodded, said, "OK," and he and Bix walked toward the gate holding hands. I lingered with Keller, grabbed his arm, twisted the sleeve of his shirt in my fingers. Father let go of Bix's hand to check the locks. He banged on the door and woke the last sleeping goats, their weird cries a mix of wailing baby and quack. Behind the din of them, the sound of a door slamming open, footsteps. I saw the flash of a lantern behind the gate, behind that, a short white man. He had a round face, like a photograph of fishermen in Norway I'd seen in the Amen library, stout and broad in the chest. He put the lantern on the ground, peered into the darkness.

"Well, my friend, you were making a big enough racket that you woke up my goats. I thought there might be another storm." He stepped closer. "The only travelers we've had wash up on our brand-new island have been dead ones."

Father straightened. "We're from Amen. We've been traveling since the storm."

"I wondered if Amen had gone. I rather thought it would

have taken everyone with it, that surge was remarkably fast. Did everything go under?"

"Yes," the weight of the flood told in his voice.

The man said nothing back, his eyes squinting in the dark. He saw Bix. "I see two of you, but I have the distinct feeling that there are more people present." He had a springlike bent to him, lit with the things he'd done before The World As It Is. He spoke like we were students. He should have scared me, a stranger, a man who liked deciding. But he was hungry for being the one who decided, and that hunger made him easy to read.

"Step closer, Nonie," Father said, "let him see you." I let go of Keller's shirt and walked closer. The man looked for a long time. Father said, "I'm Allan Mayo, that's my daughter Beatrice and my daughter Norah. We took an old canoe and got this far in it. It's beached over there and hidden under branches, if you want to check."

"You've got children," his voice strained. He cleared his throat. "But that's not everyone. There's someone else waiting there in the dark." He pointed back to the shadows where Keller stood.

"That's John Keller."

Keller stepped closer to the gate.

The man cocked his head, surprised. "Well, that's not what I expected. We haven't seen a mixed group for a long time. May I ask if you're armed?"

"No, we're not," Keller said.

The man looked at Keller. "Are you really traveling together?"

Father said, "We're together."

"May I ask you where you're headed in the wake of that monster?"

Father answered, "We're going north. My wife died, but

she had a place in the Berkshires, a sister. We're headed there."

"Good luck with that," the man said, "everything after this place is a mystery." My heart sank. "You said you have a boat?"

"A canoe, an old one," said Father. "It just holds us."

"If you'd been here a week ago, we'd have had a plan for this arrival."

Father said, "We had a place then."

"And now you don't." He was saying we were Lost now. I thought of the Lost as anchorless; maybe they were getting from their *before* to their *after*. "When travelers showed up at our gate, we took them in for at least three days, we let them work. We fed them. We learned who they were. If they were safe, of course." He looked at Keller when he said this. "Amen never took anyone new, yes? You never let a single person past your doors?" He held Father's eye. "After last night, we're leaving. We talked about it this morning while we were piling up our dead. That storm ended us." He looked past us at the water. "We'll be travelers soon."

Behind him, the goats paced on their tethers like we might be wolves. "We need a place to sleep the rest of the night, and some food. We don't even have water."

"If you're unarmed, and because you have children with you, you can come inside. But you must leave at dawn." I looked at Bix, saw relief hit her like a wave and nearly make her buckle. "That's all we can manage."

"Thank you." Father's voice broke.

"I'm Douglas."

"Thank you, Douglas."

Douglas unlocked the gate, swung it open, and we walked inside.

24
THE BATH

Douglas picked up the lantern, walked to the pile of wrapped bodies, stooped down to them. The tarp was loose. He tucked it under. "We were visited by a microburst, the wall to one of our dormitories fell, in the night, and we had no warning. We will burn them tomorrow." He straightened up and looked back at us. "I have said this so many times in the last forty years, but I've never seen a storm like that one. I wondered if there was a tsunami, though the floodgates breaching could have done all this, I suppose. Now we are like the rest of the world. Maybe they did a better job in London, it always seemed like they were doing a better job. We lost nine people last night. How many people at Amen?"

"We had fifteen left," said Father.

"Any other children?"

"A baby, she was six months. And there was another boy, but he died a few years ago."

"Mosquito Borne?"

"No." Father didn't talk about Mano.

"And these two made it through the Mosquito Borne?" Father nodded. "Lucky. We lost all our children. There are ten of us left after last night. We weren't an island before, so we only kept this boat in case of an emergency, or to hunt in the Palisades." He walked to the boat, touched the hull. "Your craft is outside?"

"Yeah," said Keller, "we hid it."

"You had better bring that boat in . . ."

"You can't have it," Father interrupted Douglas.

Douglas turned and walked back toward Father. "If I wanted that boat, young man, I'd have it in my possession by now." Douglas smiled. "You're worried about our locked gates? That's fair enough, I understand. You don't know me. But you met people at your doors the same way. Only Amen didn't shelter anyone. The lucky ones made it here. What about the rest of them? You want to come in because I've heard of Amen."

"We had kids," Father said. "We had collections to protect."

"We had children here, too, and things to protect. You are not special because you weren't traveling until last night. It might help you to remember that I am the man who opened his gates to you. Was that who you were at Amen?" He turned his back on us, said, "You need to get that boat if you don't want to lose it to the tide," walked away. "You two can go back for it when the children are settled." Father followed the light, Bix looked over her shoulder at the dead. They all disappeared through the door. Keller and I hung back.

"He's strange," I said.

Keller looked at me, face obscure in the dark. He smiled, put an arm around my shoulders. "I know."

I was frozen there, hesitating to go up the stairs, into the first place I had been since Amen. Keller felt the waiting in me.

"I'm right behind you," Keller said. "You're good." He made it sound simple. I let him.

We walked in the door, up a long, cold stone staircase in total darkness. In the dark tunnel, Douglas's lantern far ahead of us, I could feel the quiet left by the bodies in the courtyard. "It feels weird here. They lost people, too," I said to Keller.

"You know it isn't just us, right? You know that, right,

kiddo?" I listened while I looked at my feet on the uneven stone stairs. "There's a story I know: A woman lost her child, and she felt like she'd die too if she couldn't stop crying. So, she went to the Buddha, and she asked him to take away her sadness. And the Buddha told her to go and find a handful of mustard seed and he would cure her of her grief." His words gave a rhythm to my concentration. "So, the woman said, 'Sure, OK,' and the Buddha smiled and told her that she had to find the seeds from a house that hadn't known death."

"She couldn't," I said.

"You know this one. Did your mother tell it to you?"

I nodded. *"Every house knows death."*

"Every house knows death," he repeated. Bodies in their courtyard, Sergio lost in the flood, Jess too, Evangeline, Beaumont. Thinking that the world has picked only you for tragedy is looking for mustard seeds. There is the weather and there is death. You can't control them, and you can't fool yourself that your name is the only one they know. They have everyone's names in their mouths.

Douglas was ahead with the lantern, a point of light in the black cave of the stairs. "Everyone else is sleeping." His lecture echoed from far away down the walls. "I will wake Alice Winslow, and she can bring you some food and water. We moved our supplies from the basements right after the storm. Our scavenge crew kept us in luxuries here—we barter with travelers who want to stay longer. Most of it flooded out last night. We can't take the treasures that are still here, the tapestries, the sculptures. Don't know what to do with those now. We did manage to save some of our flour, goat milk and cheese, some soap." He looked over his shoulder at us. "You need to wash, get the river off you."

At the top of the stairs was a tall stone hall lit by a lantern on a desk. I could hear water echoing, the basement filling. The inside was more stone: floors, walls, carvings. "You take that light." He pointed Father to the lantern. "This way, please."

We followed him into a long room filled with art and sculptures. Lantern light flashed over paintings of saints, textiles rolled, people on cots, long tables stacked every inch in yellow notepads covered in writing, quills, plastic cups dark-stained with ink, plastic pens, a barrel stove, a pipe chimney snaking up to a hole in a stained-glass window, a grate cut into the barrel's metal belly, inside, embers in the dark. Three people slept next to the stove. The next room was empty, floors soaked and covered with glass, windows broken. On the other side of the wet, we stepped into a chapel. Inside, I couldn't hear the water. I could see plain cots along the wall, the best sight in the world.

"You will be safe as houses here for a few hours of sleep. Alice will come and find you kids. Keep that lantern for them," he said to Father, pointed to the light in his hand, "set it on that table." Father set his lantern on a table between two cots. "You keep this one." He handed his light to Keller. "I can find my way back in the dark. When you've settled them, walk back the way we came." He looked at us, his eyes had lost the edge of cool from the gate. "Saint Benedict tells us we have to take all visitors as if they are Christ." His voice sounded naked. Keller and Father exchanged a look. "I am not a monk. I do not always get it right, but the shelter is yours."

"OK," said Keller.

Douglas nodded at Keller, then he turned and walked into the dark, leaving us alone. We were in a single pool of light. I put my backpack down on the closest cot, then thought how wet it was and moved it to the floor. The blankets smelled clean. I looked at my cuts. Father saw me.

"Nonie, do you need a bandage?"

"I'm OK." I hid my hands from Father. They were shaking from relief. My stomach growled. My throat was dry. Bix sat on a cot—her eyes almost calm in their vacancy.

"Keller and I have to get the boat. We'll be back before you're asleep." I shook my head without knowing I was. "I'll be right back. I *promise*. We have to get the boat before something happens to it." He kissed the top of my head, then he turned and he and Keller took the second lantern the way Douglas had gone, leaving us alone.

Bix had her dirty, wet windbreaker over her hoodie. The seat of her jeans, Mother's old jeans, wet from the canoe, soaked the cot under her. She stared into the shadows, looking at the corners in the dark. "Do you think that they have a garden here?"

"Maybe."

Bix loved to put her hands into dark soil, loved growing things. "I want to see it." I could hear her desire for what was hidden.

"We have to take off these wet clothes."

There were footsteps on the stone and a woman came into the chapel. She held a basin of water, blond hair cut as short as Bix's, a blanket around her shoulders, bandage on her forehead, feet rattling in too-big rubber boots. "Douglas sent me," she said, "I'm Alice." She handed me the basin and I put it on the ground, she pulled a bag from under her blanket, from it she took out a flat white lump, "Soap to wash with," a cloth with a bar of hard soap wrapped in it. I unrolled the cloth, shimmering white and plain, the soap was still in its package, the word IVORY printed on it. I held it up to my nose, the smell-less smell of it, chemical and vacant.

"Where did you find this?" I asked. There hadn't been bar soap in a long time.

Alice said, "We found a drugstore no one touched, got tons." Alice took a box from the bag, handed it to Bix. "Hard-tack," she said.

Bix opened the box. In it was a row of neat circular discs, hard biscuits like ones we made last year. "Where'd you get the wheat?" Everything Alice gave us was a miracle.

"We grew it in the garden. Didn't you?" Alice kept her eyes down. I nodded but she didn't see. Scavenge found wheat seed once, and we had crops, enough to make bannock and hardtack. Hardtack kept forever. Alice took a scarred plastic bottle of water from the bag, handed it to Bix. "There's a bucket in the corner for night waste." She turned to go.

"Thank you," Bix said.

Alice looked at us under ducked eyelids for a long time. Then she nodded and left us, shy as she'd come. I put the cloth and soap next to the basin. We ate, holding back enough for Father and Keller. Bix watched me wiping crumbs off my shirt. I was shivering and filthy. "Strip," Bix said to me, "let me wash your hair." I wanted Mother, but there was only Bix. Tomorrow we would be on the river, and I'd lose her, so I nodded, took off my shirt, my wet pants, stood in my underwear in the cold, my knee swollen with a purple bruise. The skin was unbroken. I moved my kneecap around, felt the bone. It was sound. The cuts on my hand were hot and red, but closing, no infection from touching the river, no spikes of red up from the wounds.

"Those OK?" Bix asked, and I nodded. "I wish we'd saved salve, or Jess's medicine box." She moved the basin to the floor in front of me and knelt next to it, cupped water in her hands. I leaned forward and she let it run over my scalp. She wet the bar soap with her hands, scrubbed the suds into my hair. The bubbles sat on my forehead. I felt them pop. She rinsed my hair with water, then twisted it like a rope so the water poured back into the basin, pinging into the soap bubbles. She wrapped Alice's cloth over my scalp and around my head. I washed my hands in the basin, scrubbed my cuts with soap. Bix washed her own hair next, then took the cloth from me and dried off. She stripped to her underwear, used the cloth to wash her armpits and between her legs, rinsed the cloth, held it up to me, shivering. I took it and washed like she had, armpits, between my legs, quickly, hiding my body from her.

She looked at my chest. "When did those start?"

"I don't know." I looked down at the swells around each nipple.

"Wait here." She handed me my shirt. I tucked it under my armpits, covering my chest, my arms naked in the cold room. She came back with a roll of fabric from her pack. She set the roll down. "Arms up." I took down my shirt, held it in one hand and raised my arms. She unrolled the fabric around my chest, binding me tight. It felt good to let her. "This'll help. They won't rub against your shirt."

"OK." She safety-pinned the fabric around my rib cage. She was close to me, the nearest she'd been since Mother. We were reversed magnets since Mother, no holding hands, no sitting at the fire with my head in her lap. She touched like Mother, her hand stroking my back. She twirled my hair in her fingers.

We dressed shivering in our dirty shirts, our pants on another cot to dry. "You're freezing, lie down." I curled with my face to the wall, little spoon. She was big spoon, pulled the blanket over us, untangled my hair, combing it out with her fingers. "Wish we could stay here," Bix whispered in my ear. I sank into the warm bath of her. Bix and Mother mixed up, became just fingers in my hair, breath on my neck.

25
OTHER MOTHERS

Mother found other mothers for us all along. Her own mother died young. In The World As It Is, she knew she would too. Medicine gave her the life she had. Without it, her illness would take her. She knew it. She put us in the way of women who would be there after.

She gave us Jess, her long black hair back in a bun, freckles over her nose, a mix of curt Korean love and Jewish fussing, her gravity and gaze, good questions and calm. Jess unlocked things for me and kept us all as well as she could. She held the medicine we did have.

She gave us Angel, skinny and hard-boned, knuckles like snail shells, hands always pulling books down from a shelf, knobby knees, arms ropy from her muscles. Her curly hair was like Mano's, her eyes like his, as if she were his mother, not his auntie. She read to me in the library while Bix and Mano did math or biology, her voice was a creaky purr in my ear, the words musical, and the smell of her warm. She was safe but never soft, brave, and clear, said what she thought. You went where she led.

The two of them remade the library into pharmacy, shelter, and classroom. The glass doors that led into the library from the rest of the museum opened on the reading room, where the public came before the floods, where pictures hung on the wall, where display cabinets were full, where people once read at the big reading tables we used for school. Behind the circulation desk was another door that led to both the stairwell to the roof and the hallway to the offices and conference rooms and the deep stacks shelter, most without windows, where the ceiling was low and dropping out. Jess made the conference room into the pharmacy. "My *apothecary,* my lady!" Jess said.

But the classroom was Angel's place, our place, and she only let the rest of the adults use it when it wasn't school time. She brought chairs and set them in a circle in a corner between the shelves so she could read to us there. The sentence she used most often was "Why is that so?" Every time we stated back a fact to her, a detail from the history of the country or the city or the world, a way a law was made in The World As It Was, that was the next thing she'd say, "And why is that so?" And we'd have to think, make connections over time and space, not about how something was, but the reasons for it, the *why.* "Who does it benefit?" she'd ask. Even things that seemed to me as natural as any choice— the collections and the way they were and who held them, the museum and the way we wrote everything down—she'd ask, "Why is that so? Why do we have that piece of pottery here and it isn't where it started its life? Why doesn't that object belong to the people in the village that made it? Why is that statue here?" She kept a copy of *Moby Dick* in the shelter with us, and in storms she would read it to us, to me, afraid of the dark but in love with the sea, since all that ocean made Bix more fearful still. When she started it, she said, "This is really funny. No one thinks it is funny. But it is hilarious."

"About dead whales?"

"There are dead whales. But the book makes sure you know why those men were there, and who was pushing them to be there, and everything people lose when they are pushed. We see what everyone loses, even the animals. And we see what it looks like when people make a family when they think they can't or shouldn't. It explains everything."

"Who benefits? And why is that so?" When I said that she kissed me on the forehead.

I loved to hear the chapter about Bulkington, always looking to sea on the deck of the *Pequod*. I loved the language in Angel's mouth.

Know ye now, Bulkington? Glimpses do ye seem to see of that mortally intolerable truth; that all deep, earnest thinking is but the intrepid effort of the soul to keep the open independence of her sea; while the wildest winds of heaven and earth conspire to cast her on the treacherous, slavish shore?

But as in landlessness alone resides the highest truth, shoreless, indefinite as God—so, better is it to perish in that howling infinite, than be ingloriously dashed upon the lee, even if that were safety! For worm-like, then, oh! who would craven crawl to land! Terrors of the terrible! is all this agony so vain? Take heart, take heart, O Bulkington! Bear thee grimly, demigod! Up from the spray of thy ocean-perishing—straight up, leaps thy apotheosis!

The first time the Mosquito Borne came through, it was like a wave. Angel had it the first time. She lay in bed with the fever, puking into a bucket, and you could hear her all night, apologizing to Keller, "I'm so sorry. I was stupid. I can't think what I did wrong."

"You didn't do anything wrong," he said, his voice low in their corner of the room. "It can come for anybody. You can't do everything right when the government abandons you."

"What government?" she asked.

Father and Sergio and Keller went out at night then, to find medicine. On the way, they passed people who died of it, blood coming from their noses, piled bodies outside of buildings, bodies dragged to the Park. They found medicine, but none of it worked. Keller sat by Angel, and she got better, and no one died inside Amen. "It didn't get you," Keller said to Angel.

"Not yet," Angel said.

"Not ever," said Keller.

Jess added the found medicine to her pharmacy, made an inventory by expiration date, medicines for Mother and some for other Amen people too, found in bulk in pharmacies and hospitals in the chaos and after, scavenged and hoarded and brought back. In the early days, sometimes Amen let strangers in, people with children, people traveling in vulnerable groups. Those people Jess helped with medicine she had or made. People with needs that she couldn't meet left to walk north, thinking maybe other parts of the city might have stashes of thyroid hormone or insulin, inhalers or EpiPens. She made sure they left Amen with a bundle of meds to last until they could get inland to an imagined hospital or to the National Guard.

There was an old safe she kept full of antibiotics. There was nothing more valuable than the antibiotics at Amen— for every improperly sterilized cut, every time someone had to go into the basement through sewer water, every infection or illness. When the Mosquito Borne came, we thought we could use antibiotics for that. But the Mosquito Borne didn't respond to anything, not antibiotics, not antivirals, not anything, not even anything in the old books that should have been locked away. It was then Amen stopped opening the doors. Too many in need. No idea what the mechanism of disease could be, or how to keep us safe. Jess had boxes and jars of things she foraged, things she grew. She made all the salves, organized and dried herbs, made tinctures and powders, used honey from Keller's hives, made creams from scavenged oils. Meds ran low and Jess piled books on herbal medicine in the pharmacy, open on tables. "We used to keep this one locked up," she told me one day, picking up an old book with a drawing of yarrow on the cover.

"Why?"

"This is all information stolen from Indigenous folks," she said. "Some botanist in the twentieth century went to where they lived and spoke to people until they stole all their knowledge, then published it and stuck it in a book and got paid to do it and to be an expert, and here it sits. Finally, white people listened to Indigenous folks and understood that only Indigenous folks should decide if people got to read it. So, we put books like this away unless there was permission."

"And now you stole it back again."

"That's right."

"Who does it benefit?"

"That's Angel's question?"

"Yup."

"Good."

26

THE MIGHTY SCRIPTORIUM

"Nonie, wake up," Bix said.

I opened my eyes to the cold chapel in the Cloisters, Bix leaning over me, Father standing by the lantern, behind him Keller stuffing his coat into his backpack.

"It's before dawn. We have to get going. They want us in the main hall," Father said.

I nodded, sat up, rubbed my face.

"Can't we stay?" said Bix, grabbing her jeans from the next cot.

"They won't be here much longer either."

The sun wasn't up. I couldn't feel the sleep at all. We made the beds, put on our pants and shoes and packs, and walked out with the lantern. Father led the way back, the water echoing again, into the room with the long tables, the notepads and stove, the sleeping people gone from the floor. Douglas was writing, on his table a jug of water, a stack of yellow notepads, a knife, a wrinkled map, a pen with a metal nib, a jar of ink. Alice next to him, as shy of us as before. A few people worked nearby, stacking notepads into plastic bags.

"They're here," Alice said. It was dim in the room.

Douglas took a long moment looking at us from his pool of light. "Before you leave, do you have everything you need?"

"Yes," said Father. "We do."

Douglas nodded. "Alice has food for you. She has put it in bags by your boat. She has also organized a bit of fresh water for you to take, a funnel to collect rainwater. I'm not sure how long the food will last, but it is the best we can do under the circumstances."

"Sure," said Father. "Thank you."

Alice said to Douglas, "Should we show them?"

"Yes, I think we should," he said.

Douglas picked up the yellow pad he'd been working on and flipped through it, looking at the pages covered with writing. "You saw these, of course. We try to get the stories of the people who pass through here. We'd have gotten yours if there had been time. I'm more than certain that you have interesting ones. Amen must have been interesting."

"It was," Father said. "We kept records, too."

"We kept a Logbook," I piped up, my voice thin in the stone room.

"Of course you did," said Douglas. "You were natural history, yes?"

"Yes. We tried to keep working."

"Of course you did. And we're a scriptorium."

"A scriptorium?" I asked.

"In monasteries," Douglas said, "in the Dark Ages, monks were the only people left who knew how to write. And they copied down everything from the time that came before. The Roman philosophers, mathematics, poetry, the Bible, the theater. They copied it all down in long rooms like this one, where monks sat in rows and made books so all of it wouldn't be lost. 'Scriptorium,' from the Latin word for writing."

"What will you do with it all?" Father asked.

"We're not sure. We must find a way to carry them out. A boat first? A new patch of dry land we can call our own? We know all about what is south of here. We know not to go that way. We know not a single thing about what awaits if we go north."

"Or west?"

"Or west."

"It's a lot to carry."

"It is a lot to carry. To be sure. But we have something we can't take with us."

"Can I show them?" Alice asked.

Douglas nodded and Alice put down her papers, walked to the nearest wall, moved her hand over a switch, and the darkness broke into a thousand glaring shards. Light—electric light—flooded the room. I hadn't seen electric light since The World As It Was. When I was born, Old City was dark with rolling blackouts. Electric came and went and finally there wasn't any, not anywhere. I blinked in the harshness of it, and in the wonder. Bix remembered using switches, remembered the electric, and she tipped her face to the lights with a flash of joy on her face, every memory of her childhood across her features—the record player, a working refrigerator—things she remembered well, and I hadn't. She looked at her hands in the light, at Father's face. If shadows gave her mystery, lights gave her back the things the floods took. They gave her The World As It Was.

"Generators?" Keller asked.

"Our crew found them."

"We had a generator at the beginning. But then, no fuel," Keller said.

"We have had them a long time. We repair them. We scavenged diesel at first, then we cooked diesel from vegetable oil. I wish we could have had more generators. I wish we could have been more. I wish we could have been a hospital. We barely had enough antibiotics to keep alive."

"We lost all our children," Alice said softly, like she had ghosts around her. "With the light at least we can work, so there's some record."

"We are a lighthouse." Douglas swept his hand around to the room, the notepads and paper and people, the tables and the pens. "Without a lighthouse the world gets lost awfully fast."

Bix stood with her head tilted up to the light, radiating, basking. The dawn coming up outside the windows matched her. I loved the light. It birthed a shot of power from my spine to my heart, powerful as lighted windows seen from the cold canoe, powerful as water, which was neither good nor bad. Power was only power. There was power in that room, in those piles of notebooks, in the Logbook in my pack, in the *Sally Ride* somewhere.

If there was light here, there could be light in other places. If there was power in me, I could spread it. I could let that power glow and make myself a beacon.

III

THE WAY IT FEELS WHEN RAIN BECOMES AIR

<u>The Way It Feels When Rain Becomes Air:</u> Keller told me that "nor'easter" isn't a real weather word, and that at some point, there were so many storms that you could hardly call anything nor'easters anymore. Big storms just came up along the east coast, along the Atlantic, even if it wasn't winter. In The World As It Was that was all we needed to know.

—From the Water Logbook

27
HOW TO MARK TIME

For all the years of the earth, scientists name categories of time—*eras, periods, epochs*. The *periods* are *Cambrian, Ordovician, Silurian, Devonian, Mississippian, Pennsylvanian, Permian, Triassic, Jurassic, Cretaceous, Tertiary, Quaternary,* and I learned a mnemonic to remember: *Cold Oysters Seldom Develop Many Precious Pearls, Their Juices Congeal Too Quickly.* I can mark time in *periods*. The ones so far, I gave the names of weather from the Water Logbook.

There was *the Monster in the Water,* when the chaos came, and we made home out of Amen and out of each other. It was big storms and the first time the Mosquito Borne came, when the present dawned on us so solid that we began to mourn.

Then there was the time of *the Risen Sea Around Us,* the daily abandonment of expectations. There was a rising ocean and the empty city, but we had work and purpose and even joy. That lasted years and years.

The Way It Feels When Rain Becomes Air started on a day in April when Mano died. Him going opened a box of evil and ghosts, a run of losses that knocked the wind out of us, until we were saturated with rain and sadness. Mano's death was a broken case letting in rot.

The sadness made *Clouds Meant for Walking On.* The Mosquito Borne came back different. We lost Angel. There was a cascade of bigger storms. We drew into ourselves. We were in the sky and nothing of us touched the ground because the ground wasn't real anymore.

In the last period, *Light Rain You Can Open Up and Drink,* all we stayed for was Mother. She slept and changed and faded. She poured herself into us. But her light went out, and we became untethered. All it took was the storm to knock us free.

28
THE PALISADES

I t was three days before the river tried to kill us. The memories run together in watery quiet, the boat a ghost drifting into the wilderness. The canoe was our skin, a body we shared, we four set inside it like muscles working together: Keller at the bow, Father anchoring, Bix bailing, me watching for snags.

That first morning, the Hudson was all mist. "Is this water salt or fresh?" I asked.

"We're still in salt water for sure," Keller said. "The Indigenous folks around here call it Mahicantuck, which is supposed to translate to something like 'always moving water,' or 'the river that flows two ways.'"

I thought the north was only woods and fields. But the north beyond the Cloisters was not that. The towers of Old City faded and there were towns at the Hudson's edge, not empty forests—ruined and tentative, peeling roof shingles, beaten plastic signs, vinyl siding breaking off the walls of the wasted houses. We passed towns flattened by the storm, or flattened a long time before, growing over with vines, burned to the ground. The shores were thick in floating plastic and garbage, traffic lights tense above the water, the top of a lamppost sticking up, on it a ragged heron scanning the river for fish that were gone. Two smokestacks stood in the water. Rotting cement exposed their vertebrae of metal supports. They loomed over a submerged roof like the necks of the *Elasmosaurus* skeleton in the Hall of Vertebrate Origins.

"What's that?" I asked Father as we passed.

"Power station," he said.

"That made electric?"

"Yeah. It made electric out of coal."

The smokestacks made me think of Douglas standing in his bright room.

When you are stuck, you start to want things, even if you never had them—an ache for sugar or strawberries when you hardly remember the taste. You're flat, a stretch of calm ocean, but the wanting is below you, deep as the Mariana Trench. Mother worried about our wanting. People didn't make it who wanted too much. If you stopped wanting altogether, if hope left your breathing, you didn't make it either. Bix was naked in her wanting, so that it was like a skin over her skin. I hid mine.

I'd overheard Mother say, "We were all so greedy," about The World As It Was. I thought she meant me, under the whale, wanting mothering, wanting swimming, wanting the ocean, wanting the life I hoped for. I worried that wanting, and even hope, was greed in another shape. I stumbled on the blind edge of that wanting, that hope, when the lights came on in the Cloisters. Electric made experiments possible, made hospitals run, kept ships alive, made me think I could save water the way Douglas saved stories, Keller saved insects, Father and Mother saved the collections and us.

But maybe it was greed. Greed could shutter a person. I'd seen it when Sean stopped eating after Jim died from the Mosquito Borne, when he stopped working, and when he disappeared, only to turn up dead on the grass the next morning. In the library, during a history lesson to go with *Moby Dick,* Angel read to us about when the world ran its greed on whale oil, showed us pictures of men standing in heaps of whale flesh on a boat deck, sheets of fat half hanging into huge boiling pots to make oil to make lamps. The men looked certain of everything. Douglas looked that way, greedy of his light and his notebooks, of his building and systems.

But greed like that didn't start out bad. What alters wanting is what's behind it. Greed and hope aren't opposites. Greed and hope are twins grabbing for the same thing, one in fear and one in faith.

"Why is that so?" I asked myself in a whisper on the river, looking at the crumbling power plant. "Who benefits?"

"Did Douglas say what there is up north?" Bix asked.

"No. Everybody that came to the Cloisters was going away from the city; after they left the Cloisters, they never heard from them again."

"Maybe they all died," Bix said. She was lost again, but she was talking.

"Maybe. Or maybe they got safe and stayed put," Father said.

We got six hours on the first tide that morning. The tide turned at noon. When we felt it begin to pull us south, Father and Keller paddled through a wash of wreckage on the river's edge: bins and siding, upended plastic tubs, pill bottles, food containers, dead squirrels, a wall against the shore, froth and muck filling the gaps. We beached the canoe and sat in the burned-over grass eating Cloisters hardtack. "Should we make a lean-to?" Father asked Keller when we were done. "Sleep through the tide?"

"Maybe tonight," Keller said, "too much work in the middle of the day."

Keller and Bix and I slept under jackets in the daylight on the hard ground and Father kept watch. I woke in the dusk with stiff blades of grass in my hair. Father sat next to me with his first aid kit, looking at my cuts.

"What time is it?"

"Sunset."

I looked down at my hand. "Do they look OK?"

"They look fine. Not red, not hot. How are you keeping them out of the water?"

I shrugged. "I'm careful."

Father kissed the top of my head. "I know you are. You're so careful. How's the knee?"

I sat up, shrugged off my coat, moved my knee around, jeans covering the bruise. He couldn't see it. It hurt less. "Fine."

"OK." He reached out, took my hand. He scanned the distant woods, the Palisades on the other side of the river. The setting sun gave the last few leaves some gold. A single doe and fawn came out of the forest that bordered the field. The doe saw us, hesitated, turned slowly, stepped back into the woods with the fawn. "Wish I had a bow," Father said, and broke the spell and let go of my hand and went to wake Keller and Bix.

I tried to see the deer. I was glad they left, even if we needed meat. We were in their field. Keller came and sat next to me. We looked at the river. A wall of wave rolled up its surface. "What's that?" I asked him.

"Tidal bore, I think," Keller said, "comes with the tide on some rivers, a mini tsunami. I saw one in Malaysia, on the Batang Lupar. They call it a *benak*." We watched the water. "Sarawak," he said, rolling consonants in his mouth. "That river probably doesn't even exist anymore." He got up and walked to the boat. Bix woke and the four of us launched without a look back at our first camp.

In the sunset, clouds over the Palisades turned orange and purple and stacked up high. The river was perfectly still. I stared into it, watched the light change the water so that it became the sky. The paddles were soft; the ripples from Keller's strokes stirred the clouds. For the first time the river was mine, as if nothing was broken at all. The dark slid down, and the stars came out below me.

At midnight the tide shifted. "We'll have to get out on the Palisades side," Father said, "we're too far to the west."

We found a rocky shore and we climbed up the Palisade cliffs in the dark, Father and Keller carrying the canoe between them through woods. We stumbled over rocks, blind and scraped, to a stand of pines with flat ground beneath. While Father and Keller settled the boat, I stepped to the edge of the trees to see how far the ridge went. The Hudson filled every low place I could see from that vantage point, even to the west. In the woods, the leaves shivered. "Are we on an island?" I called back to them.

"Seems like it," Father called back.

Bix unpacked the boat and found the hardtack. Keller gathered sticks.

"Can we have a fire?" Bix asked.

"No," said Keller, "we can't risk it. These are for a lean-to."

I sat on a patch of bare dirt, then lay down and dragged my jacket over me, too tired to eat, pulled a patched emergency blanket from the bottom of my pack and spread it over my legs. There were so many stars. Keller laid down a pile of his sticks, began building a shelter over me. Father joined him, adding branches. "Father?" Bix asked between bites of hardtack. "Those bodies? Under the water, back in the city, that wall? Did someone build that?"

"No, Bix. That was the storm. People don't do things like that. We're all trying to get out of the way."

"Even the Lost?"

"The Lost are just people like us," said Father.

29
THE HALL OF BIRDS OF THE WORLD

Mano was never really Lost. He hadn't been in San Juan when all the buildings were swallowed by Hurricane Franklin. He wasn't there when the big melt came and Thwaites Glacier fell and there wasn't a Puerto Rico, only the tops of mountains in the ocean. Before all of that, Mano's mother gave him the only plane ticket she could get leaving the island, sent him north to her sister Angel. She stayed back to find another ticket, but never did. He landed at JFK before they closed it, and Angel went on the bus and took him back to Washington Heights to Keller. They watched on the TV in the downstairs neighbor's house while San Juan broadcast until it winked out. Then Mano was theirs.

He was eight when Angel and Keller came to Amen. Mano was eight and Bix was eight and I was younger. We were together in rooms of bones, surrounded by dinosaurs wrapped in burlap and paper tags and thick plastic, long articles describing them sealed in ziplock bags duct-taped to the outside. We played hide-and-seek. Bix held hands with Mano. When he was twelve and she was twelve, he kissed her. He liked the way Bix sought out the shadows in the rooms of Amen. He liked her bravery. He didn't mind that she was hard to predict, contradictory. It didn't surprise him that she was fearless and also terrified. Nothing about her seemed to surprise him. I was their satellite then, the older they got the closer their orbit, the farther I was outside them. He would tell her something and she'd laugh, remember it. She watched him all the time, brought him things to draw, found places for him that shone and were new, trinkets, as if she were a crow coming back with shiny objects. She found cases of untouched items, her lantern light on them. Mano brought his sketchbook.

A few months before the dogs, we went into the Hall of Birds of the World. Taxidermy was hard to keep from the wetness of The World As It Is, and no one left at Amen was an ornithologist. Angel liked the birds, going after lessons to take a bird out of a case, and slowly take it from the taxidermy frame, unstitching the careful work of the taxidermist, removing the bird skin from the form that made it look like a bird, then laying it flat in a plastic box with other bird skins and mothballs. "There," Angel said to the bird as she packed it away, "now we have your DNA!"

In the Hall of Birds of the World with Bix and me, Mano had his notebook in one hand and his pencil in another. I knew he kept a pocketknife Father had given him to sharpen the point of his pencil. "Move your lantern higher, Bix, I want to see the crest on that bird of paradise," he said.

"Where?" Bix asked, then followed his gaze to the superb bird of paradise. The light turned the feathers into iridescent beacons in the dark.

"Can you hold it there while I draw?" he asked her.

"Fussy," she teased him, "it won't be perfect."

"Not if you keep dropping the light before I've got it!"

She looked at him while he sharpened the pencil, his hands so careful, and the slowness of his gestures and the kindness of her look made a circle around them, held by the sound of the knife scraping the wood, the little hum of the lantern.

"I have an animal in mind," I said, wanting to be part of the circle, thinking they would be sure to guess the superb bird of paradise that he was sketching, the glossy black feathers, the bright blue eye shapes on the fan the males unfurled to catch the females.

"Nonie, only Keller plays that game with you," Bix said, and turned back to Mano.

Mano reached out and held my hand. "It's the bird, isn't it?" Mano was kind all the time, even when he was tired. Bix wasn't kind when she was tired. Bix was cross, short with me, short with Mano too. But, Mano, never. "Why do you like that game so much?"

"I don't know."

"You do, though. You just don't like to say," Mano said.

Bix was watching me, looking at how Mano talked to me, as if it never occurred to her to ask. I was quiet, then said, "I like it because I don't want to talk about anything."

"You don't want to talk about anything?"

"No. I want to work and to sleep and to look at the sky."

"And you want to go out to sea?"

"Yes. I want to go out to sea. And I want to have a job to do."

"Right, of course you do." Mano squeezed my hand.

"Do you ever think about what happens if that never happens?" I was quiet.

"All the time." Mano looked at me very solemnly, then up at Bix. Bix smiled at him, an older sister smiling at someone seeing me in a way she did. They were together in watching me ask something important, something grown-up, and the circle they made extended open just enough for Mano to invite me into what he said, as if he'd been waiting for someone to ask him that question for a long time. "I think about that all the time. Every day."

"I don't," I told him. "Because if I start, I can't stop. And if I start, then maybe it will come true. And I'll have invited it. I trick that thought to leave me alone with the game. And Keller lets me play. No one else does."

"No one else is as good at it."

"You could get to be."

"Maybe." He thought for a while. "Does remembering all this, all these animals, help you keep the worry away?"

I nodded. Mano nodded back.

"Ah!" A big grin spread across his face. "That's why I draw!" He started making the lines of the bird of paradise.

30
THE WOLVES

The sound of wolves in the distance woke me. It was dawn. Under the lean-to, pale sky showed between the sticks above my head where a poncho flapped free, Father and Bix asleep beside me. I gauged the distance to the wolves from their sound. They were with us on the ridge, trapped on our Palisades island. Their voices echoed off the forest, not off the water. I counted the minutes between, like counting between lightning and thunder. *Canis lupus lupus.* They didn't scare me like dogs—house creatures gone crazy in the empty streets. Wolves were meant for a forest. They didn't want humans. They wanted deer. I didn't want them close, but I didn't want them gone.

I propped myself up on my elbows and saw Keller sitting outside the lean-to, looking over the Hudson, slicing an apple with a knife I'd never seen. "Morning, little warrior," Keller said quietly. I sat up, grabbed my jacket, crawled out, sat next to him. Father and Bix didn't wake.

He held out an apple from the food bag Alice gave us, and I took it.

"Shouldn't we be getting ready to go?" I turned to Keller, took a bite.

"We shouldn't stay anywhere too long, but we can let them sleep."

"Where'd you get that knife?"

"Alice Winslow gave it to me." He smiled.

"You didn't sleep," I said, taking my mind off the wolves.

"No. I watched." He tilted his head at me, studied my face. "The wolves are heading toward sleep now, you know

that, right? Once the sun comes up, they'll be settled." I
nodded. "They're sheltering in place. *Shelter in place.*" Keller
thought for a while. "They were always telling us to do that,
like this weird tic, not admitting we needed to get out. Drives
me nuts thinking about it now." He was quiet for a while,
ate a slice of apple. "Before Amen, Angel was pregnant, and
sheltering seemed smart, seemed like the only thing to do." I
didn't know Angel had been pregnant. "The National Guard
left, and we ran out of food. Then a big storm came, and I
thought we'd be safer in the museum, maybe wait out the
worst until the baby came. On our way to Amen, Angel fell,
and Mano and I had to walk her about thirty blocks, limping." He rubbed his hand over his eyes. "And when we got
there, she was losing the baby." I stared at Keller. I had never
heard this story. "I had keys, you know, like your mom did.
So, we got in, and Sergio was doing a patrol and found us.
He knew me, we used to talk bugs when he was doing his
job. Thank god it was him doing the patrols. He told me,
years later, that walking into Amen at night was like diving
in cenotes in Mexico. Cave diving. He'd go into the cave
with a string tied onto his wet suit so he could find his way
out again. It was so dark in Amen once the electric went,
before the lanterns." Keller stopped and took another bite
of the apple. "He took us to the library where you all were
locked in the stacks for the night, Allan and Deirdre and you
kids, Rick, Jess and Beaumont, Jenny Perkins. It was dark
as hell and only Sergio had a flashlight. Angel was so sick.
Your mom took care of her, and Allan took care of Mano and
me. You kids didn't wake up. By the morning we lost the
baby but not Angel." His voice lost its steady. "I didn't think
anything could be that bad. I'm not going to let anything get
that bad again."

I finished my apple. I sat there while he was quiet, then

took out the seeds, put them in my pocket and threw the core into the forest. He cut a piece from the apple and ate it. He wiped the knife on his pants, then folded it and put it in his pocket. The wolves called again. There was a lot I didn't know about Keller. I took his hand.

He stood up. "Don't forget to drink some water. When was the last time you peed?"

"Yesterday." I'd been waiting, worried where we'd get water when the fresh ran out.

"Drink now." Keller walked away. "Don't hurt yourself with thirst."

I found the water next to the bag Alice packed. In the bag there was goat jerky, dried broth cubes, a hunk of cheese, hardtack, apples and carrots, a clean pot for boiling water, a funnel to collect rain, enough food for a week, ten days. I took a plastic jug she'd given us and tipped it to my mouth.

Bix woke screaming, her voice a needle in the morning air. I choked, looked back to the lean-to, Father bolt upright next to her. "Bix!" he yelled at her. She opened her eyes and looked right at him, panting, before recognition hit and she collapsed sobbing into his chest.

"She's OK," Father called.

"I know," I said, brushing water off my shirt. All that time on the river was bringing back her nightmares.

"Let's keep moving," Father said, brushing her hair and looking at Keller. Father pulled his cap out of his back pocket and put it on. Bix wiped her face and pulled her hood up and stumbled out of the lean-to to pack the boat. Father followed. Keller knocked the structure down behind them, so no one knew we had been there.

31
MANO

The memory of Mano comes to me when I'm afraid. That's how I hold back the dark. When the danger is bad, like in the ruin, I remember what it was to talk with him. It wasn't always wonders that Bix found in the dark. She took risks. The day that she and Mano turned sixteen, Father told us we could hunt the Park alone. Mano had a bow. He was good with it. Bix and I had forgotten our bows on the roof. Sometimes parties went out with only one bow. "Bix and Mano are in charge. Don't go too far, you three," he said.

They walked next to each other, steps in synch. Sometimes they held hands. Mano let Bix lead where she wanted, like Father did. Bix walked toward piles of downed trees, tunnels of overgrown lilac bushes, over the frost-heaved sidewalks. She pried loose the rusting park signs for scrap, flushed raccoons and squirrels. I hung back, found things in the mud. She led us farther and farther from the garden, past where we were allowed, where we could be heard if there was trouble. "Father won't know," she said. She took us to Turtle Pond to find frogs for dinner, catch them in our windbreakers. Mano looked for squirrels. We scrambled over a downed London plane tree. Then we heard the dog pack.

I froze and Mano froze, listening so we could tell which way they were headed. They were coming our way. Mano raised his bow, looked at me. I shrugged. I didn't even have a knife. Bix turned to look at us both. "Run," she whispered, but her own body bent toward the sound, as if she thought she could fix it by knowing the size and shape of the danger.

I turned to run. "Bix! Come on!" There was a tall plane tree behind me, and I ran to it. I looked back over my shoulder and then I saw the dog pack coming toward them—too fast, too many. Mano turned to follow me, but then he saw Bix wasn't with him.

She stepped away from Mano, toward the dogs. He followed her instead, reaching to pull her back as she was pulled, magnet-like, toward the thing that could kill her.

I started climbing the tree. "Bix! Mano! Get up here!"

Bix's head whipped around. I could see Mano say something to her, something I couldn't hear, and then she seemed to shake out of a trance, look at the dogs and finally see them, then turn and take off running to my tree.

"Mano!" she screamed as she ran.

Mano stood still, looked back to her, didn't run. Then he turned, aimed his bow, and held his shot tight on the pack in case it went for Bix. The lead dog ran for her, passed Mano as it sprinted after Bix, he turned and shot it. He tried to get another arrow set. A second dog jumped at Mano as he notched that arrow. His shot missed. Mano was caught by the dog, and I could hear him screaming, the pack arriving, the sound of it.

Bix gripped the tree and climbed the trunk, straddled the first low branch, screaming, trying to pull sticks off to throw at the dogs. The lead dog stood at the foot of our tree, barking and barking, treeing us. Then I held my face to the tree so I wouldn't see Mano, the other dogs, and climbed higher. "Bix," I wailed, "get up here! Higher!"

"Mano!" Bix screamed, over and over, until it was done, and we didn't hear the pack anymore, or Mano screaming or anything, until the dogs were gone, and she kept looking, staring at where they had been, the blood.

We stayed in the tree until dark started coming and we

could hear Keller's and Sergio's voices filter through the trees with the sunset, desperate, calling all our names. Bix climbed down and walked toward them with dead eyes. I climbed down and stood at the spot at the foot of the tree and found Mano and it wasn't Mano anymore, most of him gone with the dogs, back to where they denned up. On what was left of him I could smell the dogs, their dirty coats, their spit, his blood. I've never been able to smell dogs again without fear.

32

MAPLE DEATH

O n the river we came to a bridge. "We have to get to the center," Father said, "where we can portage." It was almost underwater, but in the middle the cables made a V. Awkwardly, we got the boat to it, then onto the roadbed, which was lightly underwater, carried the canoe over, then launched again. Hills gathered up and marched away, forests thickened, broken by storm gashes, bald in places with dead trees. Where the trees were living, the leaves were thick, waxy brown and orange, scorched by summer heat. The weather flattened. The sky turned a hot white. We covered our heads, drank water, rested when the tide went south, got on the river at sunset. We didn't see towns or any other person. We stopped before midnight and walked shakily through the dark into the hills on the west side of the river. Father and Keller portaging the canoe, we stumbled into a dead forest, had a meal, sitting together in a circle without a fire. Around us the trees were tilted and gone, an interrupted thought, bark peeling, deadfalls everywhere like a skeleton arbor.

"Why are the trees like this?" I asked Father.

"The trees? Maple Death. It got too warm for them. This must've been a sugarbush once. You remember that taste, Bix, maple syrup?"

"Yup," she said, then went back to staring at the hardtack in her hand.

"We had some maple syrup before we left Tenth Street. I was sad to run out of that. Grandma Ida used to sugar at the farm in Tyringham, before you were born, before their grove died. They had a boiling pan in the clearing, and they'd boil the sap down right outside since there was no sugarhouse."

"What was the taste like?" I asked.

"Sweet, but something else, too, like you could taste the tree in it."

I sat with the taste of *never* in my mouth. Through the open branches of the forest, I saw across the water to a flooded power station, two giant domes of what Father said was a nuclear plant. Near it was a town. I thought I saw the flicker of lantern in a building. Then it was gone.

"Where is it?" Keller asked, surprising me, as if he'd seen the light, too. "The farm, Deirdre's farm in Tyringham? Where is it, exactly? You said it's in the Berkshires?"

"Yeah, east of the river. I think we can stick to the water as far as Hudson." Father ate his apple like an animal might, not stopping for the core, right down through the seeds. "The town of Hudson, I mean. That was the train station we used to visit Deirdre's parents at the farm. We have to go east from there. There's a bridge at Hudson, the Rip Van Winkle. We have to be on the east side of the river, so we won't take that one. But that bridge is for a state road that could take us to the Taconic Parkway, then the Mass Pike. All of that's highways, on foot. We take the Pike to Lee and then walk up into the hills to Tyringham. The farm's on Fernside Road, south from the Pike, up this big ridge, that's Fernside. I've done that drive from the train station a hundred times. The farm is right on top of the ridge, a white house on the high side of the road, a big white porch, a bunch of barn buildings on the other side of the road. I'd be able to find it in my sleep. Easy." His voice was warm. I memorized everything Father said. The places he named sounded imaginary; still I clung to them.

"Oh, yeah," Keller had the first grin I'd seen in a few days, "easy as pie. You should draw me a map." He laughed.

"Sure. As soon as you find me a pen." Father laughed too.

"I'll take that dare," Keller said. He reached into his pack and took out his notebook and the pen that wrote upside down. "Draw."

"OK, OK. Got it. In case I get river madness, you'll have a map."

"Look. Nostalgia can carry you through, fine. But you know better than anyone that it's the redundancies that save you." Father laughed and took the notebook.

The next morning there was early heat. Bix was awake, looking at the boat, checking the seams with her fingers, dull-eyed, fearful, obsessive. We got a late start. The morning was still. We came to a bridge at midday, just under the river's surface. We had to stand on the bridge railings to portage over the submerged structure, drag the canoe full of all the gear over it. The heat pressed me down like I was under a pile of rocks. We sweated through the work, hovering over the ugly water. We stopped early, before the tide changed, exhausted. Father and Keller carried the boat to the shade, I lay next to it, but I gave up trying to sleep. Bix knelt by the boat, the gear dumped out, checking the caulk, inventorying food. She counted, counted again. Father watched her from the shade.

I went to sit with Keller. He looked across the river to a city made of pale stone, a rotting cathedral tower at its center. "What is that?" I nodded at the city.

"I think that's West Point, the military training school." Worry in Keller's voice. "If I wanted a fortress, that's where I'd go."

I could hear Father get up. He sat on the other side of me. "If that's West Point," Father said, "World's End is up there—people used to wreck their ships trying to make that turn."

I looked up the Hudson; there was a curve past the city, an illusion that the river stopped at a tall hill at the bend.

"Looks OK," Keller said.

"Yeah, maybe it is." Father studied the river. "At least it's calm."

The river had turned strange, placid to the point of seeming motionless. But something in the air had changed. The nerve endings in my body woke up all the way, my barometer, Jess would say, the mercury in me moving to the changing air pressure. I could feel it drop fast, like there was a front coming up from the ocean to the south, pushing a wall of silent, heavy air, behind that wall, a storm. I felt water gathering into clouds. In my skin a dozen sirens sounded. I looked around for birds—they went to ground before a storm. I couldn't see any. I turned to look at Father. "Storm's coming."

"How bad?"

"Big and fast."

Keller looked at me. "Will it be like the one that got Amen?"

"Doesn't feel like that. Maybe a nor'easter?"

Father ran a hand over his face, looked at Bix, then out at the river and the cloudless sky. "OK, Nonie. Let's look for shelter."

"Where?" I asked.

"Anywhere but West Point," Keller said.

33
MAGICAL THINKING

"What do you think it is like out there?" I asked Jess. It was sunset, and we were standing on the edge of the Amen roof and looking out over the view to the towers to the west. It was hot and we were moving the water from the rain collectors into jugs. Jess walked away from me, came back with a milk crate, four empty jugs inside.

"On the ocean?" she asked.

"On the ocean."

"On the *Sally Ride*? The research ship?"

"The ship, the fleet. Do you think the fleet is still out there?"

"I think so," she said. "I mean, I hope so. I had friends out there. They signed on for a long-term mission, you know."

"Mother said that, too. You didn't want to go?"

"I met Beaumont. Hard to go out long-term unless you were both in the same work."

"And he was in computers."

"Yeah, and not the right kind."

"What if the storms got them?"

"Well, that could've happened. And if we really do get hypercanes one day, it might." Jess modeled that question in The World As It Was, the idea that hurricanes could turn into hypercanes, monsters in the water. "But they were careful when they built those ships, they made them extra sturdy and ballasted, and huge, like cities."

"I hope they're still out there."

"Me too."

"I hope I find them."

"Me too."

"Can I have another lesson?"

She filled up the last jug. "Before we distribute these?"

"Yeah. Before. Before the light goes."

"OK. What was the last one?"

"Dead reckoning."

"And you feel like you get that one?"

"I do."

"That lesson was hard to do up here. It is way easier if you have a map, and if you are moving over a big distance. Like if we did that one again, but in the Park, it would be better. It is better walking, or in a car, you know. It would be *best* if we had a boat."

"I know."

"And what are the three pillars?"

"*Heading, speed,* and *time.*"

"Right, OK. Good. Next clear night we'll do some celestial navigation, OK, and I'll show you the sextant? But that one's useless unless you're on the water."

"Right. And the *Sally Ride* would have instruments."

"That's called GPS, and I can't teach you that. Not anymore."

"No screens."

"No screens."

"But at least I can teach you the sextant, in case you are ever on the water with one."

"OK."

"That's navigation stuff, basics. But weather stuff ends up on ships, too. Want to know how to use the barometer? Because Deirdre always told me you were like a human barometer. So that one should stick."

"It'll stick."

"And where do I keep the old barometer?"

"In your shelter. In the box with the other tools." Jess took all the weather tools she could find and used them gently and with reverence. She couldn't help herself, like a magpie.

"And where do they belong if we put them back some-day?" she asked.

"In the library archives. Except for the sextant from the cases by the planetarium."

"Where we don't go because of the break-ins, right? OK, run and get it."

In the early days of Amen, people weighed all the op-tions for storage. Pottery and textiles were hauled up to the top floors, stacked along in rows. The big bones that hadn't already been moved to storage in Jersey were stored on the higher floors. Some halls were empty but for the skeletons of rusty armatures and placards where the animals had been. Some tools were relocated and used—microscopes, collec-tion jars, prep solutions.

Inside the shelter she shared with Beaumont, there were piles of under-repair textiles from the collections, notebooks, a case where she kept salves and tinctures, piles of books she'd borrowed from the library. I found the barometer in the box.

"This is a Torricellian barometer, Nonie," she said when I came back with it, "and I'll start with this because you can always make one like it with an old plastic cup. I'll show you how another day." She led me through the reading, made sense of the way the mercury could move. The mercury in it was steady, because the weather was steady. "What you feel in your body when the weather changes," she said, "it's like this, like the air pressure changing displaces things inside you. In another thousand years we might figure out how all kinds of senses and perceptions in humans work, scientifically speaking. But for now, we have to accept the mystery of what you can do."

She handed me back the instrument, and the globs of floating mercury shimmered as the sun set, tiny planets in space. I liked the feel of the barometer in my hands. It was heavy and solid, compact for use on a boat. The liquid in the instrument turned orange with the sky. "This is so pretty."

"I'll teach you the aneroid barometer, too. But I like this one. I like that all the parts for it were around for a student of Galileo to make it in 1643. No point in us giving up on our tools, Nonie," Jess said. "They worked once. Now we need them back again."

If the people on the *Sally Ride* were saving the water like we saved the collections—keeping the records, making the observations—then they'd look like Amen. They'd be people from everywhere: African scholars, Danish professors, curators with grandparents from Japan. I could picture the boats better if I thought of the people, the tools. "And if I were on the *Sally Ride,* this would help."

"This will help. And so will what you can do without it."

It took Father a long time to see me. Maybe it was that children were invisible for a while, after Old City started falling. Maybe it was that the adults didn't see us except as something vulnerable or dangerous. Or maybe we made them confused, in a fog of panic like a mother coyote if you get between her and her cubs. Mother didn't take any time at all. When I told Mother bad weather was coming, she stopped anything she was doing, squatted down to my height and listened hard, then told everyone else what was coming. "Nonie knows," she always said.

Father called any predictions "magical thinking," didn't trust them unless they were backed with evidence, like what

Jess could do. What I could do he didn't want. One day when we were leaving to harvest the garden, I told him a squall was coming. He went to the garden anyway, we all did, but then we were all caught in a downdraft of hail, hiding under park benches, running for shelter. Rick got his arm broken by a falling tree, and half the harvest was ruined. Then Father listened.

34
WORLD'S END

We passed West Point before the storm. "You never know who is camped out there," Keller said, "waiting. If they have ammo from that arsenal, we'd be dead before we hid the boat."

We rounded World's End's tricky currents. One moment, we were pointing at what looked like a hill that was the terminus of the river entirely. The next, we could see the river turning left, as big and powerful as it had been. The current asked you to keep going straight forward, preferring that you crash into the trees. Keller and Father pushed hard to make the turn with the water. We moved past the insistent pull of the current. I could hear their strokes change, tension ease. We passed a half-submerged village. "No towns," Father said as we went by.

"Why not?" Keller asked. "That town's abandoned. We have to find a roof."

"If we're not going to West Point, we're not going to the town nearest West Point."

There was a wave of feeling between them like on Ninety-Third Street. I saw Keller try to shake it off, then he called back to me, "I have an animal in mind."

"All right." I was scanning the hills around us, looking for a place with a roof. I wasn't thinking of animals.

"And this animal in mind is an insect."

"No surprise."

"Hey, I've got a few things on my mind!"

"Fair," I said. I could feel the storm building. It felt like panic.

"They predict the weather. They swarm when the weather is warm. They try to get into houses and structures when it gets cold outside. Little dots on their backs. There is a kid's rhyme about them. About houses on fire. 'Fly away home.'"

"Ladybug, ladybug, fly away home . . ." I said.

". . . Your house is on fire, your children are gone," finished Bix.

Night was coming, the hills on either side were very tall.

"That's Storm King Mountain, I think," said Father.

"Can't we wait in the woods, in the trees?" I asked.

"We can't be exposed like that," Father said. I'd seen the Park during windstorms, dying trees could be as dangerous as lightning. Being on the river was the worst place, worse than a bad shelter, worse than a forest. The sky shut down under a black wall of clouds. I'd never seen a storm without the city for balance. It was a naked feeling—the big sky, the waves tearing at the bottom of the boat, the wind making the zippers on my pack click like chattering teeth, and nowhere to go.

35
THE RUIN

The rain began, heavy and warm. Bix scrambled to cover food bags, to pull on her waterproof jacket, to bail the boat. I grabbed Alice Winslow's cooking pot, turned it to the sky to catch rain, put up the hood on my raincoat. To our west was the empty skull of Storm King Mountain. The banks had no towns, no houses.

We got soaked like that for forty-five minutes of paddling; then, in the middle of the river ahead, I saw the shell of a building.

A flash of lightning stretched horizontal across the sky, and its light showed the outline. Surrounding it, there were scraggly treetops, a nest of twisted branches, dead leaves whipping in the wind and rain. Amid them were the broken tops of walls like pillars sprouting out of dark water, not an island, not a landing. It was hard to see detail, rain got in my eyes. I took off my bandana and wiped my face.

"There," yelled Keller. "What's that?" Pointing at the mass of drowned trees and bricks.

"No idea," Father yelled above the wind, "but it might have a roof. It looks empty."

I looked back at him. Rain dripped off the bill of his cap. He couldn't see any better than I could. I was hot, T-shirt soaked against my skin. The hulk of the ruin didn't look like it had a roof. That building looked like the biggest snag I'd ever seen.

"Empty!" said Keller. "Empty's good. You think it was a house?"

"I don't know," Father said. "Maybe it's an island?" The

wind hit the boat hard and there was another horizontal burst of lightning. I could feel Bix shivering behind me, spasms of terror. I couldn't tell whether they were for the water or the ruin.

"We've got to get out of this!" Father yelled at Keller.

"That place is drowned!" Bix yelled back. "We're better off in the woods!"

"One more gust and we're swimming," said Father. "We need shelter!"

"Unless it's rotting!" Bix's voice neared screaming.

"Worth the risk!" Father yelled.

"No choice now, Bix!" Keller sounded frustrated with Bix's panic. His hand slipped on the wet grips of his paddle. He pulled his field hat lower and dug into his stroke.

The hull scraped the branches surrounding the ruin. Lightning illuminated the warren of trees under the water and us in the middle of it. In the light I could see that only the top floor of the ruin was above the water, like a drowned man with his hat showing above the waves. There were words picked out in the brick of the structure, BANNER-MAN'S ISLAND, and below that what looked like the tops of the word ARSENAL. Whatever the thing had been—house, factory, armory—it was a shell now, big empty windows, rot lacing the walls, a sheen of fungus and moss climbing the brick. It had been flooded for a long time.

"That does not look good," Keller said.

"Maybe there's a room we can pull the canoe into!" Father yelled.

The building was covered in scaffolding, as if someone had been repairing it in The World As It Was. The scaffold had rusted, parts falling off, loose. The wind scraped the metal against the brick with a banshee sound. Lightning coursed ropes around the ruin, the breaking waves buckshot with raindrops. Underwater, a tree limb rose up in our way and the lightning let me see it. "Left!" I shrieked. Another strike showed a chunk of old wall. "Right! Now! Right!" We barely missed the wall.

I looked back at Bixie. All I could see were her eyes. "What if it's just water inside?!"

"This boat is going under if we stay together, we're too heavy!" Father screamed over the wind. "You two can climb in if we help you!"

"Climb in without you?" Bix yelled.

"We'll go around, find another way in. We'll find you inside!"

"What if it's just water inside?"

"No choice!" Father yelled. We pulled along the wall of the ruin alongside the scaffolding. Father back-paddled. Bix and I scrambled for packs. "Leave them!"

Keller clawed the wall to anchor us, reached back his free hand, and said, "Climb on my shoulders." I climbed, shaking, onto Keller's back. I put one foot on each shoulder, grabbed the window ledge. It was wet, and I was wet, and my fingers slipped on brick. Keller put a hand under my slipping foot and pushed. I pulled up and kicked against broken wood, my knee half in and half out the window. Lightning flashed. I saw a floor littered with construction pieces, pipes and wood.

"There's a floor!" I yelled, looking back down at the shifting boat.

"Go!" Father screamed.

I vaulted, sliding in through the frame.

36
HUNGRY GHOSTS

In the ruin, I scraped my legs on the empty window frame and came down hard, hitting rough planks in a wet ball, breath knocked out of me. Pain shot from my knee, from my bruised leg. I got to my feet, turned to look back out the window on tiptoes. It was dark inside, dark outside. Lightning showed the canoe twisting backward against the wind. Keller got the boat close again, then Bix climbed onto his shoulders. Bixie landed on me, her elbow digging into my side. I rolled away, heard her panting, trying to catch her breath. I was dripping on the planks.

"You hurt?" I asked.

"No." She breathed hard. "Rattled."

Wind pushed rain through the window. In more lightning, I saw that the room was larger than it looked from the river. There was a ceiling, a floor, patchy and dangerous, made of wide planks, some covered with wet, giant gaps between them showing the glittering black of the Hudson beneath my feet. The window amplified the sound of the scaffolding.

Bix wasn't getting up, so I grabbed her hand, wet and cold. "Father said to try to get to the other side of the building, out of the wind. They might be able to get the canoe in there."

There was just enough light to see Bix's eyes in the dark. In the darkness, just us, all of her came back, the contradiction of her, fearless in the shadows, walking toward darkness, frozen in the water, curious, brilliant, and clueless sometimes. My neck prickled. I always felt a little fear alone with her in the dark.

"I wish we had a lantern." She stood up, still holding my hand. Bix put her free hand against the wall, pulled me along after her as if she'd remembered, inside a solid building, that I was younger. She moved, feeling on the rough brick of the walls for a door. I followed. My fingers hit bent nails, tufts of rotting wallpaper, splintered boards.

Bix tripped. "What's that?" I couldn't see what she'd hit. "It's soft," she said, then lightning flashed, and I saw a bedroll at her feet. Bix and I stood still. Lightning flashed again and I scanned the room, breathing fast. I could see cans, boxes, mess stacked in a corner, a fireplace on one wall, crumbling but with cinders. The smell of wet and ozone had masked the smell of ashes and humans. Black shadows along the walls were so sheltered I couldn't see into them. It went dark again, and fear singed my limbs like lightning tunnels through soil, irregular and fierce. The Lost were here.

Bix squeezed my hand, turned, put a finger to my lips. I nodded. I closed my eyes, stilled my body. That bedroll, that room, was a mystery, danger, and I was afraid of it, but I was afraid of Bix too. She wanted to know what was in the dark. She walked toward the deep shadows, farther into the mystery.

The next strike of lightning had thunder right after. In the brightness, faces emerged from the shadows. Two tall men, cheeks shining slick with rain and sweat, beards longer than Father's, coats and jackets on, knit caps. They moved so fast it was clear they'd been listening. Dark fell. Arms reached out. A hand closed on me. I made myself an otter and wriggled, dodged, got behind them in the sudden dark.

"Come here," yelled a voice. "Where are you, boy?"

I heard Bix scream, "Let go!" Then her voice was covered by a hand.

"It's a kid, Mike," shouted the other, "a girl."

I heard her feet thrashing on the plank floor. I ran into a wall, felt for an opening. I found a doorway. I was so noisy. The second man said, "She fell right out of the window."

"There's another one somewhere," the first man shouted. Footsteps came toward me.

I didn't move. Silent. Silent. I heard Bix's feet against the boards, her voice. The second man yelled, "She bit me!"

Bix screamed one word, "Run!" There was the sound of a punch landing.

In the dark someone said, "Mike, you get that other one."

I didn't move. *Father,* my brain shouted, *go for Father.* My body wanted to go to Bix, but I stilled it. I was half the size of the men, the grip on my arm had been strong. I swallowed, went through the door and left her.

37
THE PARLOR IN THE RAIN

I was in a hallway. I crashed through the dark. The floor under me was worse than the one in the first room. I heard no steps behind me, only Bix screaming, quieter and farther away, then, "No!"

Ahead of me there was a waterfall of rain: a ladder led to a hole in the roof, water poured through the hole. I looked back while I ran. No one was following me. I tripped on a plank and went down, chin scraping the floor, hands out to keep my chest from the ground, cuts opening up, my foot through the boards, dousing my shoe in river. I sat up in the dark, still in case I was heard. Warm blood trickled down my throat from my chin; I swiped at it with my hand, and I pulled my foot free, splinters in the heels of my hands. No one was coming.

I stood and walked, hands out along the walls, splinters stinging, felt another opening in the maze, went through. The corridor widened onto a room. I was in the rain again; the room had no roof and was missing a wall, open to the river like it wasn't a room at all, waves washing the floor. There were arched windows in the remaining walls, scaffolding hung on the outside. Tied to the scaffolding was a boat, battered and dirty, tossing in the high waves, bashing against the bricks. Across the river surface, I saw our canoe coming toward the open room.

"Father!" I shrieked. "Father! Keller!" I waved my arms over my head.

"Nonie?" Father yelled. "Bix?"

"They took Bixie!" I screamed, waving.

"What!" yelled Keller, paddling hard to pull closer. "What?"

"Men! There were men in the room!" I yelled, hysterical. They got close. We could see each other. "Father!" I screamed, waves drowned the edge of the floor, my sneakers soaked. "Hurry! Hurry!" They paddled closer, glacial, painful minutes. They reached me; I met the canoe at the edge of the floor, grabbed the bow to steady it. Keller got out, then Father, stumbling in the weird space, the walls, the rain. They took the gunwales and hauled the canoe out, laid it on the rotting floor. "Hurry!" I yelled.

Father took hold of my shoulders, saw the blood from my chin. "You're hurt!"

"It's nothing! There were men in that room, and they took Bix and I got away!"

"Where is she?"

I pointed up the corridor. "Up that hallway, in the room!" I turned to lead them there.

"Nonie!" said Father. "Nonie, you have got to stay here!"

"No. No, I have to come! They're going to hurt her! *I couldn't stop them!*"

"Nonie! You have to stay. If you come, they could hurt you. You have to stay here and wait for us. You have to stay by this boat. If anything happens you have to stay by this boat, use it to get away."

"Without you?"

"If you have to. You have to keep safe," he said.

"Keep the boat safe, little warrior." Keller bent down, grabbed two of the paddles, handed one to Father. There was one paddle left in the hull. "Wait here."

Paddles in hand, Father and Keller ran the way I'd pointed, up the corridor and into the ruin.

38
THE WOUND

I looked up the corridor after Father and Keller. Then I remembered the other boat I'd seen. I went to where it was, looked down at it in the water, broken gunwales, hole where the engine should be, cracked, dirty, pounding the building, no paddles. It would sink with too much weight. It might sink in the storm. We'd be faster if the men chased us.

I went back to our canoe, knelt on the splintered floor next to it.

I heard a gunshot. I heard another shot. I heard a scream, high-pitched, carried by the wind. I heard two more shots. I heard a man's yell cut over the rain. I heard two more shots and voices. I stood up and walked without realizing it—to the corridor, back to the canoe, pacing.

I thought I should get the last paddle, go after Father and Keller. I tried to shift the gear, reach the paddle, pull the canoe by the gunwales. It moved the way a buck would if it hadn't downed completely, weight all deep mystery beneath your hands, looking to get away from you. Then the canoe slipped down the incline of the floor and slid into the river, a buck into brush, an otter down a bank.

I froze and watched it go, then grabbed for the gunwales, my hand skittering wet along the edge until I gripped the last end of it, my splinters stinging. I held it as it pitched in the water. I heard footfalls.

"Nonie!"

Father.

I let go.

"Father! I'm here!"

I turned back and saw the boat slipping away, out of reach. It had everything in it. I couldn't let it get away. I stood up and leapt for it. I landed on top of the gear. I drifted into the waves on the canoe, digging for the paddle under my belly. "I'm here!"

"Nonie!" Keller yelled.

"I launched!"

"Come back, Nonie! You've got to get us," Keller called.

I was tangled in the gear, the paddle tangled in my legs, slick and heavier than I thought. The waves moved me sideways, tipping the boat in the troughs. Now I could see the ruin, now I couldn't. I got the paddle in the water, but I wasn't strong enough for the weight of the boat and the force of the storm.

"Nonie!" I followed Keller's voice and saw him and Bix on either side of Father. He was dangling pale between them. Bix curled toward Father, free hand up to her chest holding her clothes together. Bix favored one foot. Keller was at the edge of the water. "Nonie, get that boat back here." He dropped the paddles he was carrying.

"Wind's too hard!" I heard the fear wild in my own voice.

They lowered Father to the floor. There was a stain down Father's chest, it stood out in the storm, the dark center of the worst night, made my heart beat harder in my chest. The next wave cut off my view.

"Nonie, get that boat back here!"

"Help me!" The wind pushed me farther.

Bix and Father had sunk. Keller was standing. His skin and clothes were soaked. He was poised over the edge of the floor, his body tense, looking for me. He kicked off his boots and dove into the water, cracking the slick skin at the top of the violent waves, splitting them like a knife, disappearing.

Bixie screamed "No!" raw and high, "No!" like she sounded watching from the tree while Mano died.

39

BREAKING AWAY

Keller was strong, even in that evil, riled-up water. The days he spent at the public pool in The World As It Was were still in the shape of his arms as he swam. He surfaced, rode a crest, ducked through the wave crown. But his strokes felt futile, we all knew that water could do things to a body. I lost track of him in the tall waves, then felt the canoe shift when he grabbed it. The boat wanted to capsize. Keller lost balance, his hand slid off the gunwale, his head went under the river again.

"So, you could go swimming?" I asked him once. "There was enough water that you could keep it in a pool? What was swimming like? Was it like being in the rain? Or like after a bath, when you pour the bucket over your head?"

"It was a big room, high ceilings. The tiles were cool against your feet, no moss, no mud. And the air smelled like chlorine . . ."

"What was the chlorine doing there?"

". . . you had to put chlorine into the water to keep it from getting algae, to keep it clean. That's the way you can have standing water and have it be safe, you know, not to drink, but safe so you could be in it and not get any kind of infection or sickness. The pool rooms were usually humid, and it was always echoing in there. Every kid learned swimming. Sometimes there were pools at schools and kids learned to swim in gym class."

"Because you could swim in the ocean?"

"Because you could swim in the ocean. And in ponds, and rivers, and everywhere. Well, OK, not always everywhere. My mother took me, because we lived not too far from Lake Michigan, and in the summertime, we went there as a family for barbecues and spent the whole day. There were lifeguards, you know, people who kept you safe in the water. But she didn't want to take any chances."

His head popped over the waterline. He was coughing and spitting out water he'd swallowed. He pulled himself up into the canoe and I backed up to steady it. He took my paddle, clambered into the stern seat, and dug deep with it; slowly we turned and headed right for the ruin.

Bix was kneeling next to Father. I could see her mouth moving, chanting *no* like a prayer, but I couldn't hear her over the wind. She rose to standing. She tucked a gun in the back of her jeans, picked up both paddles from the floor in one hand. One of the paddles had blood on it. She leaned down to Father and put her free arm around his back to help him stand. He stumbled, she limped, but they walked to where the floor met the water. Keller drew the boat up and steadied it.

Bix tossed both paddles in the canoe, helped Father in. Her jeans were filthy with dirt and blood, there was a stain of blood on one leg, her shirt was ripped, her jacket gone. She had a cut on her face, a bruise along her jaw, her eyes were black holes. She climbed behind Father and leaned him up against her knees, wincing. Father's skin shone in the storm light. He breathed ragged. He had twin stains on his chest, front and back: gunshot wound.

"What happened?" I asked.

Bix looked up at me. "I don't know."

"Go," Father said, very quiet, "I think one's still alive."

Keller looked at Father, pushed off the planks with his paddle and sent us back into the storm, spat out water, coughed. The ruin slipped behind us, blocked by a wave crest.

Sometimes what looks like shelter is only menace.

We weaved and pitched through the forest of snags. There wasn't lightning to see by. When we were free, the Hudson was going south, so we went south too. The tide was strong, the waves still high, the rain easing. Keller directed the boat, but the river took us mostly where it wanted. I took up a paddle, shifting Father's leg to get it, to help. Father lay in Bix's lap. Keller hacked and spat, wet and ugly sounds. Bix sat stone quiet. Father had his head down. Rain fell into my eyes, washed down Bix's hair, sank into the hull. I looked back past Keller's shoulder, the river empty and wild behind us. There wasn't a boat.

"No one's coming," I said.

"I think they're dead," Keller said. "Bix got one gun. One fell in the water. Nobody was left to follow, I think."

"You don't know," Bix said.

40
THE OAK TREE

The wind died. Rain striped the water in patterns. The current pushed for Storm King Mountain, the slope's fine skull above the water. I could feel the grab of tree limbs under the belly of the canoe, hear the rocks under us, and looked up to see the forest, the wrecked shoreline of downed trees. Keller got out, the canoe tipping, splashed into the water, pulled the boat higher, Bix got Father out of the boat, and they leaned on each other and staggered up into the woods. I splashed into the cold branchy water.

"Grab the gunwales, Nonie. Let's see how high up we can get." Keller took most of the boat's weight. I stumbled, couldn't see anything in the forest, hit my shins on tree limbs, misdirected the bow. Keller pushed the boat from behind. The branches scratched my legs. My arms ached. We followed Bix and Father up a ragged deer path.

I listed what I knew: Father was shot. Bixie had a limp. Keller had a lungful of river water. We were in the forest. It was raining, Bix was hurt. I had splinters and cuts and bruises.

At the top of the ridge there was a clearing, and in the center was a broad oak bigger than any other tree in the forest. It had used the extra sunlight to grow, and luck had kept other trees from competing. It had its brown November leaves, and they blunted the rain underneath. There was an outcrop away from the tree, and it had a view of the Hudson. Bix lowered Father down onto his side under the oak and sat next to him, her face close to his.

"Lower your end, Nonie." Keller let down his end of the canoe and I let the weight fall to the ground. Keller took out

Father's pack, dug for the first aid kit, put it on the ground next to him. "Nonie, help me. Bix, you first, then we'll move Allan." He got a water jug out, walked over to Bix, rolled up her pant leg, splashed water over it. A pool formed below her foot, hard to see, dark from blood.

"What did that?" I asked Bix.

"Could have been worse. Keller bumped the shooter and he missed, grazed me."

"Oh." Father and Bix both shot. "Did you shoot the men?" I asked.

"No. Bix did," Keller said. "When we got to her, she had one of their guns. One guy shot Allan, then Bix was fighting with them. We were trying to hit them with the paddles. I caught someone, changed the angle of the shot, knocked his gun to the floor—sounded like it fell through, into the river. Then Bix shot them both. . . ." He trailed off, poured water over her wound. "It was too dark to make sense of it." He thrust the jug to me. "Drink some, wash your hands."

He picked up the kit and turned to Father. He peeled off Father's jacket. Bix watched; the black centers of her eyes went nowhere. Keller started to lift Father, get his arm out of his coat. "Hold him up while I do this." I got behind Father and held up his body, shifted him so he was leaning against me, stripped off Father's shirt and undershirt and hat. The clothes had holes in them, were soaked and sticky, even after the rain. Bix took them and folded them slowly like laundry off the line at Amen.

The wound was neat and round, and blood oozed out of it, not as fast as a wound in a deer. It was high, away from his heart, maybe away from his lungs. I was covered in blood where Father leaned on me. Then he coughed and so did Keller. "You can hear me, right, Allan?" Keller asked. Father nodded. "Get him some water, Bix." She snapped out of folding, got the jug and held it to Father's mouth.

He swallowed. "It's cold," he whispered.

"Hand that jug to me," Keller said. He poured water over Father's shoulder and Father shuddered. Keller grabbed a roll of bandages from the first aid bag.

"We don't have enough salve," Bix said.

"Salve won't take care of this. We need medicine. We'll stop the bleeding tonight, maybe we can find someone tomorrow, some settlement. It looks like the bullet went through muscle, not organs, so we can get him somewhere in the daylight. Got to stop the bleeding first." He packed the wound with bandages and wrapped them around Father's torso. "Bix, get an emergency blanket from my pack." She did. "Now fit it under him. OK, Nonie, lay him down." I rested Father's weight back until he lay on the blanket over the humid earth. "Now, we make a fire."

"They'll see us," I said.

"Doesn't matter, they're dead," Father whispered.

"Or close enough," said Keller. "Get him a shirt, Bix. Nonie, help me get sticks."

We got sticks for a wet, smoky fire, enough big ones for a lean-to. Keller made a fire while Bix found a wet clean shirt in Father's pack, draped it over him. "Maybe the heat will dry it out," Bix said. She folded the bloody shirt into a pillow, laid his jacket over him.

The fire was smoky. Keller took a drink, stood and worked a lean-to over Father. The blood was dried on Bix's face and hands, her hair was wet. Random drops of rain came through the branches of the oak.

"Your face is hurt?"

"Not like that." She lifted her chin, indicating Father.

"You need Jess's salve."

"No, save it."

"For what?" I took a bandage, watered it, washed the blood from her face, around her mouth, her hands, finger-nails torn, knuckles raw. I painted her cuts and bruises with salve on the end of my finger. "Did the men hurt you?"

"They tried." She touched her clean hand to her mouth and the blood. "They were stupid, couldn't get my pants off. They didn't think I could fight." Her voice was closed off. It was like Mano, like how she never talked about that day again.

"You killed them?"

"I don't know. It was dark. It was all fast. I don't know what I did. I don't know."

I felt as numb as her voice, but under that a flare of anger. Father and Keller left us in the dark, Bix walked into the mystery like she did at Amen. I knew the storm was bad, and the ruin was bad, and no one listened. Rage made my voice come when I didn't know it. "Just like with Mano. You always go where you shouldn't."

"Don't say that. Don't say this is my fault."

I hadn't meant that. The World As It Is had dogs, and sometimes they chased you. Sometimes they killed you. It had storms and men. You didn't cause those things to be there. "I didn't. I didn't mean that." My words sounded too small.

"If I know what's in the dark, I can fix things. If I'd had a gun, Mano wouldn't be dead."

"You can't fix it. We can't fix anything. Guns don't fix any-thing."

"I fixed it with those men. Some things we can fix. It's hard."

Keller coughed in the distance.

Father took a deep breath, whispered, "Nonie's right. Guns made this bad in the first place, Bix. And you would have fought no matter what. No matter how it happened, we're alive. Sometimes you have no choice but to walk into the dark. Being brave is what fixed it."

I could feel Bix soften. Bix lay down next to Father, curled toward him with her hand on his shoulder. I lay down, too, and drew toward her and curled her like a shrimp inside the spoon my body made. She was pliable and silent, and she let me. I was shorter than her, and it was awkward, but I rolled her up: pill bug, fiddlehead fern, seed inside a husk. I put my tummy on her back, a hand on her forehead, another on her arm. There was something sharp between us. I found the gun in Bix's back pocket, took it out and sat up and set it at our feet. I lay back down, and she cried, a hand resting on Father next to her. We all breathed together, fighting the cold while the rain slowed down and the light came up.

"Bixie?" Father whispered. "Do you know where we are?"

Bix startled at the sound of his voice.

"No," she whispered.

"I've just remembered." He coughed wet and very hard, which made Bix's whole body tighten. "This is Storm King Mountain."

41
STORM KING MOUNTAIN

"Remember?" Father whispered. "Remember? We can't be four miles from where I first kissed your mother."

I could feel Bix soften as I held her. I could hear Keller walk closer to us to listen to Father's voice.

"When Deirdre and I first knew each other," Father whispered, "we were friends. I didn't want to be friends, but she wouldn't talk about it. Things were hard, no one talked about anything except how hard things were. One weekend I found a gas ration card on the subway, talked her into going out of the city. She didn't want to go, told me I was wasting gas. But I wanted something normal. I took her to a sculpture park, Storm King, close to here.

"In the park there was a sculpture like the stone walls farmers make through the woods, but when you followed it, it circled in on itself until you realized you were always inside it. It even went into a pond and came out again on the other side. When you got to the end, you saw that it held you the whole time." His voice got stronger. I could hear Keller sit down outside the lean-to he made over us, could feel him watching. He reached out and held my foot.

"It made me understand what she was doing, not admitting that she loved me. You can't pretend that the world is so hard you aren't allowed to love. I knew that wasn't the kind of person your mother was. When she decided to love, she loved with everything. If anyone knows that, you do. That wall made me think about how your mother kept me out, afraid of risking anything with the world so hard. But that wall told me we should keep each other in no matter what.

So, I said, 'You already love me, and we can make something inside here,' and I put my hand on her sternum and I kissed her. And here you are."

I could feel Bix crying against my stomach, feel her hold Father tighter.

"Bixie," he whispered, his voice fading, "sometimes you need to make a wall to keep what's good inside with you and decide to be alive." I put my arm over Bix's, so we were both holding Father, and Bix took my hand with her free one and held it tight, my splinters burning under her fingers. We lay together like that for a while. Then Father's breathing shallowed. It sounded like him falling asleep.

"Keller?" I asked. "Is it OK for him to sleep?"

"Let him rest, he lost a lot of blood," Keller whispered, still holding my foot. One hand on Bix's leg, patting her next to her bandage. "We've got to keep him warm, get him to medicine." Keller paused. "You OK?"

"Mm-hmm." I closed my eyes. Keller squeezed my foot, stood up, and went to get more sticks.

I could feel that Bix was restless. She pulled free of me and of Father. I sat up and watched as she crawled from the lean-to, walked to where Keller was standing, next to the oak tree in the rainy predawn, holding a bundle of sticks, his face in deep shadow. She took the sticks from him, then embraced him. He put his arms around her. I hadn't seen them do that since Mano. She led him to the fire, got the food bag and the water, and started making soup, finding something to hold inside the wall Father reminded her to build.

42
IN THE COLD

I woke up under the lean-to, next to Father. I was cold. I could hear the fire going but couldn't feel the heat. Father lay on one side of me. I stretched and curled away from him. Bix was sleeping on my other side. I turned back to him, put my hand on his bandage. His clothes were damp. He felt cold.

I have to get him more clothes, I thought.

It was light out. I looked out at Keller by the fire with his head on his chest, snoring. I looked back at Father on his back in the lean-to shade. His eyes were open.

I was about to ask if he was cold. But I knew. He couldn't see, staring eyes set in a white face, freckles painted on, hair wet, skin damp and waxy. The shirt that Bix draped over him was off, the bandage on his chest exposed, stained with blood, under his body, the emergency blanket covered in blood. Everything of him, the flint and spark of him, was flown out. He was dead.

Bix and Keller slept while I looked at him. I could hear the fire pop like a heartbeat.

It was so true, his being gone, that it stopped the progress of the world. The trueness was bigger than anything and familiar, like I saw it coming, every day, from a long way off. I thought Father would stay. Mother was gone, so I thought he'd stay. I was wrong.

I reached for him but reaching was moving through water. I said, "Wake up, wake up," but my voice was somehow distant from my ears; it woke Bixie and Keller. They came to him. Keller felt Father's skin, his wrist, called his name.

Bix called, too. I couldn't hear them through the water feeling, so I watched. Keller picked him up, held him, felt him cold and stiff and put him down again, looking at blood on his hands. Bix laid her head on his chest. Keller's voice was like coming through the water, "Bled out, bled out, he bled out. It must've hit something." He was crying, his face a blank. "I was asleep." Bix was crying. I was shaking. I didn't know when I started shaking. I clenched my teeth so they wouldn't chatter. Keller was looking at the blood again. "He was alone, that's my fault."

Bix lifted her head from Father's chest. "Don't say that! Don't talk like that! We don't say *fault,* we don't do that! We don't do that to him." Keller stared. "We keep together!" She put a hand on Father's chest, wiped her eyes. I was crying, and she grabbed me and hugged me to her. "We keep together."

Bix let me go and we sat and looked at Father. My brain wouldn't catch up to time. Keller closed Father's eyes. I closed mine too. I fell into the void, until I was alone, away from what was waiting when I opened them again.

43
GOING OVER JORDAN

I opened my eyes. When I did, I saw Bix touching Father's hand, his cheek. She got up and untied Father's boots, took them off his feet, took off his socks, dried the skin of his feet with the cuff of her hoodie. My heartbeat and the fire popped. His toenails were long, the balls of his feet callused. She put his boots aside; he wouldn't want us to bury them.

His face was still. His closed eyes were lying. He wasn't sleeping. He was emptied out. He would empty more the longer I looked at him. I forced myself to memorize a picture of the last minute I'd have him. I had a photograph of Mother, none of him. But it already wasn't him there, and so I stopped.

Keller said, "We can't leave him out here. At night, it'll draw scavengers. We could put him in the river. Get off this mountain."

Bix looked at him. "Not the water," she said.

He nodded. "OK." Keller was exhausted. "Then we have to dig a hole."

"With what?" I asked.

"Paddles," said Keller. Bix nodded. We had nothing else.

I went to where the paddles were. My feet were separate from me. My hands weren't real. The boat was a shell. My eyes were, too. Nothing worked. The afterimage of Father's face shivered behind the world.

I walked back with the paddles. Bix and Keller left the lean-to. Father's bare feet stuck out of the shelter, but I looked away from them. I gave Bix and Keller paddles, and we went to the oak tree. We used the handles to break up the wet dirt. There were roots, we had to try two spots before we found a good place, near the shade of the branches, but clear enough to dig. When the soil was loose, we used the flat ends to move the dirt out and dug deep. Keller coughed the whole time. I was sweating but the cold wouldn't leave me. I wasn't hungry. I wasn't anything but hands moving dirt.

When I looked up from the soil again the light was low, late afternoon, and we had a hole, and it was deep enough.

Bix limped to Father in the lean-to. I followed her. I stood outside and watched while she checked his pockets for his knife and compass, smoothed back his hair, took his folded jacket, and put it on. She used a piece of bandage to wipe his face. "He'd know why we didn't wash him," she said.

We didn't have a rope or cloth to set him down slow into the grave, so we lowered him ourselves. We were covered in dirt, using the paddles to push the earth back over him.

At Amen, when someone died, two people would carry the body to the cool stacks. When night came, grown-ups would go out and dig a grave. If we wanted, we could come. We couldn't use lanterns. We couldn't sing. We didn't want to draw the Lost. We didn't have enough water to wash the dead. We didn't grow flowers. We had shovels, and cloth saved for a shroud, and we made sure that the hole was deep enough to keep the dogs away.

Father was the one to say things by the graves at Amen, whisper a poem, he said he couldn't remember the poet:

So, we'll go no more a roving
So late into the night
Though the heart be still as loving
And the moon be still as bright

After, he'd say things about the dead. And we'd speak quiet so no Lost would hear us. We'd all go home through the tall grass, in the doors, through dark marble rooms to beds waiting for us on the roof.

The sun was setting, the woods already shadowed. It hadn't rained all day, and I'd never looked at the sky. We were silent. Then Bix sang. She hadn't sung since Amen. I forgot how her voice was. It was Mother's, deep and scratchy.

> I am a poor wayfaring stranger
> I'm traveling through this world of woe
> Yet there's no sickness, toil, nor danger
> In that bright land to which I go
> I'm going there to see my Father
> I'm going there, no more to roam
> I'm only going over Jordan
> I'm only going over home

That was a Mother song, one she kept for bedtime. I hated it when I was small. Bix told me when we first came to Amen, I wouldn't let Mother sing it. The lyric hurt my heart, the loneliness crawled in and bruised it. But on Storm King Mountain my heart was already broken, and the song didn't hurt.

I sat down next to Father's grave and cried until the sun went down. I didn't notice Bix stop singing. I didn't notice the dark come on. I didn't notice Keller asking me to eat or making a fire. I fell asleep there and woke in the deep night curled on the ground, stiff and dirty, with a fire going back by the lean-to, my hoodie laid over my shoulders.

44
LUCA

We brought Mano back to Amen once we were sure that there weren't any dogs left to chase us. We came in through the big doors, into the dark of the great hall. Bix and I didn't know what to do except stand by Mano, where he was, wrapped in a tarp that Father and Keller carried. We waited for someone to tell us what to do. We waited for someone to come and clean us up, feed us. We didn't know we were waiting. I am waiting still for him, for someone his age, for anyone we could love like that who was a brother and a friend and what he was to Bix.

When I think of Mano, I think of the last day that was ordinary before the dogs, the day he was drawing a dog while we talked on the roof. The dog was short-haired and relaxed, soft eyes, mouth drawn back, panting. I sat down next to Mano on a blanket on the rooftop stones, close to the edge, looking toward the Park where the sun rose in the morning.

"Luca," he said. "My dog, in Puerto Rico."

"You had a dog?"

"My mom got it for me when I was little. It was a *sato,* do you know what those are?"

"No."

"Those are dogs that are born on the street, and nobody takes care of them. They live in garbage dumps, gross beaches, bad parts of cities. There used to be these people who made, like, clubs, that would go out with ropes and cages and raw meat and catch the dogs. And then they'd bring them in to the vet and clean them and teach them how to play and remind them that they liked humans."

"And Luca was a *sato*?"

"Yup. My mom found him in the garbage, and she helped him. He was really nice."

"You left him with her."

"I did. Maybe they kept each other safe."

"Maybe they are still together."

"I think so," he said. "Sometimes you have to remember that The World As It Is changed things, but we can change them back."

At Amen we used rocks to mark where someone was buried. It showed the place, not the name. The only one different was Mano's—it had a cross. Angel roped together two-by-fours, carved them with a tool she found in a curator's lab. She worked all day on the roof. "Papi would know if I didn't do this," she told me. "Papi would know." Her hair untucked from her bun, the curls waved in the humid air like fern fronds. She was beautiful in the haze, her cheeks pink, sweat on her upper lip, sawdust on her dark eyebrows from carving: *Manolito Rivera. Loved boy.*

45

LEAVING STORM KING

I sat up beside Father's grave and saw Keller by the fire. He waved me to come to him, so I did. He had a pot next to the fire, and he handed it to me. There was broth inside, made from dried cubes that Alice Winslow had put in our bag in a clay jar. "Drink some."

"Where's Bix?"

"Sleeping. She made this. Drink some." I drank straight from the pot, and let it warm me up. "Here," he handed me a wet piece of cloth, "wipe your face." I put down the pot and ran the wet cloth over my skin and then over my hands until they weren't so dirty. Keller coughed, then looked at me. "What's on your chin?"

"Splinters. From the floor."

A knife was sitting next to him on the ground, Father's pocketknife, not the one Alice gave Keller. "Let me get them." He picked splinters from my chin with the tip, dabbing the blood with the cloth.

"How'd you get so many bits of wood in your face, little warrior?"

"Don't know."

He finished and put the knife down. "Tomorrow we have to move." He coughed.

"You should take something for that. If we had antibiotics."

"Anything left around here is probably expired."

I shook my head in the dark. "Jess said the expiration dates don't matter."

"Bix needs some too."

"Yes, she does. Maybe we can find some."

"Maybe. You should sleep."

"What about you?"

"Not tonight."

I nodded and left him there. Bix lay rigid, avoiding the blood on the ground under the lean-to. I tucked myself next to her, my arm across her stomach. In the night I woke to the sound of Keller coughing, a long rattle of wet in his lungs, then fell asleep again, stiff and cold and close to Bix.

Keller woke us, handed us hardtack, and said, "Pack up, we need to catch the tide."

Keller scuttled the fire and covered the ashes. He stood by Father's grave, covered it with sticks and dead leaves, covered the dark soil where Father's blood had soaked in; it looked no different than another fall of branches anywhere in the forest.

"We have to go," I said. I felt my knees weaken, exhaustion of the kind they say the drowning feel, I was about to sink there and never walk away from the oak tree. "Keller."

"OK." He kept working.

"No. I have to go. Keller, I have to go *now.*"

"She has to leave here, Keller," Bix said, looking up from packing. "It's good enough."

Keller looked up—saw the look on my face. "OK. OK, we'll go."

46
IN THE BOW

"Nonie, you have to go in the bow," Keller said. The Hudson was still and soft, as if there was never a storm. Mist rose from the surface of the water. In the distance I could see the ruin. "When you see a snag, put your paddle on that side of the boat, OK? That'll help me know how to steer." He coughed.

"OK." I nodded at him, took the paddle I'd used to dig the grave, and sat down in Father's place in the bow.

"Bix, you take Allan's paddle, take the middle seat." Bix shook her head out of reflex; she didn't want to paddle, the spell of the canoe settling back on her. Keller coughed and Bix started, looked at him. "Take Allan's paddle," he repeated with tenderness so deep, and reached out and hugged her. She softened in his arms. She had done things since we left Amen. She shot someone. She left the ruin alive with Keller and Father. She took Father's language in her mouth: *we keep together*. She cared for Keller. She dug the grave. She'd have to act in the face of the water now. We were only three.

She looked at him, her face like weather moving, a storm moving off. She reached into the hull and took Father's paddle, then took her place in the middle of the boat. Keller pushed the canoe into the shallows and took his place at the stern. Father was alone on that mountain. The mist lifted and the color of the sky reflected on the still river. My skin itched where the dirt was, hands hurt from digging the grave, blisters starting. I imagined an *Archelon* below us, a late Cretaceous turtle three times the size of our canoe, carrying the boat under the mist. We passed the ruin by. It was quiet. I stared at it until it was gone. No one was following.

47
FEVER DREAM

We broke for rest that night above a submerged town. When the boat was onshore, Keller stood for a minute, then buckled and knelt in the grass. Bix dropped her pack and ran, limping, to grab him. I got to Keller first. He tipped back and lay on his side, shut his eyes as a coughing fit hit him. I put my hand on his forehead. His skin was hot and damp with fever. I put my ear to his chest, his lungs full.

Bix sat down next to us, she put her hand on his forehead. "He's burning up. Nonie." She laid Keller on his back, but that made the coughing worse, so she twisted him onto his side.

"Should we move him?" I asked.

"Can you carry him?" she asked, and I shook my head. "Then we should stay here."

We made a fire and broth, fed him and gave him water, Keller shivering from his fever, we covered him in blankets and clothes, and he kept saying, "I'll be up in a minute. Just need to rest a minute." He closed his eyes and he slept, the sound of his wet lungs loud, his eyes moving sharply behind closed eyelids.

"He won't get better just with sleep. He's got a lung sickness. I wish we had goldenseal."

When the Mosquito Borne came, no one was ready. The bugs changed, the warmth didn't leave in winter, we had to go everywhere for medicine, keep it close. Everyone wanted antibiotics. Rick was good at finding them, always in the backs of big store pharmacies. They didn't work on the Mosquito Borne. People still tried them. Then we didn't have any for the bronchitis, abscessed teeth, fever. We wasted medicine that way. We had some left in the stacks in the medicine kit, but they went the night we lost Amen. "You have to ignore the dates on the bottles," Jess told me. "Suggestions for a world with plenty of everything." Jess made goldenseal salve with olive oil and a plant she found growing wild in the Park. Rare, she said. I watched her cook the oil in a pan, set the powdered root in it, mix it and set it to cool in used jars of shea butter she used to ask Rick to find for her. She set that salve on everything from a raw tooth to a scrape, made us smear it in our noses to ward off strep, said it was almost as good as antibiotics. The salve was back in the stacks, too.

"I know," I said. "We don't have any and he got a lungful of that water."

We watched him in the firelight until we fell asleep.

In my dream Father walked into the water, stepped onto the *Archelon*'s back, stood, sat with his legs crossed, lay down to sleep; the turtle swam away, and I ran past the roofs of the drowned houses, screaming for him.

48
FERAL HOUSE

Wrestling Keller into the boat the next day was not easy. The day made it worse. By the tide break, he was barely awake. "He needs a real rest," Bix hiss-whispered to me in the canoe, "a roof." Once we got to shore, she left us by the gear, Keller able to stand and move from the boat until he sat, leaning on me, in the dead grass. "Stay put," she told us, and I stayed with Keller and rubbed his hands to keep him warm. Behind us was an old road. There were two rusted cars, crashed into each other, locked, their bodies pale from the weather; old age found them of one flesh. I tried to imagine the accident that brought them there, then turned to see her coming out from the tree line, running across a burned-over meadow. "I found an empty house!" she yelled. "We'll be out of sight." The three of us stumbled into the woods—Bix limping, Keller between us as if we were crutches—then into a clearing to Bix's house.

It was melting, weather had beaten it in, half the roof was gone, siding peeled like sycamore bark until the bones were showing through. It was a big house, too many rooms, irrational windows, details of columns, pretending to be a mansion. Next to it, the garage was plain, buckled, its door ripped off, the frame a pile of sawdust, nothing left inside it—no cars, not even boxes, only a lawn mower slumped in a corner. The front door hung open and we entered a hallway with skylights, now the broken conduits for rain and seeds, the floor covered in young trees, their roots tearing up floor-boards, their limbs reaching back to the windows, trying for reunion with the forest. The house had forgotten tap water and light bulbs. We walked through the trees, a carpet of moss under our feet; through a doorway was a large room with a high ceiling, a kitchen, the inner walls covered with dark mold, vines, nests at the wooden frames of the windows. More vines half covered a television built into one wall, the black surface in the black frame unbroken, the same color as the mold. We were inside the skin of the forest, cocooned. Bix helped me lower Keller to his knees in the moss. He lay down on his side, face on the soft green, retreated into his body. Heat shone on him, shimmered like a mirage on the water.

"He needs a drink," I said. Bix looked at me, motioned me to step away from Keller until we were close to the back wall. She leaned in and whispered, "We're nearly out of water and food." My heart sank. "Nonie, don't start looking like that," she whispered. "We have water enough for him, just not too much for us. Don't tell him." I looked out the windows, up at our first roof since the ruin. The boat was far away; so was Father. The room smelled like the amoxicillin mixed with apple mush Mother gave me when I was sick in the apartment on Tenth Street. Bix sat in the moss, and I lay down next to her.

"Can we have a fire?" I asked.

"Not inside the house," said Bix. "You cold?"

"No." I was, but I didn't tell her. "Let me look at your leg. You got water in that wound."

"OK. Can you get the salve? And bandages?" I got them. Bix rolled back the cuff of her pants. I saw the dirty bandage. She peeled it back. Her leg was red and streaked.

"That's not right," I said. "How are you going to walk like that?"

Bix shrugged. It was infected. We both knew it. "Don't worry about it," she said. "We'll figure it out."

"Antibiotics. We need to find somebody who didn't run out," I said.

Lying still on the moss next to sleeping Keller, Bix asked, "How do you play it?"

"What?"

"Your game with Keller."

"Animal in Mind?"

"Yeah, that one."

"You think of an animal, and you try to describe it so that the other person will get it, but you make it kind of hard."

"Any animal?"

"Anything."

"I have an animal in mind. This is the biggest animal on planet earth."

"Blue whale."

"Right."

I thought of all the days we spent under the model at Amen, swimming in imaginary seas. "You think the whale is underwater now?" I asked.

"Probably," Bix said. "Where it was always supposed to be."

"You're good at this, at the game." I took an apple from my pack. "Will we leave at the tide change?"

"Yeah. We've got to get to medicine," Bix said. "I'll take watch, try to sleep. We should try to sleep until the tide change."

"I can't sleep here."

"Why not?" She watched me eating.

I finished the apple. "Too crowded." I couldn't tell her I was afraid of lying down here in the moss and not being strong enough to get up, melting like the house was melting.

She smiled. "Not as bad as it could be. We can make it worse. Want to plant an apple tree?" I raised my eyebrows.

We used to harvest apple trees in the Park, Jess and me. "There's a big stand of apples over by the Met. But it is such a long walk. And I like these better," Jess said, walking into a secret grove not far from our garden.

"Why?"

"They're, like, an old variety, I think, wild from when the Park was first built. They taste like bananas. And foxes like them. So maybe we'll see a fox." We walked off the trail behind the Ramble. She had a gun over her shoulder. "You have to remember that the Park is more than just dogs, Nonie," Jess said. "There is so much here. Did you know it was a village first, a village built by and for Black people? Then the city kicked them all out. I wonder if there are apples left from them here somewhere." She walked behind a shed and down a deer track, and then up a ridge. We were nowhere near where the dogs had been. "Get your pack ready so we can load up on apples when we come to them," she said. "They're going to be delicious."

Jess's apples didn't taste like the ones from Alice Winslow.

"Give me that." Bix took the apple core I'd been eating, picked out the seeds. "Give me your hand." She put the seeds into my palm. They were black and shiny. "Throw them."

"Here?"

"Why not?"

"It's too full to be an orchard."

She shrugged. "Apple trees are tough."

"OK." I tossed the seeds into the moss.

"Nonie Appleseed."

"What?"

"Nothing."

49
WHERE THERE'S SMOKE

The last day we were on the river I couldn't have told you it was the last day. At our campsite, north of the feral house, Keller woke me, screaming Angel's name. Bixie held him down while he thrashed, and he looked at her like Angel's face had settled over hers, a mask of memory and fever. "Angel!" he yelled at her. "Get him into the ditch, roll him over! Run, Angel! Mano's there!" His arm struck out and clipped Bix on the ear.

"It's Nonie, Keller. I'm Nonie, it's Nonie." I didn't tell him that Angel was dead. Angel wasn't with me, but she was with him. I sat up, stroked Keller's forehead, listened to his lungs, heard him setting into sleep.

Keller kept saying, "Allan," as if they were still sharing the canoe.

We went north again. There was the river. There was Keller sleeping. There was Bix in the stern. There was me in the bow. She was in Keller's place. I was in Father's. We gave almost all the last water to Keller. Fog came up on the river, a shroud like the repeating motions of the days and nights since Father died. Every hour bled into itself in numbness until fear and sorrow burst up into my chest from nowhere.

"Nonie, you've been dead reckoning, right? Like Jess taught you? How far have we come?" Bix asked.

"I think ninety miles. Hard to tell. I think we get ten miles a tide."

"So, we could be close to Hudson?"

I remembered the map in Keller's notebook that Father

drew, *Rip Van Winkle Bridge, Hudson, Mass Pike, Lee, Fern-side Road, Tyringham.*

"How will we walk to Tyringham now?" I asked.

"We could make a travois."

"A what?"

"A travois. Remember in the Plains Indians room, the stretcher, the two poles and a bed made of a blanket between, hitched to the back of a horse or a dog."

"We'd need a horse. Or a dog." I thought of dogs. "How can we stay safe?"

Bix got her pack. "I don't know." She opened it, got out Father's cap, put it on. There was a smudge of his blood on the brim, but I didn't tell her. "If we're not, the gun's in here. I checked it out. It's eight-chambered, takes three-fifty-sevens, maybe thirty-eights, too, and there are two rounds left." She was quiet. "Why haven't we seen anyone else since the ruin?"

"Too close to the water? I don't know."

The fog was a second river over the river. My spine tingled with rain. "We should use the compass," I told Bix. "We won't see anything in the fog. It was in Father's pack."

She dug in Father's bag and held up his beaten metal compass. "Safety Pup. Remember? Keller called him Safety Pup?" She put the compass in her pocket.

I asked Father once, "Why do you have that compass in your pocket?"

"I've carried it since Scout camp," he said.

"Scout?"

"My dad gave me this compass to go to Boy Scout camp in Michigan. I went out with friends, after dinner, when most of the Scouts were up at the fire. Two friends walked off with me, Jerry and Andy, we were going to climb a ridge and look at the Perseids. But they got tired and went back, and then I was wandering through this ravine that was by a lot of marshes, no one stream to follow. Navigating is easier when the biggest landmark is a lake the size of an ocean. I kept getting turned around, fell down an embankment, wasn't paying attention, got winded, sat at the bottom of this swale, terrified I'd never get back, or fall again in the dark. Nobody knew where I was. But I remembered Dad's compass in my pocket. I figured out I was walking the wrong direction, away from the campsite. I turned the right way and found my way back."

Over Keller's sleeping, feverish body, Bix handed me water. "You need it."

"You too," I said. She nodded. Only a few swallows left.

"Might rain," I said, "maybe we can collect more water."

"Is it gonna rain hard?" she asked. She'd never asked me like that before.

"No," I said. "It is gonna be a soft rain. The kind you can drink."

Bix kept the compass on her knee, looking down while she steered. The chill lingered. Keller was shivering. I leaned over him, rubbing my hands on his arms. I unzipped my hoodie, fingers numb, and covered Keller with it. It started to rain.

"That was fast!" Bix called as the first drops hit her. She dug in the packs. "Where's the emergency blanket? Father's emergency blanket?" She looked up from under the brim of Father's cap, the letters AMNH dirty, hit with raindrops. She found the blanket, ragged, smudges of dried blood from Father still on it, draped it over Keller to keep some part of him dry. I took the bailing pot and tipped it up to try to catch the rain.

The fog dissipated in the shower. I could see the river. Islands loped on the edges of the water, a maze of them, roads disappearing into the Hudson, reappearing on another shore. Bix looked for somewhere to get Keller out of the rain. I saw a double camelback of metal ahead in the water, a bridge blocking us. There was no room to go under, like most of the bridges we'd portaged, there were spars in the way. It was too high to go over, a barrier to going any farther north without leaving the river and hauling the canoe over land.

"Nonie, you see that?" I turned to look back at Bix, thinking she meant the bridge. Bix was staring, not at the bridge, but to the east, pointing to shore.

I followed her gaze to an island hill with a high brick tower poking over the trees, arched windows on the sides, and below it the long roof of a main house, decorated with tiny cupolas and arches patterned with colored brick, gray slate on the roof shining in the rain, a house, a huge house, a mansion above the river. It was beautiful. A twisting funnel of smoke rose from a chimney on the western side. I couldn't take my eyes off that smoke.

"Someone's home," said Bix.

IV

CLOUDS MEANT FOR WALKING ON

<u>Clouds Meant for Walking On:</u> Some days there is low fog everywhere on the ground, in the valleys in the Park, in the valleys between the towers of Old City. I asked Mother about it, and she said that there was a kind of fog that rolled down from the Berkshire Hills, or not from the hills, not down but up, up out of the trees as the trees breathed, and into the air, like clouds being born in the forest, like new sky somehow, and they became so thick while you watched in the morning that you started to think you could walk on them all the way over the mountains.

—From the Water Logbook

50
THE WOMAN WITH WELLS FOR EYES

I almost sank the boat on the edge of a billboard, looked down and saw the ad rippling under the murky water, a picture of the orange autumn hills and a road and a car. We beached the canoe on the island. The house we'd seen from the river was huge up close, standing on the hilltop without fences or barricades, alone, surrounded by grass.

Keller woke and stood, unsteady and coughing. "I can do it," he said. Bix put her shoulder into his armpit to steady him, he buckled, but began to walk, halting, toward the house, Bix and Keller both unsteady on their feet. I checked my pack; the Logbook was still there, wrapped in oilcloth and untouched by the rain. I carried all our gear, the food too, but left behind the empty water bottles. Shivering, wet, we came before that house and its woodsmoke, stopped in front of a tall door that faced the Hudson. The house was perfect, ornate, covered over with patterned brick and tiles and stained-glass windows.

Bix faltered. "Nonie, he's listing." Keller stood, tipped like a falling tree, slid gently to his knees. I knocked.

"Nonie, wait!" Bix said. "Nonie."

"Hello." I knocked. "Hello?" I said hello instead of scream-ing like an animal.

I heard a key turn in a lock and the door rattled and opened. The space inside wasn't lit. A figure stepped for-ward from the black rectangle of the doorway, a woman, tall and stern, her black hair curling past her shoulders, a streak of gray running from the part in the center. She came into the light and gravity came with her. She was a gate carved

out of woman, soft until you tried to move her. She held a
hunting knife, the kind for skinning. She took us in the way
an animal will when it isn't sure whether you mean to eat it.
I felt damp and small, not someone with a scream inside her.

"How did you live?" she asked, staring at us, not seeing
Keller at all.

"What?"

"You didn't get the fever, the mosquito fever."

"No."

Something made a deep well in the woman, and the water in it went right up through her until it rippled below the
irises in her brown eyes. Around her house there was no
fence, no wall. Somewhere there were more weapons than
her knife.

"We need help. He's sick," I said, touching Keller's shoulder, "his lungs."

"I can hear," she said. "Fever?" I nodded. "Any boils, any
vomiting?"

"No," Bix said, "nothing like that."

"There's a new fever," the woman said, "and we don't have
the CDC to tell us what it is. It started west of here, and
people have been dying all summer. There's a quarantine. I
couldn't let you in if he had that." She put her knife into a
holder at her belt.

"He doesn't have that," Bix said. "None of us have that."

She looked at us with the water in her shivering at her
eyes, the deep need she held in that gaze. She decided
something. "Come on. Get him inside."

51
PETRA

She limped into the house. Bix limped in, Keller between us, through the pitch-back hallway, into a room with a grand staircase, busy with objects and paintings and color. Orange light poured through the window over the stairs.

"You have extra clothes?" she asked. "Anything that isn't wet?"

"No," I said.

She led us to a room with a fireplace along one wall, over it a painting of a city carved into a narrow sweep of cliffs: Petra. I recognized it from a book. She dragged an upholstered bench to the fire. "Put him there." He shivered and coughed, his teeth chattering, his eyes closed. "We have to get those clothes off him before the crew comes back." The room was abundant, my eyes were not used to abundance indoors. On the chair next to me was a blanket, on the blanket a copy of *Moby Dick*. "Come on," she said, "give me a hand." We were careful with Keller's modesty until he was under a blanket, wet clothes in a heap. "How long have you been like this?"

"Three days," he said.

"Nightmares? Sweating? Chills?"

"Yes," said Bix.

"I can't breathe right," Keller said. "I got a lungful of water." He started coughing.

The fire warmed my back, my clothes dripped. "We're from Old City. They killed our father, some of the Lost, in a ruin on the river," I said. The woman's face paled. I thought of the hole on the top of Storm King Mountain. "River water, he got a lungful of river water."

Keller tipped to lying on the bench and she got a pillow for him. "So, pneumonia. Bacterial. Viral. Probably both. Names? I'm Poppy." We told her. Poppy put her hands under Keller's back while he coughed. "He needs water. You need water. Stay with him." She limped out of the room, locking the door behind her.

Bix and I looked at each other over Keller. I listed what I knew: a house, a fire, Poppy's knife, Keller had two kinds of pneumonia, he was naked, we could hardly lift him.

"Is this her house?" Bix asked.

"She lives here?"

"But do you think it was hers? Before?"

"Don't know."

Keller coughed. Bix adjusted his pillow, she took off Father's wet jacket, took off Father's cap. "It's like nothing ever happened here."

"I know. Who's *the crew*?"

Bix shrugged.

Poppy unlocked the door and came in carrying a jug and a cup. "Keller," she asked him, "can you sit up?" He nodded, eyes closed. She gave him water. "Mary's our medic, she's coming with the crew. Let me talk to them. They don't trust the Lost and they won't like him," she said, lifting her chin toward Keller. "We haven't seen any strangers all summer, or any Blacks since the refugee wave. Our tower is the highest point around. I saw you coming up the river today." She paused. "It's extra work protecting a Black man. One traveling with children?" Her voice caught when she said "children." "Jared hates extra work. People come here for medicine—for Mary, before the quarantine—and we don't have enough." She rubbed a hand over her eyes, looked at the wet carpet where we stood. "Bix, stay here, I'll take Nonie up for dry clothes before they come back."

Poppy limped out the door and I followed. We went through the big hall, past a dining room lined with formal paintings, another fireplace, another fire, an iron pot balanced over it, up a staircase, past rugs and sculptures and the window of orange-colored glass. At the top, she turned in to a bedroom. From a trunk, she pulled clothing, handed it to me. I followed her to a room with a child's things, dusty toys and books and a bed. In there was another box, from which she took out smaller clothing. "Will these do?"

"Yes."

"Poppy."

"Yes, Poppy."

Bix was right, nothing had happened here, no storms or flooding or crowding. I walked to a shelf, picked up a teddy bear with mottled fur, brown and tan, and two black eyes and a matted ear, soft, covered in cobwebs. "Please leave it." Poppy's voice was brittle. I put it down, next to a picture of a younger Poppy, two children in her lap, dark curly hair like hers.

52

WILLOW TEA

oppy and I brought the clothes back to the Petra room. I heard voices outside the house, people coming up the hill, four of them visible through the big window in the room, a man at the head of the group with black hair and a pack.

"They're back," said Poppy. "Get dressed." She went out the door, locked it behind her.

Bix and I dressed, put our wet things on top of Keller's. Bix put Father's cap in her pack. My ankles and wrists gangled below the clothes. Bix rolled her cuffs. I sat on Poppy's chair, Bix stood over Keller, moving the blankets to warm him. "Stop fussing," he whispered.

"Fussing is my job now," she said. We heard footsteps. Bix looked at me. "Is that Poppy?"

I shrugged. The lock turned, the door opened, a woman came in, putting the key in her pocket. Her face was round and shallow, eyes brown with wrinkles in the corners, jeans with the knees torn, army boots, army jacket, black T-shirt under, red scarf around her throat, hair damp and loose, straight black. She didn't talk, smoothed her hands over her hair, pulled a cord from around her wrist to tie it into a ponytail, a blade the twin of Poppy's in a sheath on her leg; her skin smelled of the rain. She took Keller's wrist in one hand, pressed the other against his chest. She lifted the blanket, looked at the sheen of fever on Keller's skin, put the blanket back down, turned to leave without a word, locking the door behind her.

Bix and I stood in her wake. "Mary?" Bix asked.

"I guess?"

When she came back, she carried a bowl and cup in one hand, a lantern in the other. She locked the door behind her, pointed to the armchair in the corner with a free elbow, said "Pull me up that chair," put the lantern on the mantel behind her, said "Get me that blanket."

Bix limped over with the blanket; the woman looked her up and down, assessing, noting the limp for later. I brought over the chair, then stood close to her, looking at what was in the bowl and cup. In her bowl there were hot water and floating herbs.

"You're a pack of ghosts. Shoo." Bix and I stepped back, and she sat down. She poured the bowl's contents into the cup. "Willow tea. For the pain. For sleep. Take the fever's teeth out." Bix looked at me, worried. Mary caught it. "You'd better keep that eyebrow lowered." Keller took a drink from the cup she held. "This'll get you comfortable. Not as good as antibiotics, but a start."

"Do you have antibiotics?" Bix asked.

"We'll have to see," Mary said.

53
ONION PLASTER

There was a knock and Mary let Poppy in and she sat down on a chair by the window and watched us. "Jared wants to talk to you."

Mary went into the hallway. I could hear her talking low at first, then a man's voice, muffled. Then, "We *have* antibiotics," Mary said.

"We'll run out if you take care of him," the man said. "If we run out then you'll go to Hancock to barter. In fact, you can't do it unless that's the plan. I'm saying that's the plan."

"You want to order me around like we're still in the service, fine, see how well that goes." Mary opened the door and came back in. "If he makes one more rule about who I can treat," she said to Poppy. "Makes Hancock look appealing."

"You don't want to be there. Think about what Esther told you, about Childs. You want to be in debt for the rest of your life?"

"No. You know I don't. What is it breaks them like that? How do they stop making sense?" Mary walked to her pack, took out plastic pill bottles and baggies of medicine, a first aid kit. She laid them down on the floor next to Keller. "Making rules about what I can do is going to make everything worse."

"I know."

"Help me get these antibiotics into him."

54
VENISON STEW

Mary checked Keller as the medicine began. Keller fell into the first easy-looking sleep since the ruin. Poppy brought a tray with bowls on it. She handed them to Bix and me, pointed to a pair of high-backed chairs in the corner. She lit a candle next to us. We sat close together and ate. The bowls held stew with turnips in it, herbs, venison; the fat in the meat disappeared into my tongue and made me embarrassed by the wealth of it.

Mary sat next to Keller, ate fast, set her empty bowl on the floor, listened to his chest.

"What's Hancock?" I asked.

"Settlement. East of here. Only place with real medicine supplies for miles. They have a doctor. You'll have to get him there."

We finished the food. Mary said, "Prop him up and give me that water cup. Hold him so I can get him to take this. Come on, Keller, time to wake up and have some food and medicine." She handed him big pills, a cup with some stew. Then a cup with tea. "How are you feeling?" she asked him.

"Exhausted."

"We need to do one more thing for your fever, Keller. And then you need to sleep. Can you set him up for me?" she asked us. We put down our empty bowls and came to her. "Get his legs higher than his heart. Leave him on the bench, but like with his legs suspended over it," she made a gesture to show us how it should look, "like this." We nodded and she went out and Bix and Poppy and I used chairs, suspended a blanket as a hammock for Keller's legs to float over the bench. Mary came back with a cast-iron pan covered in dried ground corn and a bowl of mush smelling of onions, a brush handle sticking out. She set down the bowl on the floor, scooped black and red coals with a fire shovel and stirred them into the black pan until the corn caught and burned, set the smoking pan of corn onto the bench below Keller's knees, heat radiating up to the undersides. "Blanket. Not over his feet," Mary directed.

Bix took the blanket, covered Keller, left his feet stuck in the air. She looked sweaty.

"You OK?" I asked.

She shook her head and wouldn't meet my gaze, but she said, "It's hot by the fire."

Mary tucked the blankets in around Keller. "He'll sweat out the fever. It'll help break it while the antibiotics do their thing. Onion plaster next." Mary picked up the bowl and the brush and painted the soles of Keller's feet with the smelly mush. She settled on her haunches. "Now we wait."

Keller fell asleep like that, legs in the air. But as the hours went on, the sweat came on him. He coughed and shook. The fever raged until the dark was full outside the big windows. Poppy came and went, people walked past the closed doors, arguing. Mary made willow tea. I sat on the floor, ten paces back from Keller in a nest of blankets, the fever more frightening in that pretty room than out in the open. It filled the space and me and Bix. Mary sat and watched. Her manner, so quick and hard, kept her separate.

Keller dreamed. "The fridge, get some milk, I'm thirsty," he said. "Mano, where's the blanket." I moved closer to him, lacing his hand in mine.

Midway through the dark hours, Poppy pulled me back to lean on the far wall, gathered the blankets around my legs, inched closer to me. I rested against her, muscles aching from paddling, from digging Father's grave, from carrying our packs, from helping Keller and Bix limp into that house. I smelled her clean skin and clean clothes, smoke in her hair. She was soft, and I shut my eyes.

55
THE ARMORY

I woke next to Bix, squeezed into the warm arc she made. Mary and Poppy were gone. Keller slept without shaking or sweating. The pan of corn was gone; his legs were lowered and covered with a blanket. Bix was shivering, moaning in her sleep. "Bix?" She woke up and looked at me, her face tense with pain. "What's wrong?"

"My leg hurts. A lot. A lot more than last night."

"You cold?"

"A little."

"Can I look at it?" She nodded, reluctant. I scooted down to her leg, rolled back her sock, she winced. I kept going. It wasn't good. Lines of red streaked down the foot from her ankle. I took off the sock and she flinched, then started rolling up the fabric of her pants. The wound was seeping, full of yellow pus, and the red streaks radiated out along her calf. "Bix! This is bad!"

She gritted her teeth. "Infected?"

"Septic."

"I was worried about Keller."

"Poppy and Mary aren't here; can you walk?" She tried to move the leg, then looked at me and shook her head. "I'll go." I checked the doorknob, unlocked. I went back up the stairs. At the top, I saw that the room with the big bed was open, the bed empty. I walked into the children's room. I saw the bear, the pictures, heard a footstep overhead, saw in a corner an open door, inside, a staircase, walked up it, through wood-lined hallways to another open door. Through that door was a huge unfinished room, the tower room I had seen from the river, plain brick, bare floor, and columns, through its arches the Hudson. The sky had the pale, flat light of coming rain. The floor of the room was littered with ammo casings. There were boxes, a table in a corner, a folding nylon camp chair. By the window a shooter's nest, a gun propped on sandbags.

From the shadows on the edge of the tower room I saw movement. Poppy stepped out into the light. "Nonie?" She smiled at me, binoculars around her neck and a cup in her hand.

"I need Mary. Something's wrong with Bix's leg." I saw a gun at her feet. "That yours?"

"Yes." She prodded it with her toe. "It's mine. Part of the job."

"Are you an army?"

"Some of us were in the army, like Mary, and Jared." Poppy moved the rifle farther into the shadows with her foot. "But I'm a good shot. I was an archery teacher a long time ago, at a summer camp."

"You don't have a fence." I took a step closer to the windows.

"No." She pointed to the wall. "We have those." She pointed to a row of rifles. "Those are our fence, the armory. Jared was a sniper, before, in the army. Anyone coming up the hill, he did what he had to do, so people learned to leave us alone."

Jared was the fence. Bix was wrong. Something happened here, it just happened to the Lost. I could feel my face flush, my skin prick like when I heard the wolves howl on the Palisades. Maybe Clare made the mistake of coming here without children on the way to the farm. Maybe her bones were below us in the tall grass of the meadow below the tower. We barely made it up the hill. We lived because Jared was out, because we were children. I thought about what Poppy said last night, that Jared wouldn't want to take care of Keller, that it was harder with Black men. Maybe she meant that there wasn't anything but our skin that got us up that hill alive. I had to get Bix and Keller away from there. "Can we find Mary?"

56
O BULKINGTON!

The second time the Mosquito Borne came through, Beaumont got it. He was sick, but he lived. Then it came for Angel. She lay down on the sleeping shelf Father set up for her in the longhouse. Maybe it was losing Mano that made Angel weaker. Or maybe it was the first time she had Mosquito Borne that made the second time worse. The longhouse stank. Keller was up all night, placing a wet towel on her skin to cool the fever. He drenched it with tepid water from a bucket at his feet, wrung it out, wiped her face and neck, wafted the cloth over her, back and forth, back and forth. I watched him from my bed. The Mosquito Borne moved fast when it came, and two days later, Angel died, lying in a pool of her sweat, her mouth as open as her eyes, seeing pain in the molecules of the air.

Father and Keller carried her, zipped into her sleeping bag, down to the cool stacks to wait until her grave was dug. When Keller came back up, he lay down on his bed, Angel's loss a giant zero to fall into.

At Amen, everyone knew Keller kept us safe. Keller let Father plow through things, get people moving. He was a good motivator, Father. Keller kept us steady and balanced. Keller never was seduced by nostalgia, or greed. I saw Keller show Mano how to plant, how to sketch a bug, how to tell the body plan of one kind of beetle from another: *This one has an oval abdomen. That one's is round. What's the head shape? What's the mouthpart?* He sat with Mano, showed him how to use a whetstone to sharpen his pocketknife. Father wouldn't have done it that way. Father would do it all for you, so fast you wouldn't learn, impatient, ready for the next task to conquer. Keller took time. He stood behind your elbow. Told you that you were good. He walked you through dressing a deer, sat a few feet back while you made the cuts so you knew you could do it yourself. He taught us like someday we'd be alone, like a Jared was waiting in a tower a long way off and in his future, in ours, and you could only trust yourself. I thought he'd stayed at Amen for us, so Angel stayed safe, so Mano lived, so Mother had food brought to her when she was sick, so Bix and I learned to hunt. But maybe he stayed because he knew about the man in the tower. That's what he knew at the ruin. He knew it. He knew that man was always waiting. And now I knew it too.

I wasn't there when Father told Angel that Mano died. I wasn't in the great room when she came down to see his body. I was with Mother on the roof, her bathing me and bathing Bix and giving us warm food and a bed. "There will be time when we bury him," I heard her say to Father. "Enough time for them to process it."

Keller faltered when Mano died, but he'd thrown himself into work. With Angel there was no bottom. You could see it almost hurt him to look at us, the ones who survived.

There was no school without Angel, so Jess was kind, took us out to the garden. "Best thing for you." She took us to find elderberry in the Ramble. She took us to black-cap bushes where you could pick fruit while you stood in the grass. She took us to collect honey from the hives. She took us to the pharmacy so we could watch her make salves. "Think of it as an internship." She showed us the books in her piles and had us read them aloud to her. "What is best for pregnancy?" she'd ask.

"It says, 'See childbirth,'" Bix read.

"OK, so, see childbirth."

"Trillium," Bix said, "along with other stuff. Didn't you show us trillium last week?"

"It was blooming, yeah."

"We should go and get some, just in case."

"I like your optimism."

I took *Moby Dick* and sat in the crook of one of the windows of Astor Turret. The sun came in the window and warmed my legs, and the room was cool behind me, the marble floor picked out in washes of shadow light from the trees, sparkling. I had my binoculars resting next to me, I had the Water Logbook. *O Bulkington,* I read, imagining Angel's voice.

Below me in the grass I could see movement. I picked up my binoculars and looked, adjusting the focus until I could see Keller. He had a spade and a bag of seeds. He dug into the healed earth over Mano's grave, and scattered seeds in the fresh cut. Then he took the spade and turned over the fresh earth of Angel's grave. From his pocket he took out a sapling and buried its roots in the ground. He covered over the spots with earth, cozied the sapling into the soil, then lay down next to the graves and looked up at the sky.

57
A LONG WAY OFF

When we got back to the room, Poppy checked to see that Mary was there, then went back to the tower. Keller was sitting up. He looked alert, himself. Bixie sat with him, cup in her hand, blanket over her shoulder. Mary sat on the floor next to them.

"Nonie," Bix said, "look at Keller."

"I see," I said, and started crying.

"Nonie. Don't cry." Bix waved me over.

"I don't mean to."

Keller grabbed my hand. "Where were you?" he asked, so quiet.

"Up in the tower," I said. "Where were you?"

"A long way off." I held Keller's hand, he coughed.

"You OK?" I asked him.

"Don't know," he whispered. "Breathing hurts."

"Fever's down," Bix said.

"Now we can make it to the farm," Keller said.

"Farm?" Mary asked, and the tone was like the one Douglas used when we told him we had a boat. There was greed in there, or hope, hard to tell.

"That's where we're going," Keller said. "Their mother had a farm in Tyringham, in the Berkshires. We have a map. We were going to start walking when we got to the Rip Van Winkle."

"Well, that's where you are," Mary said. "Don't tell anyone else. OK?"

"OK." Keller looked worried.

I wanted to talk to Bix, tell her about the tower, the army.

But I blurted out, "Mary, Bix's leg is bad! You have to look at it."

Mary gave Bix a sharp look and Bix ducked her head. "Get over here," Mary said. Bix limped to Mary and pulled up her pant leg. The leg smelled when she revealed it, and it looked worse than it had when we'd woken. "Jesus, kid. That could kill you. Is that a gunshot?"

"Yeah," I said, "gunshot. Those men on the river. Same time as Keller."

"I haven't seen one of those in a long time. I bet you didn't even have any disinfectant. And you were in that canoe with the water right up on you. You're lucky you can still walk. That's the last of the antibiotics right there, even if Keller didn't need them all. And a way more complicated trip to Hancock. Esther has got to help us save that leg."

"Esther?" Bix asked.

"Hancock's doctor. One of the few around here. She's a wiz. This is beyond me."

"Wait, save the leg?" Bix asked.

"And you. Sepsis. We have to leave tomorrow. One dose of antibiotics is all I've got left, and it might not be enough."

Keller opened his eyes. "So, I'm not the hardest case anymore, is what you're saying?" He whispered, grinning, "Stealing my thunder, Bix?"

Bix, sweaty and stricken, looked back at him. "I didn't know."

"Bad joke. I'm sorry. We've got to take care of each other, kid. We're all we got."

58
THE MAN IN THE TOWER

The way ahead was like the edge of a cliff, like the drop out the tower windows. The way ahead was full of all the things I didn't know. *Sometimes what looks like shelter is only menace.*

Poppy woke up at dawn when I did, Mary gone somewhere. Keller and Bix slept next to the fire. I asked, "Poppy, is this your house?"

"No. This isn't my house. I came here like you did. It belonged to a painter. He collected a lot of this stuff overseas, and had this place designed. He called it Olana. Jared was stationed in Hudson, protecting the bridge, but then things fell apart, and he started our patrol up here. He'd been looking at this place from the bridge for months. He wanted the high ground. This place was all closed up, none of the hurricanes touched it. Jared was pretty smart about it. People squatted here. They sold off the things in it, burned furniture in the fireplaces. Then Jared came in with a few guys from his unit and cleared them all out. Mary was in the service with him. When the army broke up, she was stationed at the Camp in Pittsfield as a nurse. Met Esther there. Not too many medical folks left. They got through the Mosquito Borne. But she left there after the riots, came looking for him back here. I stumbled in. Any house with a chimney is worth a lot to people." I stared. "What?"

"My father, he was in chimneys."

"What?"

"He said that. He studied houses with chimneys, said that they would be worth something."

"He was right. You can live in a mall if your house floods, and you can scavenge the stuff there, but you can't heat a mall unless you make a hole in the ceiling or smoke yourself out. Here, all we had to do was unblock the chimneys, make hand pumps to get the well water out, chop wood. Until this flood, we could come and go as we liked in case something bad came in from the south, or from the west."

"Is west bad?"

"Yup. Maybe not in the Catskills, not right away, but Albany, the highways, the flatland, the Great Lakes, the Rockies. It is a burning plain all the way to the Pacific. Of course, the refugees went there, makes sense, right? Farther from the sea. That's what people say anyway, the ones who come back." I wondered if this was the story Jared told Poppy to keep her scared or if this was how things really were.

"I like the water. The ocean."

"I used to feel like that once. My husband taught me to like the mountains."

"Where is he?"

"Gone. Mosquito Borne. With my kids."

I was quiet. "Mother told me there were boats. For scientists. I want to get on the boats."

"That's the most sensible plan I've heard." She stood up. "You're never far from the sea now."

I looked back at Keller and Bix; he was sick, and she was shot. Jared was a man in a tower. Poppy lived here and knew it, and all the talk between us couldn't change that. *Why is that so?* I found myself thinking, like Angel whispering in the room. *Who benefits?*

I saw how we must look to the man in the tower. For our sake, Father and Keller pretended that the world outside Amen was better than it was. Maybe they wanted us to think that we all had to worry about dogs and starving no matter who we were. But it mattered who we were out here, and it mattered if we could find medicine.

"Mary said we needed to get to Hancock," I said to her.

"You do. It's two days' walk, east from here, overland. Mary's going with you, to take care of Keller and Bix and get you to Hancock safe. Jared didn't want to spare her. He's worried there's another refugee wave coming behind you from the city."

"No one's left."

Poppy shrugged. "Anyway, Mary insisted. She knows the way, and she'll tell Hancock who you are. Hancock's in the Berkshires, a big settlement. I want you to be careful. If they ask you to stay, don't do that, OK? Hancock isn't a place to stay. They have this debt system. If you take medicine or food or a place to sleep, you're supposed to work it off. I get it, but it can be difficult to get out. We don't do that. We've had troubles with them. There's a pact now, and we need them for things—"

"Medicine?" I asked.

"Medicine," she said, "and other things. Safety. There was a refugee camp in Pittsfield, close to Hancock, and there was trouble."

"What trouble?"

She hesitated. "The Camp was there a long time, in The World As It Was when we took in people from the Maldives, from Syria, Turkey, the Caribbean. It was the holding spot—Puerto Ricans, Dominicans, Haitians—but then the military tightened it. They rationed the food and the medicine. The town would raid it for supplies, they never liked having refugees up here. They burned part of it to the ground, killed a lot of people. The hospital in town didn't have enough for the residents. It was the same story all over the place. Finally, the army fell apart, the townspeople came in, there was a massacre. The raiding parties left for the hills. Hancock took the leftover stuff, the ammo and medicine. Like they were waiting for the end of things. I don't know. Hancock has ways of keeping order that I don't like." Everything sounded different from Amen: armies, camps, settlements. She was describing so many places made without care. Amen, the Cloisters even, were made entirely around love.

There was a knock on the door and Jared came in. "Can I talk to you?" he asked without looking at me. He looked so ordinary: average tallness, average bulk, average age, trimmed brown hair, shaved face. No uniform, black pants, a gray shirt, waterproof jacket. I tried to memorize him so I could see another Jared coming, but my eyes slid off him as off the surface of a tinted skyscraper window.

Poppy left with him. Bix woke up. I wanted to tell her everything I knew about the man in the tower, about Hancock and what Poppy told me. But I asked, "You OK?"

"Leg hurts."

"Rest."

Bix closed her eyes. "Do we have to go back in a boat?"

"Only a little."

Keller woke up. "Well," he said. "I feel like I might be alive again."

"Antibiotics," I said.

"They're a hell of a drug." Keller smiled.

"We're leaving. They're out of antibiotics, and Bix needs them too."

"That leg?"

"Yup."

"She's gotta learn to lean on people."

"She does?"

"Yeah. She does. You too, little warrior."

The door opened and I could see Poppy and Jared and Mary. Jared had his hand on Mary's arm. She pulled it away. She walked angrily into the room, left Jared glaring from the hall, collected blankets, walked back through the door without speaking to him.

"Something's up here," Keller whispered.

I looked at him, afraid I'd start talking and not stop. "Yes," I said. "I think it isn't safe."

"Mary's safe."

I nodded. "Mary's good. I don't think Jared is."

Keller raised an eyebrow, smiled weak. "You learning to smell predators, little warrior?"

"Maybe."

"Better than smelling rain." Keller shut his eyes.

"Same thing," I said.

59
LEAVING HUDSON

We packed, dressed in our own dry clothes, folded our borrowed clothes and left them on the floor. Bix checked her pack, touching the gun inside it without taking it out. I checked the Logbook. It was dry, and I peeled back a corner of the waxed canvas around it, looked at the cover. Father's handwriting was there, and I felt the cold rain of Storm King Mountain open up a hole in me that I was trying not to feel, like ice cracking on the center of a frozen water jug on a cold day, leaving the edges thicker and intact—the opening that will destroy everything solid and turn the whole barrel to liquid again. Even in that room— dry walls, paintings, rugs, fireplace, bowls of stew—I felt the darkness of the ruin, Keller's leap, the dirt still under our nails from the grave.

We left the way we came, through the halls and out the front door, only Keller was on a stretcher and Bix was limping with my shoulder as her crutch. We walked into the tall grass, my nostrils full of the rain at the edge of the sky, down the eastern slope of the island on which the mansion sat, the Hudson surrounding all of Jared's high ground. Jared might have been watching us from that tower through his scope.

At the edge of the river was a boat. They settled Keller and the gear in the bottom.

"Where's our canoe?" I asked.

"It's too small for this job," said Poppy.

"Oh," I said. I hadn't said goodbye. It felt strange to leave that part of our bodies behind. At least it was finally closer to home.

"Nolan's on the other side, Union Turnpike, with Pumpkin," Poppy said to Mary. "He left at dawn; he'll get the Whaler back."

"Whaler?" I asked.

"This kind of boat," Mary said, then nodded to Poppy. "Thank you."

Poppy petted my hair. "OK," she said, kissed the top of my head, forgot she didn't know me. I leaned into the kiss until I remembered Jared, the shell casings on the floor. Bix and I sat on a bench in the Whaler above Keller, leaving a space for Mary. Mary and Poppy grabbed the gunwales to push the boat into the river. Mary jumped into the back. Poppy kept pushing from alongside, wading into the Hudson, "Come back, OK?" she said to Mary. "He doesn't mean it." Mary turned away from her and didn't say anything. "Be safe," she whispered to me.

The boat was deep enough now that Mary lowered the outboard motor and started it. They had fuel. Poppy stopped following us and started waving.

I shut my eyes to make sure I didn't look back at Poppy. I didn't want to see her growing smaller, the need on her face, didn't want the anger it made me feel.

I waited a long time, until I knew I wouldn't see her, then looked back over my shoulder. From the water, the house was small enough to be a toy. I couldn't see Poppy, only a tiny roofline in the flat haze.

"That bag next to you," Mary ordered, "there's fry bread in there."

We opened the bag and got out the food, Keller waved food away, but we ate and drank. Keller fell asleep. Bix looked out at the water.

We rounded a peninsula, the top points of a church poking out from the water, a town in the distance. "That's Hudson," said Mary.

This was the town Father meant us to find, the end of our time on the river. We'd found it and we hadn't known. There were roofs and steeples, traffic signs and billboards, all the bases of their buildings underwater, roads slid down from islands. It started raining, woke Keller up, Bix pulled a tarp over him, "Thanks, kid," he said. Mary put up the hood on her rain shell. It got cold again. Bix had Father's cap on under her hood, rain dripped off it, then the cloud passed, and we were under dry gray skies. We passed between two patches of land split by the river, on one side a rotting diner laced with burn marks, on the other the tops of headstones marking a cemetery, Hannah Putnam 1935–1992, Arthur English, 1974–2020. There wasn't anyone to remember the people in those graves. Father didn't have a headstone; nothing marked him at all. The wrought-iron fence of the cemetery trailed off into the river, the bodies under the water now, along with the town. An auto-parts store was next to it, a bullet hole punctuated the name of the shop on the plastic sign: Mal*one's. The shore ahead was a green meadow, not a building nearby, the blacktop of an old road and a worn track beside it through the grass, on the blacktop a horse and a man standing next to it. On the back of the horse was a frame that looked like the travois I'd seen in the Hall of Eastern Woodlands. The river shushed under the boat. "Welcome to Union Turnpike," said Mary. "Nolan, you got her ready?" Mary asked. He nodded, quiet as Jared. "This is Pumpkin," Mary barked at us, pointing at the horse. "Bix, you have to ride." Nolan took the Whaler from Mary and cast off to go back to Olana. Mary fussed over gear and the travois for Keller, Bix's placement on the saddle. "We've got thirty-seven miles to go, give or take. Stop tonight on Hartigan Road."

The road was buckled like the sidewalks in the Upper West, years of frost heaves and weather on it. In some places it ran true, a picture-book version of a highway, but it was broken so long that, no matter the condition, there was a dirt track big enough for the horse to walk running the length of it. Mary took the lead and Pumpkin's reins, knife on her leg. My muscles didn't remember walking, my knee still ached from the bruise I got in the hypercane on the Amen roof, the scrapes from the ruin scabbed over and tight. On the river, we were a small craft in a big space. We were quiet. On the road, the horse stamped and puffed, the travois wheels bumped the ground, Keller coughed and woke and talked. We were a parade, moving bait. An hour in, Mary asked, "Is Keller sleeping?"

"Yes, ma'am," I said.

"OK. When he wakes, we'll get him some tea."

I looked up at Bix on the horse. "Winter wheat," she said, pointing to a meadow. "I read about it. It must have self-seeded. Farmers used to plant it late in the year. It would live through the freeze and ripen in the spring. The ground froze solid. Can you imagine that?"

"Nope." When the wheat moved, it shirred up a silver tinge under the pale green. In the sweep of it, the color changed back and forth with the light, almost like water. "I like that color."

"Me too," said Bix. She liked that it was growing. I liked the sea of grass.

We kept to Union Turnpike, away from towns. "More trouble than they're worth," Mary said. Mary's back tensed at every building. She walked like Keller paddled. When Keller woke, we stopped in a dry meadow for food and drink. Keller sat up on the stretcher and Bix stayed riding Pumpkin.

"She's got the march down," Keller whispered to me when I tucked his blankets back in. I smiled. "Ever think you'd see me on a travois?"

"No, I did not."

"Keller," Bix said, "she says we've got thirty-seven miles to go."

"That's a long way to travel on my back."

60

LENOX HILL HOSPITAL

We always looked for meds for Mother. She took things to keep her blood pressure down. She needed antibiotics when she got a bladder infection, a kidney infection. She took painkillers and vitamin D when we could find it. By the time Mother was sick, Old City was scavenged so many times that there was not much chance of finding anything she needed. But it made Father feel better, to go out, along with Keller, to go deeper into the canyons to where there might be a clinic or hospital, a doctor's office on a high floor. I went once with Keller and Father and Oliver and Jess to scavenge Lenox Hill Hospital. Inside was empty of people, echoing rooms, screens pulled from the walls, overturned carts, boxes in the halls. Keller and Oliver and Jess went to the basements, to check in supply rooms and mail rooms, to find the old pharmacy. Father and I climbed the stairs and checked in the dialysis center and the nephrology department, and finally wandered halls of patient rooms, looking for nursing supply closets. None of Mother's medicines were there, only a blood pressure cuff, splints, a cane. A fridge in a lab had injectable painkillers, all smashed.

"People left so fast when the army said this was a sacrifice zone," Father said. "But it is still strange to see how they left things."

Father went to the left down a long corridor, I went to the right. There were a few towels left in a closet, some pillows, some trays and cups, no medicine. I circled back and found Father inside one of the rooms, sitting on a hospital bed.

The light came in cool through the windows. There was an old recliner in the corner, and I sat in it, looking at Father. "There's nothing here, is there?" he asked.

"It's pretty empty."

"I thought so."

"We still had to try."

Father looked at me. "You know, don't you? That Mother's not doing OK?"

"Bix told me. She said you said she's not OK."

"Come here," he said. I came to sit by him, but I didn't want to talk then. I wanted to find medicine. I wanted to fix her. I sat stiff next to him. He tried to put an arm around me. I could tell he wanted me to put my head on his chest or start crying. But I sat so still. "She's not going to get better, Nonie."

"What can we do?"

"We're doing it now, trying to help."

We sat for a while, and he tried to rub my arm, tried to look into my eyes. I didn't want him to. I knew I was supposed to feel something, but I didn't know how to feel like Bix did, or like Father did. I felt, but I didn't know how to show it like they wanted me to. The feeling would come out sometime, and I wouldn't have any say about how.

"Can we go?" I asked.

"Yeah. OK, sure. We can go." He stood up and picked up his pack. "You're always so distant, Norah." He never called me that name. I made him feel alone, even when I was right there.

61
DEVIL'S CORKSCREW

Roads led off the highway, like there were houses down them.

At Amen we had a *daimonelix* on display in a case in the Hall of Primitive Mammals. A *daimonelix* is a type of ichnofossil. Ichnofossils are not fossils of organic matter—bodies, bones turned to rock—but rather fossils of behavior. That behavior can be in the form of tracks, footprints, a pathway, a burrow, a boring, a scat.

A *daimonelix* is sometimes called a "devil's corkscrew." It looks like a huge corkscrew standing upright, with a lump at the bottom. It is a spiral fossil of a burrow, long and twisted, tall as me, made by a *Palaeocastor,* an extinct land beaver, less than a foot tall and fur covered. You could tell it was a fossil when you saw it in the case. It was solid and clearly rock, but comic, as if a cartoon snake had jumped up from the ground and in its twisting, wild energy been turned to stone. There are devil's corkscrews that are fossilized with the *Palaeocastor* still inside, trapped in the path they made to keep themselves safe from harm.

Maybe behind those roads there was a spiral as curved as a devil's corkscrew hiding people burrowing away from The World As It Is.

Through the woods I could see the light changing in a clearing ahead. "Tornado did that." Mary nodded at the broken trees. "We came on this mess in patrol." On the other side of the woods the trees opened on a highway. "The Taconic." Mary named the place like a talking map.

"What?" Bix asked.

"The highway." Mary gestured ahead of us. "The Taconic Parkway."

"I thought we were taking the Pike," I said.

"Not today."

Most of the Taconic was empty. We walked a dirt track between the river of ruined blacktop on one side and a twin river of it on the other. We passed piled-up broken vehicles left where they fell, a single car, undamaged, tires airless, rust painting the metal, highway road signs ripped from their posts. Mary looked back over her shoulder. "We'll be there soon. Hartigan Road. There's a farm."

My feet ached. I was thirsty. Mary led us off the highway, smaller tracks along smaller roads, past a burned farmhouse. The dark came down in earnest. To the left of the road, a flicker of light came through the trees. Ahead of that was a driveway, and we walked up the dirt track of it, to the side of a ragged farmhouse. The white clapboard was dull in the low light, chunks of the planking and some windows covered with plywood. A candle was burning in an upper room. People lived here, but it was very quiet. The barn behind the house was rusting metal, its tin roof a quilt of galvanized pieces left after storms.

"I'm gonna find Dan," Mary said, "you take Pumpkin." I stood holding the reins, shy of the big animal, watched the door where Mary had gone. I wanted to lie down on the farmyard grass and take off my shoes and sleep. Mary came out, didn't look at us, took the reins from me and led Pumpkin to the barn. The sliding metal door screamed when she opened it; inside was total darkness. Still holding Pumpkin's reins, Mary felt along the wall to a lantern on a hook. She handed it to me, and dug in her pocket for a box, fumbled a match to burning and lit the wick. There was hay all over; stalls on the far wall, tractor in the corner, horse blankets and plastic drums on the floor. Mary and I settled Bix and Keller and Pumpkin. The barn was cold.

"Can we have a fire?" Bix asked.

"No," Mary snapped. Then, "Dan says no," softer. She took willow tea from her pack, got out a baggie with two pills. "This is the last of it. Hopefully we make Hancock tomorrow. I know the pace is hard, but we don't have a choice. We don't have anywhere else to sleep, so we have to get seventeen miles a day. Tomorrow will be the same." She handed pills to Bix and Keller. Keller coughed, the sound stored up in his chest the whole walk, deep and rattling and wet.

Keller looked at me. "I'm OK, Nonie."

"No, you're not," Mary said. She dipped a cloth in water, laid it over Keller's head, poured out more tea. "Better for you both if you tell the truth."

Mary got me food and a blanket from her gear. The weight of my skull pulled me to lying down, rain pipping the galvanized roof, straw under the blanket under my cheek, scratchy and smelling like hot field. Mary sat between Keller and Bix, ready with food and water. She took the wet cloth, wafted it back and forth to cool Keller, like he'd done with Angel.

62
ARCHIE

Then it was light out. I'd slept with my mouth open, and drool had made the wool wet against my face and the straw smelled cold and green now. I rubbed my fingers over the wool, wiped my face. Keller was asleep, Mary awake beside him, right where she'd been. Next to her was a dog.

I sat up, terror lighting my chest. But the dog looked at me and wagged its tail. It looked at Mary; its mouth looked like smiling. Mary was too tired to see my fear. "Nonie meet Archie, Archie meet Nonie."

Archie walked over to me. I felt the nausea coming up, the smell of him making me retch, put my hand over my nose and mouth to stop it. He sniffed me, wagged his tail, looked back at Mary, and walked out the door. When he was gone my body relaxed, my stomach sour.

"Just a dog," Mary said.

"I know." A bead of sweat came down my neck. "Is there a pack?"

"Of dogs?" She shook her head. "He's a pet. Dan's pet."

"We had packs, not pets."

Mary looked at me. "Where'd you live?"

"Amen, on the roof, near the Park." I didn't know how to say it all. "In Old City, in the Park, there were dogs. I don't like them." I swallowed, the nausea leaving. "How is he?" I nodded to Keller.

"Not great. He'd be dead without the antibiotics, but the pneumonia isn't gone. He might need antibacterials or hydration. Esther will know."

"What time is it?" asked Bix, sitting up, her short hair a pointed wave on her head.

"Early," said Mary, "past dawn. Find a place to pee, load up. We have to go."

Bix covered her hair with Father's cap. We put on hoodies. She leaned on me to walk. I saw Archie resting on the farm-house steps, head on his paws, tongue out. I froze, but Bix squeezed my hand, and I looked up at her and she pumped my hand like I'd done for her in the boat in Old City. "Just a dog." She smiled.

We found a place to pee behind the barn. The farmhouse had a terrible quiet to it. No fence here either, high up on a dead-end road, a *Palaeocastor* burrow. The grass was wet, the driveway a mud meadow, the sky tall with thunderheads sweeping the cloud line. A day like this, you could think the weather was safe.

We left the farm, a woman's face watching us at the back door. Archie followed, that dog grin still on his face. At the highway, Hartigan Road behind us, Archie stopped, know-ing the edges of home. We kept on walking without him.

63
TO THOSE WHO REMAIN

"I don't know how to help Keller," I told Mother after Angel died.

"You can't," she said. "He has to go through it."

"He can't look at Bix."

"I know," she said. "He will again."

"He won't even look at bugs."

"Then you'll have to remind him. Ask him about bees."

I went to the library, because I remembered a lesson Angel taught us, about bees and about the symbol all over Europe. It was in a decorative art and architecture lesson, one that helped us know what was on the buildings around us, the building we lived in. And in that book, there was a passage about what bees meant. I found the book on the shelf and ignored the places where Angel's notebooks were left on tables and desks, her handwriting still sharp in the dark room. I found the book and took it back to the longhouse, where I read it until sleep.

We walked to the garden the next day, all of us for safety. Jess peeled off to forage, and Bix went to work inside the fence with Father, and I followed Keller to the bees.

I sat in the grass watching him tend the hives. He didn't speak. "Angel told me that people painted bees all over Italian buildings, and made sculptures with them," I said. "And that there were bees in mosaics and frescoes. And also, that the people who held the Dead Sea Scrolls loved bees. They called their priests drones or bees or something, the Essenes. And also, that Napoleon used bees as a symbol of the resurrection of his kingdom."

"Is this reverse Animal in Mind? Where you give me the answers?"

"This is something that made me think of Angel."

"I never stop thinking of Angel."

"I think, bees mean so many things."

"I know, Nonie." Keller stopped working and sat on his haunches. "I know. Angel said so many things that I can't stop thinking about her ever. And I want to tell her things, right now even. Like, I want to remind her that she did a good job with you, teaching you."

"She was a good teacher."

"She was." He wiped his hands together, as if they had dust on them, or dirt. Then he looked at his nails, then at the sky. "She told me about the Essenes too, you know, when she read about them. They were communal. They made communities that favored peace and combined government. They always worked together to keep secrets about God, and they wouldn't eat animals. And that's why they loved bees. Not just for resurrection. Not just because of God. But because they worked together like bees do, to keep things going even if they lost part of their number." I looked over at him. He looked back from the clouds to me. "But maybe you remembered that, too."

If Angel was another mother, I wonder what it meant to Mother when we lost her. Maybe she could already feel her body shutting down as the days got harder. I could feel the way she began to pour herself into me. She took every single chance to tell us anything she could remember. She read us books. She held us so close. She made lists I couldn't read in a notebook she shared with Father. She tried to say everything. When Angel died, the number of people to care for Bix and me shrank.

64
MASSPIKE

We came to a big highway. A sign said MASSPIKE, a black hat next to the words. "The Pike," I called to Mary. She didn't turn around, but I saw her nod.

There was a semi on its side like a stranded turtle, rotting boxes drifted into the forest from the open container. Cars melted into the pavement, a tree trunk across the hood of one, the dirt track littered with toys, food wrappers, blankets, a stone cairn maybe marking a grave, every item a catalogue of what could go bad. The Logbook was a weight in my pack that felt purposeless, the worst thing all that work could be. Bix listed in the saddle. Keller slept.

"You don't carry a gun?" I asked Mary.

"No. Never. Just a knife, and only because I was told to."

"Why not?"

"Don't like 'em."

"That's it?"

Mary walked in silence for long enough I wasn't sure she heard me. "I made a pledge. I promised not to do any harm, to always be a helper to human beings. I don't want things to have gotten so bad that I have to go back on a promise I made."

We left the highway and walked past a burned-over ruin. "What's that?" I asked.

"That was the high school," Mary said. "It was a storm shelter. They were using it when it got hit. They sent us to help, over from the Camp in Pittsfield. We had tanks then, the unit got the bodies out, but we needed earthmovers for some. Lots of bodies still inside when we left," said Mary.

"Then there was lightning the next winter, took out the last of the walls, timber. When that fire came everyone was glad. No one wanted to look at it anymore."

Behind it was a meadow broad as the path a twister would cut, that stretched over a mountain in front of us. "Is that where we're going?" I asked.

"Yeah. Up that old right-of-way for the power company. They cut this path over the mountain, buried electric under it. It never grew back. We use it to get to Hancock, so we don't go through New Lebanon. The Camp went down five years ago and if you didn't get to us or Hancock you were dead. There are plenty of the people left hiding in these towns, taking their chances. Some make it, like Dan, because no one wants to touch them. But the towns aren't like that. I've patrolled this route for five years. This way there's nothing but forest. If anyone's coming, they'd have to take this same path and we'd see them. On the other side of this mountain there's an old house where there's fresh water."

When I couldn't sleep, Mother told me hikes, her mind a library of all the places I'd never see, hikes she'd taken before the airplanes and cars stopped—Uchisar's desert houses and olive groves, the Olympic Peninsula's tree moss, the Absarokas' high snows, the Twelve Bens' quiet green, Conejos Peak's ice-blue lake.

"Stone Barn!" I'd beg.

"Well, that was the last time we went back to visit your father's grandparents, when they were still alive, and we came with your grandparents to see some cousins out in Illinois. This was all when we were first married, and hard to organize. Your father and I took a break from family for the hike. We parked on the side of the road, because the prairie around the trail was fenced off for the bison. We got out of the car, and we put on our packs, and we left the

road. We started up the trail. At first, it was only a young forest of skinny oak trees on a ridge, but the trail forked. One
way you would stay on the high ground and make a circle
through the woods. The other way was the way we took.
And the trail was gravel in loose loam and sand, unstable.
But it went around a hollow, almost like a kettle in the land,
until it came to a low place between two hills with eroded
limestone."

"And one of them looked like a stone barn?"

"Exactly! Now, no more questions or you won't fall
asleep."

Once, she told me a hike she'd taken near the farm on
Tyringham Cobble when she was a girl. It was a story of
rockfalls, beetles, rattlesnakes, ropes of princess pines, cathedral maples, wild blackberries, jack-in-the-pulpits, laurel
bushes, tree trunks marked by buck antlers, wild turkey up
in the brush. That kind of forest wasn't in Turkey or Arizona
or Canada or Ireland. It was in her own place, the place we
were going. Her hike was all around me as we climbed the
right-of-way through the forest.

Halfway up the hill, Bix was listing in the saddle, and
all at once she folded forward. I ran up alongside her and
grabbed her arm so she wouldn't fall. "Mary!"

Mary turned back and looked at us. "Jesus." She went
to one of Pumpkin's saddlebags and took out some paracord. "Bix? I'm going to secure you to this horse, OK?" She
checked her forehead. "Shit."

"She's not OK." I must have looked at her with exhaustion that looked like suspicion, maybe. There was sweat
down the hollow of my back, jeans hot, knee aching. "Why
is she falling?"

"She's getting sicker. We're going to the right place. You
have to trust me."

"Why?" I said it before I thought. Keller was asleep, Bix passing out, I was alone with Mary, and I'd known her four days. All the worry of the tower bunched up under my chest, all the things I hadn't been able to tell Bix and Keller. "You and Poppy work for Jared. He would have shot Keller if he'd seen him coming. Keller's some Lost man to you, some Black man."

"You think I care he's Black?"

"Keller's too much work. Poppy said it."

"Then Poppy's the person you should be yelling at!" She pointed at Keller. "Jared's got some idea that there's an army of Brown people coming to take over his house. You think I don't know who Jared is? You think I didn't fight to be allowed to take you to medicine? You figured out Keller's in danger? Smart girl. Why do you think I was in the god-damned army?"

"Why?"

"I'm Mohawk, Kanien'keha:ka. Half the kids from my town went into the army. It's how we got to college. That's how we got back any power at all. I wanted to learn medicine. I did all of it to help." She took out a bandana from her pocket and wiped her forehead. "Nonie, you idiot, can't you tell who to trust? Jared kept me because I'm a medic. He needs me." She pulled the paracord around Bix, tied a knot, straightened. "Doesn't matter. I'm not going back."

65
THE GREAT BLUE WHALE

There wasn't much time between losing Angel and Mother. That April, that last April at Amen, was hot and raining and we couldn't work in the garden or collect, there was no school and no foraging. Mother and Father were inside the office in the library writing things down, Bix and I were left to wander the museum without purpose. I followed her to Warburg Hall, past Yankee towns in all four of the old seasons. We walked past dioramas of maple sugaring, past the huge tree-ring wall, deep into the shadows, the wet smell of rotting basements coming up the stairs. "Did people like this room?"

"No. People thought it was boring. Who cares about maple syrup when you can get it at the store?" I followed her.

"Is this where we came when the city flooded?" I wanted her to tell me again.

"This is where we came. And you didn't talk. And we slept right there," she pointed to a carpeted corner by the diorama of winter, "until Sergio and the others showed up and we made a plan."

"And that's what winter looked like?"

"You know that's what winter looked like."

"And you used to eat the snow?"

"Yes. We ate the snow with maple syrup."

We walked to the Milstein Hall with the dolphins and the squid, the fish everywhere, the great blue whale hanging over all of it. Even though the room was about the sea, she loved it because it was dark. I loved everything else, the deep stillness like being underwater. We stopped at the foot of the stairs, under the whale. "Can I swim now?" I asked.

She looked at me. "You go ahead. I'll be back."

I nodded. "OK. But come back quick."

"OK." She looked softer. "No time at all. Just swim with the whale."

She wandered off to the squid diorama in the far corner of the room. I lay down on the floor. The room was a huge, pooled blackness outside my lantern light, ringed on all sides with dioramas of ocean life, of polar life, of dolphins and otters and kelp. I could hear Bix's footsteps. I'd been in every corner of the room, knew all the edges. My lantern light reached the pale belly of the blue whale, the huge model that the museum erected in the 1960s. Mother told me that it was wrong at first, since scientists were using pictures only, from a female whale that they'd seen in the 1920s. She told me about it the first time she took me there, in The World As It Was. Then, the whale was clean and bright, the low light of the room artificial and soothing. "See, they put in the belly button later!"

"It is because they are mammals!" I parroted what she'd told me on the subway ride there.

"That's right! That's my girl! Whales nurse their babies like we do."

Under my back, the rubber floor tiles were cold. Above me, strings of cobwebs fluttered down from the fins. I squinted until the whale faded out. I thought about swimming, something that, despite all the water in The World As It Is, I'd never done. It would be calm, I thought, deep under the water under the whale. Maybe I would have a scuba suit and hover there, like flying. If I could swim, I could swim in any sea I wanted.

I imagined water flooding down the long twisting staircases, the course of the Eocene sea slipping away under my tailbone, under the marble of the Amen floor. I slipped the features of the *Basilosaurus* over the whale: long teeth in its long jaws and always hunting. Around me and through my squinted eyes, the seas shifted back and forth through time—now the Eocene, the Devonian. A *Dunkleosteus* covered in bony plates seemed to bump against the upper railing of the room. The water became the Ordovician sea; an orthocone with pointed shell and eight long tentacles pushed itself backward toward the ceiling like a nautilus. Trilobites scuttled around my ankles and under my socks, every size of them, every ribbing pattern, ready to curl up and make themselves into marbles I could shoot along the floor until they hit the edge of the wall in the dark, plinking their tiny brittle backs.

I could hear Bix's footsteps while the seas rolled around in my mind, hear her settle next to me and sigh. I looked over at her face, half in lantern light, the shadow side away from me. She closed her eyes. "Are you imagining the sea?"

"Yes."

"What period?"

"Ordovician."

"I like that one."

"Me too."

"Mother has good stories about that one."

"You're awake for the stories?"

"I'm always awake for her stories."

I closed my eyes, and the imaginary trilobites settled around us like sleepy cats, snuggled under my knees, head-butted themselves under my clenched hands.

"What will we do when she isn't here for stories?" Bix asked.

I opened my eyes. "What do you mean?" I asked.

"When she's gone? What will we do then?"

"When she's gone?" The trilobites unsettled. "Where's she going?"

"Mother's dying." Her voice was settled. "You know."

I sat up. "She has good days."

"I know, some, she has some good days. But her kidneys aren't working right."

"I know that!"

"Right, of course you do. But they are *really* not working right. It's been too long without a doctor. Jess can't find her any more medicine. If there were hospitals, they could have given her a new kidney like replacing a generator part. But there aren't. Not here, anyway. And that's how it goes, with the thing she has, that's what it's like. It keeps hurting her until she's gone. Father told me." I stared at her in the dark. "He didn't tell you? I'm sorry, I thought he told you."

"She has good days."

"I know. She does. But you've seen her skin, Nonie. She's yellow. It's worse." She tried to reach for my hand. "She's dying."

It drained into me like the sea, the things she was saying. I'd seen them, I had. I filled up with liquid dread, like water of the wrong level, too hot or cold or with the wrong chemical balance. Inside my skin wasn't the ancient sea, but the one from outside of the Old City seawalls, the one with the leachate and nukes and disease, the human filth and the dead things, the sea we weren't supposed to touch. The trilobites started sinking in it, the weight of the water overwhelming.

Bix reached out again, rolled over and looked at me. "Stay with me, Nonie. I'm here. I thought he told you too. I wouldn't have said." I let her take my hand. She reached up and pushed my hair back, like Mother did when I couldn't sleep. "We'll be OK," she said. "We'll be OK. We're together. We're OK." Above me the whale hovered—her belly button, her pale belly where she'd nursed her babies, her fins slicing through air that was really sea but was really air. "I've got you. I've got you."

The broken sea was inside my veins, as if I'd breathed it in through gills and made it my own, my blood, my future. I could feel tears. I hadn't known I was crying. "You'll drown if you don't sit up," Bix joked, then brushed the tears from my face, from my hair. "Your hair is wet."

"Sorry."

"It's OK. I'm sorry." She draped herself over me for a hug. "Can we go?"

She stopped hugging me and sat up. "Yeah, OK, we can go."

I sat up, too. We walked back, the light disappearing from the room behind us, the whale floating back into the dark ocean, a parade of creatures trailing after me up the long staircase.

66
THE PUMP AND THE BEAR

We reached the bottom of the hill in a honey-wash of setting sun, Bix tied to Pumpkin by the paracord and sleeping, Keller on the travois. There was a house, set in a deep meadow of grass, the forest around it warm as firelight, the house itself cold, one story, a solid black box of windows and walls. A smell I knew but couldn't name was in the air around it like fog, stronger as we got closer.

"There's well water in the back."

In the back garden, there was a black, iron-handled water pump, a dark lily rising out of the ground. "That's funny." I pointed to the old pump, out of place next to the modern house.

"The pump? I know. It was the only kind they could get installed. Still works."

As Mother poured herself into us, the stories of the farm were more detailed, maybe so we'd recognize it if we ever went to find it. I had a picture in my head of a place I'd never been, a place I'd never seen in pictures. Mother and Clare grew up on the farm. They came to Old City for college. They were girls in the woods and on the dirt road where they were born. She talked about sleeping in the narrow beds. She talked about the rugs Grandpa George collected. She talked about the fireplaces. She talked about the pump in the yard. She talked about the blueberry bushes. She talked about the barn swallows under the eaves of the porch. She talked about the forest. She talked about the deer grazing the meadow at twilight. She talked about how snow was soft, not like the sharp hail we got. The house seemed distant as an airplane.

When she was too tired to walk, she sat weaving a blanket in front of the longhouse, working a loom cribbed from the Hall of South American Peoples, her hands fast, the shuttle slipping over under over under over under, a prayer of back and forth. "We used to pick blueberries all afternoon on the hot days," she told me. "Clare and I would stand in there when the berries were ripe. We'd stand there and eat our way up one side and down the other. There was no trying to save any for later. We'd take the berries to the porch; we'd hull them. You picked out stems with your fingers, threw the rotten berries over the rails where the birds could get them. Then you washed them at the pump."

"What kind was the water?" I asked.

"The water was like a hailstone—that cold. I'd drink from my hand. After dinner Grandpa George would get the ice cream maker out. He'd fill it with ice and rock salt from a bag in the barn. And then Grandma Ida would come with the cream and sugar and other things she'd mixed up, and she'd pour that into the barrel. Then we'd crank the handle on top for, like, an hour, until your Aunt Clare and I never wanted to see that ice cream maker again. And then, it'd be done."

"What was the taste?" I asked.

"It tasted like winter and summer at the same time. I loved it. But the farm wasn't like Amen. There wasn't any work to do. I got older than you and I started feeling like if I didn't meet more people and be somewhere that kept me interested, I'd lose my mind. I knew that something was waiting for me."

"Like how I want to be on the *Sally Ride*?"

"Yeah. Like that. I knew I had my *Sally Ride* waiting, and it wasn't at the farm."

"What about Clare?"

"Clare wanted to stay at the farm. She only came to the city for me. She missed me."

"That'd be like Bix coming on the boat."

The pump at the house at the bottom of the hill stood out as black as the one I imagined at Mother's farm. I wondered if the water would be cool like hers.

Mary woke Keller. "Time to get some water," Mary said.

"Can I stand up?"

"If you want to try."

Keller stood and tested his weight on unsteady legs. Mary shook Bix to wake her, checked her fever, undid the paracord from around her so she could sit up.

"Where are they? The owners?" Keller asked, looking around, stretching his back.

"The family was from Old City. They built the house before the floods. Some of them took the refugee walk. One died on the road. We stayed here sometimes. The last time we came through, we found them. Buried them in the back."

"What happened to them?" Bix asked.

"People came over from New Lebanon looking for food."

Mary and I got the pump going, dumping in water from our jug to prime it, the water flowing out at last good and very clear. I filled jugs. I cupped my hand, brought the water to my mouth, cooling sunburned lips. "Mother said there's a pump on the farm," Bix said.

A loud, sharp rustle sounded in the woods.

"Hear that?" I asked. We four turned as a single animal, looked for the sound, there was a second rustle and shake. Pumpkin whickered. The black head of a bear peeked out from the dry trees. It was not like the bears in the cases at Amen, sealed in from beetles, glass eyes catching glints of lantern light. This was a real bear, hit with time and weather and heat, thin and dark, patches of fur missing, mange eating it, the sleekness native to it fled before a thousand days of hunger.

"Just let it pass." Mary was quiet, walking up to me at the pump.

Under the sparse coat, where muscle and fat should be, were skin and the pokes of bone, a skeleton frame, a puppet bear, a starving deer wearing a bear suit. It crossed parallel past us, walked to the front of the house as if it hadn't seen us at all.

"That one's gonna die soon," said Mary.

"Wish I had an arrow and a bow," Keller said.

"You don't want it. It's got worms—sick on the inside."

"He should be hibernating," I said.

"Never gets cold enough," said Mary. "We see them drunk on hunger every winter."

We left the bear and the house, the smell and the blank walls and the empty larder, the cold water and the hill. We passed driveways, farms, a store, an inn—all dead. Curls of dry vines covered light poles, cracks in the road sprouted tall grasses, thornbushes and thistles. I had pictured the north full of people, but it was as empty as Old City, yawning and broken, silent farms with locked doors, houses with blind windows and unused pumps, rotting bears, grown-over roads. Fog settled into the crooks of the hills, the light falling. Mary pointed ahead to a parking lot blurry in the dusk, full of tree trunks and stacks of cordwood, rusty light poles listing in the concrete. At the eastern end of the lot was a fence as tall as three men standing on each other's shoulders, so long it vanished into the woods, in the center a gate wide enough to admit horses.

"That's Hancock," Mary said.

V
LIGHT RAIN YOU CAN OPEN UP AND DRINK

<u>Light Rain You Can Open Up and Drink:</u> There is one kind of soft rain that comes in the summer. This is the kind of rain that will fill the rain barrels without knocking them over, so you can drink clean water for a few days. Always remember to put the rain barrels out when it comes. If it begins in the late afternoon when it is very hot and you feel tired, when you are walking home and all you want to do is be in your own bed, if, just then, the rain starts, and it is this soft kind of rain, the kind that falls like it wants to be your friend, then you can tip back your head and open your mouth and let it fall onto your face and your lips and fill your throat, and you can feel cool and satisfied. It is like being at home already.

—From the Water Logbook

67
LIQUID ORACLE

O nce I knew Mother was dying, I started carrying the pictures of her in my pack. I started carrying the Logbook, too. I started making time into periods and thinking of how to name them. I started making myself a kit for when we let go and washed out to sea. The idea of losing Mother and losing Amen were both so big that they became mystery and nothing else—endless space and water and creatures, unknowable and impossible to control, not the trilobites I corralled in the room with the blue whale, not the creatures that visited me in my imagination—a real, overwhelming mass of the unknown.

I would take the pictures of Mother out all the time, out of the plastic baggie. I would take them out so often that they got faded by the oils from my fingers, by the change in humidity when they were viewed in the fog or the haze of a summer on the Amen roof. I looked at them so often that I memorized them. I knew the picture with the microscope. In one, Mother was younger than I'd known her, her hair long and dark, curling, her skin freckled, sunburned, warm. She was alone in the picture, and there was a flash, a halo of sunlight behind her, and there was a stretch of water over her shoulder that I didn't recognize.

I asked Father once, "Where were you?"

"The last time we flew anywhere," Father said. "We were at the beach, on Crete's south coast, a taverna, the food cleared away. It was the best place in the world to be, on a research trip with your mother, in Greece. She was terrible at having her picture taken. It was like trying to catch a cat. So, I caught her by surprise." He took the photograph from my hand and stared at it. "We knew we wouldn't be able to travel again. I mean, we didn't know it, but we knew. Everything was getting so hard. But we loved it. We loved it. We scuba dived with octopus. I never knew how to love the ocean until I met your mother."

That place was lost. And Mother too. And even the ocean that they swam in. But her joy was in the picture. That joy seemed like what I could reach for, what I could find, what we were all reaching for.

In California, there are huge kelp plants that reach from the seafloor to the bright surface of the water, making forests that stretch many stories high. Or there used to be. In them, sea lions and other animals played in filtered light like the light from trees in full leaf in full sun. When the end of their growing season came, the anchored plants released their grip on where they clung to the rocks. They let go of their anchors and they floated out to the deep sea, fading and changing, feeding the sea as fertilizer. Their children came back another year to make a new forest. The anchors that held them in place were called holdfasts. They slipped them. They slipped their holdfasts and let go, and then the tide carried them away.

At Amen, when those we love died, we slipped our holdfasts. It was gradual, but as Mother was dying, I knew we'd slip the holdfast of Amen once she wasn't there. I knew that we'd pack the Logbook and ourselves and we'd leave. I never saw the storm arriving. I thought we'd have to leave Amen behind as it was, waiting to be found and tended again, just not by us.

Mother started to falter. All water for so long, her skin swelled in the heat, her face pulled across the humid storms inside. I think she hurt all the time. I think she wanted to leave, take us all in a boat. In the end, Mother could barely make it down the stairs when I felt a storm. Father fireman-carried her to the stacks. Two days before she died, Bix and I were with her, curled on either side on her pallet, unable to part with the warmth of her body. She stroked Bix's short hair from habit, pushed the bangs so Bix's freckled, high forehead was clear. Mother slept and woke, slept and woke. Her eyes closed, hair unwashed, combed smooth into a bun. I stared at the light blond hairs on her ear, wanted to blow on them, make them wave like the feathered feeding strands of a barnacle.

Dreaming, she said, "I know you'll get there. Go back, butterflies."

"Go back where?"

"Back north. The Berkshires. The farm. Clare. Higher ground. Go north, it's yours now. If Father asks you—go," her eyes a bottomless liquid oracle. "Do you remember when Angel used to read from *Moby Dick*?" she asked us when she woke, and as if she'd never leave, she sounded herself, alive.

"Sometimes I remember," Bix said.

Mother closed her eyes. "'And there is a Catskill eagle in some souls that can alike dive down into the blackest gorges, and soar out of them again and become invisible in the sunny spaces. And even if he for ever flies within the gorge, that gorge is in the mountains; so that even in his lowest swoop the mountain eagle is still higher than other birds upon the plain, even though they soar.'"

The words washed over me. "I remember that."

"I love that," Mother said. "I think it means that for some people things are harder and they don't know it. But then also things are more beautiful because they are harder, and they don't know that either."

On the last day, Mother slept in the longhouse. That's

how she'd fade, Jess said. It would be very quiet. And it was. I fell asleep, and when I woke up, she was gone. Father carried us to Jess's tent so he could be alone with her. And when we buried Mother, I wanted to lay my body over her body, asking her to rise through the dirt like the reverse of making a fossil.

68
HANDS TO WORK AND HEARTS TO GOD

We crossed the last of the broken parking lot to stand in front of the gates. There was a flash and a noise, electric light flooded the whole landscape, the gate, the fence, the trees, the broken parking lot.

"What's that?" I asked Mary.

"Solar," she said, "they have solar guard lights."

I rubbed a hand across the flash ghosts, the view of the gate fixed even with my eyes closed.

"Wake up Bix and Keller," Mary said. "Tell them we're here."

I did what she asked. I looked back and saw that the gate had a hatch. It opened on hinges, revealed the face of a young man not much older than Bix. "That you, Mary?" he asked.

"Yes, it is, Byron," she said. "You've been spying?"

"I have. Got to use those binoculars for something. No need to send out the dogs, then?"

"No, not yet, but a day will come, Mr. Byron." Mary smiled.

"You carrying the dead?"

"No. No, we are not. But you have to get Esther. We need all hands."

Byron nodded, looked behind him into the world past the gates, then back at us. "Mosquito Borne?" He pointed to Keller's travois.

"No."

"Not the new thing?" He tensed, shifting his weight.

"No. Pneumonia."

"Oh." Relief and energy passed over his face. "OK. Come in."

The hatch shut. Bix looked at me from the saddle, groggy, but with purpose, maybe thinking like me: Mano would be the boy's age now. We never saw anyone that age. *I know,* I mouthed at her.

The gate opened onto a stone courtyard between two red buildings. The courtyard was lit; beyond that, a solar panel array to the right, cables leading into darkness. Byron stood inside. His gold hair swept back from his temples in ring-lets, haloed Afro, a little dirty, but someone cut it for him. His skinny frame in a pair of loose pants and a T-shirt with a picture of a fox, his skin light tan, neither Black nor white, dotted with freckles, his cheeks rough from shaving and high pink, a cherub, green bright eyes looked like they had extra light in them, awkward, tall. We never saw Mano tall. Behind Byron there was a group of men clustered inside the wall. Everyone but him had a gun. They drew back when they saw the travois. "Darling will be glad to see you, but this isn't your week to trade," Byron said.

"No. We had this sickness. Get Esther." Mary eyed the pack of men.

Byron nodded. "I'll run." He took off into the dark.

Mary followed him into Hancock. She didn't rush.

69
BROTHER SISTER HOUSE

We walked down a path, past a sycamore, past railings like where you might tie a horse, past a water tub of shiny metal, past black electric cables. The settlement had multiple buildings. Where there wasn't a path, or a piece of cultivated ground, there were shacks and tents. Solar panels ranged in banks next to buildings. There were lots of buildings. It was a village. There were rain barrels, stacked tools, chickens. It smelled like Amen, like cooking fires, fry bread, drying meat, garbage, night buckets, dirty clothes, laundry, water. There were goats, a sweet smell like in the barn on Hartigan Road, manure, woodsmoke. It was the diorama from the Hall of Eastern Woodlands. You could practically see the pumpkins and smoke.

There was lantern light coming from the open windows. There were people; I hadn't seen so many since I was tiny. After the smallness of Amen, empty country, the river and the forests, the quiet dead farms and houses, the people were strange.

Mary stopped at a building, brick and four stories with white window frames. Black electric cables ran in through the basement windows, stone steps led to open double doors, light spilling on the grass, inside, another stairway, this one clean and white, steps of wood and dark railings.

At the door were two people, Byron and a tall, dark-skinned woman, they moved toward us like we were on fire, and they were the only water.

"What's he got?" the tall woman asked Mary, pointing to the travois.

"Pneumonia," Mary said.

"Bacterial or viral?"

"Don't know. Both? River water in his lungs. And she's got a leg wound," she gestured to Bix in the saddle, "gunshot, infected. Got here fast as I could." Mary tied Pumpkin to a post next to the steps while the woman undid all the fastenings on the travois, picked up Keller's stretcher and lowered it to the ground.

"This fever isn't the new thing?" The tall woman looked up at Mary.

"No. He needs fluids. They've had the last of the antibiotics at Olana. Two doses."

"I'm Keller. I can walk."

"I'm Esther, it's a couple of flights of stairs. We'll take you." She looked up at Bix.

"Bix," Bix said.

"OK, let's get you well. Byron, get the other end. You three follow us up."

Mary helped Bix down from Pumpkin, and Bix put an arm over each of our shoulders so we could be her crutches up the stairs. Behind us, Pumpkin was left alone in the darkness, bottomless eyes, brown coat spattered in mud. My eyes stung from the brightness of the lantern light as we came into the building. There was a long white staircase, a hallway, another staircase, another hallway. Noise and random talk came from the rooms we passed. Esther and Byron turned in to a room, backed up, shifted sideways to make Keller's stretcher fit in the door. Mary and Bix and I limped in after. We were at the corner of the building, the walls split with tall dark windows on two sides. Three single beds were lined up on the wall, wooden pegboards above, two red wooden chests on another wall. A black iron stove hunched between two of the beds like a dog. There were a big round hospital light and a pump with tubes in a corner, a stand for medicine. A wide black cable came in through a window.

Esther and Byron settled Keller into a bed, and she stepped away, standing at a worktable by the window, framed against dark glass. Mary and I settled Bix, and then Mary joined her. She came only as high as Esther's shoulders. Esther was thin, her collarbones picked out under her shirt, bony knees and elbows visible through her clothes, bony knuckles. Her skin was lighter than Keller's, darker than Byron's, some freckles on her cheeks and chest, her hair in short, tiny, matte brown locs. She looked as rested as Mary looked tired.

Esther walked to Keller's bedside. "Well, you made it. This is Brother Sister House, our hospital, such as it is."

Keller closed his eyes. "Good. Thank you. Can't think of anywhere I'd rather be."

Esther laughed. "We'll see how you feel after more than a minute. Now comes the hard part."

70
WHAT ABOUT THE LEG

"What's the hard part?" Keller asked.

"Shut that door, Byron," Esther said. Byron closed it quietly.

"The hard part is Childs. The hard part is Hancock," Esther said, looking at Keller.

"How long until Childs gets up here?" Mary asked. "Can we start Keller on a drip before he gets here? Get the meds so it's done?"

"Warren probably went to get him right from the gate," said Byron. "He'll come up here to see you as soon as he knows. We have ten minutes, maybe less."

"You need to get the antibiotics now. If you have any left," Mary said.

Esther looked at Byron and Mary, then at Keller. "We have them," said Esther, "of course we do." She rubbed a hand along her jaw. "But I can't get them until Childs says. Byron and I don't have final say on how that stuff gets used anymore, and we only have a little that we stashed without Childs knowing."

"So, it's the same as Mary's place?" Keller asked.

"Olana? No, things are done differently here. Childs likes to think he's running an official refuge, building something that can anchor this part of the state, be a beacon from here to the New Sea. We are self-sufficient. But it all runs on debt, on who can pay off what they eat with how much they work. We're OK, Byron and me, we have valuable skills."

"Since you taught me," Byron said.

"Since I made you a fine nurse practitioner," Esther said.

"But when someone new comes, they have to prove they're able-bodied. And now he has them sign a contract in order to get food and lodging and care. There're no courts around to enforce it, but he doesn't care. And he doesn't take people who can't work. So, if I treat you, we have to behave as if you can work and stay."

"Poppy told me not to stay, told us not to stay," I said.

Mary looked at me. "We're not staying. But we don't have to explain that. Esther, I think Bix's leg is bad, septicemia. I don't know if you can save it."

Esther walked to where Bix lay on the bed, pulled back her pant leg; the smell was bad. "That's a lot of meds right there."

Byron walked to the door, put his ear against it, listened.

Bix said, "Wait, Mary, save it? What did you say?"

Mary talked over her. "They have a place you can go, if you treat them, they have a farm."

"They do? Then we have options. For them at least. Childs is so worried about that new illness that he keeps counting the boxes in the pharmacy like it's going to be the Mosquito Borne all over again, checking antibiotics as if there's a war on . . ." She trailed off. "If we use all those meds on them, and they leave, I don't want to think about how Childs will come down on us."

"Slow down," Bix said. "What did you say about the leg?"

Mary spoke to Esther like she hadn't heard Bix. "You have any pleurisy root left?"

"Some," said Esther.

"We can start him on that. Childs might think that's all," said Mary.

"Maybe. Maybe play down the leg. But Childs is gonna figure it out."

"Cross that bridge later."

"OK," said Esther. "Byron, you hear that? Don't mention the leg, just the pneumonia."

"OK," said Byron. "Darling's coming. I saw him on the path."

"He'll help, that's good." Esther covered up Bix's leg and stood up.

"I don't understand," Bix said.

"Jesus, Bix," Mary said, "your leg is bad. It's infected. It might be septicemia, that's why you have the fever. Esther can operate if we don't let Childs know you need it. And if she can clean out the tissue, debride any infected flesh, you'll be fine. But we don't have any tech here, and we don't know how bad it is until Esther can get in there. So, try to pretend you are fine for a little while, OK?"

"You didn't tell us about Hancock on the hill, on the road," I said to Mary. "You said to trust you."

"Nope," said Mary, her voice iron, hands on her hips. "Nope, I didn't tell you, because, you know what? This is what we have. And I had to get you here. OK? This is it. And I would rather give you this. If I'd told you what Hancock is, you would never have come. You don't have a good shot without Esther. And that is exactly why you can trust me."

Things were happening without us. The storm on the roof, the men in the darkness, the bullet in Father, the poison in Keller. We had to listen to Mary like we'd listened to Father on Storm King Mountain, *sometimes you need to make a wall to keep what's good inside with you,* even if we didn't understand yet what she was building.

71
CHILDS

There was a hard knock on the closed door. Esther shifted to face the doorway. Mary settled all the blankets, walked to the worktable by the window. *Childs,* she mouthed toward Bix and me. The urgency was gone from the set of her back, she'd made it disappear.

"He in here?" asked a man's voice on the other side of the door.

"Yeah, Childs," said Esther in a voice so calm, "come on in."

The door opened, a man of almost six feet stood there, blond hair low to a jaw covered in blond beard, wearing a red waterproof coat zippered to his chin, carrying a bag in one hand. "I heard there were some complicated visitors," he said, pushing a long thin nose into the room first, the rest of his knife face following after.

"There are," said Esther.

"Warren tells me that this man isn't the usual Lost, and that he doesn't have the new thing." He looked square at Byron. "Which is good, of course, since, if it was, Byron shouldn't have let these people through our gates."

His eyes were kind, the softest eyes I'd seen in The World As It Is, softer than Mother's or Poppy's. Soft like there was never anything wrong or unpredictable. Eyes that expected to be able, by force of will, to make The World As It Is what they wanted it to be. I could see how eyes like that got to be in charge. They were eyes that could trick you into thinking you were safe with the man in the tower.

"You know we'd never let that up here," Esther said to Childs, smiling.

"Good. Good, Esther." He looked at her like he wanted to touch her, wanted her close.

"It's just pneumonia. We're starting some pleurisy root for his fever." She walked to the table where Mary stood, not letting go the string of his gaze. "I don't think he'll keep anyone up with the cough."

"Good. Has he got any needs besides that?"

"Maybe," she said, shrugging. "Might need a box of anti-biotics before the night's up. Just in case. Something for the pain." She looked away out the window. "Maybe enough for the night. And the generator, for a bit."

Childs laughed. "You know that's only for people who plan to stay," he said. "Or for people who can work. Dead men don't pay debts, sick men don't either."

"No, they don't." She started grinding a root with a mortar and pestle. "He'll be up and working if we get the antibiotics in him. Just pneumonia."

Childs walked to where Keller lay. "Name?"

"Keller."

"I heard you came in by travois." He looked over Keller's body, over the blankets, over the packs by the wall, the stretcher, looked right at Bix. Bix looked at the floor, then back at him, and there wasn't a soft place on her.

I remembered hearing Mother talk to Bix one night. She thought I was asleep. "This is important for you, and one day for Norah," Mother said. "But not until she's older. You know Father was out locking the doors? Part of why we do that is because of men. You remember we talked about sex, right? And we talked about how it is really important, and supposed to be fun, full of pleasure and desire, and all the good things, making babies and connecting people? And we talked about how love was like that too, that it was supposed to make people closer and safer and happier together. Right? You remember all of that?"

I could almost hear Bix rolling her eyes in the dark. "Yes, Mother. I remember all of it."

"Well, the thing is that men can use sex to hurt people."

"They can?"

"Yeah, they can be bigger and use their weight and their bodies and a kind of broken desire to force people into sex. And if that ever happens to you, you have to tell me. Even if it is someone here, someone you know. Sex should never feel bad like that. And people can use their love like that too, their way of treating you, to make you feel hurt and scared. We have to watch out for that from strangers *and* from people who look safe. OK? You understand me?" I could feel Bix nodding in the bunk. "You might have to help Norah remember this, or someone else, OK? You have to know the difference between the safe and not safe when someone loves you." I could feel the broken love, broken way of treating people pouring off Childs.

Childs scanned Mary and Esther at work, Byron by the door. He stared at Esther a long time, then made up his mind and turned to go. "Byron, they can eat tonight. Get Warren to start the generator. In the morning we'll see how it stands." No one said anything. "Night, all." He slipped from the door and was gone.

We stood still a long time, listening to his footsteps go back down the hall. Then Mary looked at us. "How do I put this, Esther?"

"I don't know, Mary." Esther put her head down. "How

do you explain that you fear for your life when there isn't a scratch on you?"

"I think you just say that," Mary said. She looked at me. "Childs wants to make sure that Esther—*especially*—does everything he wants her to do."

72
MAKING READY

Esther stood with her head down at the table, wriggled her shoulders like whisking a swarm of gnats off her skin. "Move those chairs back, it'll give us more space to work."

She took a bag from the floor, pulled tools from it: blood pressure cuff, thermometer. Mary made tea of pleurisy root, a plaster for Keller's chest from mustard root. Byron left, came back with blue-and-white boxes of anesthetics and antibiotics from a refrigerator in the basement. But he also carried a lot more in a bag. They didn't talk about it, and Byron hid the bag under a spare blanket. Esther made an IV and put it in Keller's arm and Keller fell asleep.

Then Esther worked on Bix's leg. It was swollen, an ugly wound under a dirty wrapping. Esther held it in her hand, her bony, careful fingers skirting the shape under the bandage. Mary held Bix's heel to balance the leg with her left hand, ran the long fingers of her right along the naked skin to the top and bottom of the calf, where there was no bandage. Checking for heat, for swelling, for how taut the skin might be, undoing the bandages, unchanged since we started on foot, rolling them back off the leg. A smell emerged from it, the wound colored, a red pulse along the rip, the flesh gray and wet with yellow pus.

"I saw a lot of gunshots in Boston," Esther looked at the wound, "and then here after the Camp went crazy. Don't see so many of those anymore."

"Not enough ammo left," said Mary.

"Or enough people." There was a knock on the door, as soft as Childs's had been hard. Esther looked at Byron.

"Darling?" Byron said. "Come in." The door opened and a tall older man slid into the room through the doorway, ducking under the opening as if his body never fit anywhere. It was hard to tell his age; his hair was gray, his unlined face a record of any number of ancestors in the Americas before whites. He had bright red cheeks, like Byron, even if they looked nothing alike. He was a shadow of a desert in gray clothes, scruff on his face and neck, and below his jawline a badly healed gash across part of his throat, an old scar. Darling nodded at Byron, who got up to hug him, then nodded around at all of us without speaking.

"Did you hide out from Childs?" Byron asked him.

Darling nodded. His eyes lit up at Mary, who came to hug him too. "'Turning, turning / We come round right,'" Darling sang into her neck. He hummed until they parted, holding hands.

"You can help in a little while," Byron said to him, and Darling nodded, and sat on a small stool by the window, taking off a knit cap and holding it in his hand.

Esther looked at him with tenderness, her hands too busy to touch him; she looked at Bix's leg then back at Darling. "I haven't seen an untreated wound in a while, not since Darling wandered into Hancock out of that freak freeze with half his toes off, carrying Byron in a blanket." Byron looked at Darling, and Darling looked at the floor. Esther took the focus off him: "I think you're right, Mary," she said, "the leg is septic."

"What do we do?" Bix asked.

"We have to cut out the bad stuff and clean it, and hope there isn't gangrene started, and hope you keep the leg," said Esther. "But we can't wait. If we wait, and Childs knows, we

won't have a chance to do it at all. We have to start now."
Bix's face was just as white as it had been the first time Esther suggested she could lose the leg, but she nodded, and
everything started to happen.

Esther and Byron got their hands sterile and dressed in
gowns. Darling helped like he'd done it before. It didn't look
like a hospital, that room in Brother Sister House. There
was a stove, wood moldings, ancient chairs, jars of herbs,
tincture bottles, a mortar and pestle, and wavy window glass
with bubbles in it. The modern equipment, big electric
lights, blood pressure cuffs, needles and vials of morphine
and antibiotics, all looked out of place. Esther gave Bix an-
esthetic but put a cloth in her mouth to bite in case it wasn't
enough. There was a white cloth over her body, a pottery
basin to catch the blood. Mary made a fire. Darling went
out for more wood. Byron got water to sterilize instruments
boiling on the stove. They had masks for us, rubber gloves.
The light in the corner plugged in to the cable snaking from
the window. It made the room hot and glowing and more
incongruous still.

Darling went out to sit on the stairs and keep watch. Byron told me to stay by the door in case Childs came, or anyone who heard Bix if she screamed. Outside, I could hear
Darling singing softly in the hallway, an old hymn Keller sang
sometimes in the garden. "'Though like the wanderer, the
sun gone down / Darkness be over me, my rest a stone / An-
gels to beckon me,'" he sang, "'nearer, my God, to Thee.'" Inside, the cutting was loud, the sound of it not like anything,
the way flesh is when you cut it. The way it makes a noise
that hurts your own skin. That is something I wish I did not
know. I watched all of it. Bix was awake while they worked.
There was blood, and I know there was tissue lost. But then
the noise was over. She didn't scream. The drugs were good.

Childs didn't come. Esther and Byron were painted in blood and sweat. "You'll keep it, I think," Esther said to Bix. "It's good you rushed," she said to Mary.

"I thought it would be," Mary said.

Everything in the room held still for a moment and breathed.

73

THE TIDAL BORE

The medicine worked in Keller and Bix. They slept. At dawn, Esther and Byron went for food and Darling went for water. Esther's stethoscope sat on Keller's blanket. Mary slept. I slid off the bed where I'd watched all night, sitting up like Keller with his knife the first night on the Hudson, on the Palisades ridge with the wolves. I put the plastic ends of the scope in my ears, put the metal disc against his chest, my head on his ribs like he was a warm boulder in the sun, rested there, making sure of his heartbeat, drifted while the sun rose.

His voice woke me. "Nonie?"

I thought it was a dream of him. "Uh-huh." I sat up. "Mary, he's awake. You're awake?"

"I feel good."

"Keller? Feeling better? That's good." Mary walked to him, put an ear on his chest, felt his pulse, his neck, both sides, took his pressure, checked his fever. "OK." She closed her eyes, as if the lids were heavy. She got up and went to Bix, picked up the blanket and checked her leg, removed the bandage and got up to find another one. When she turned back to wrap Bix's leg, she saw me staring at her. "What, Nonie?" She kept looking, waiting, I couldn't ask, I couldn't talk, like the time with Father on the bed in Lenox Hill Hospital. It was too much to tell her I was terrified that I'd lose them too. She kept in the silence with me, kept letting it unfold until she understood. "Oh," she said, "I get it. He's OK. His pulse is good. The medicine's doing what it's supposed to. His lungs sound crap, but better. He'll make it. Bix's leg looks OK, like they got the bad stuff. She'll heal. She'll be OK. Don't cry, Nonie."

I didn't notice I was crying. "I know. I don't mean it."

"It's OK. I'm sorry I said that. You can cry."

"I can't usually." A sob shook my shoulders. Like Keller's tidal bore, it rose up, a wave over the wave of feeling I usually had, a tsunami, so big it changed the shape of me, of the river of me. I put a hand over the flat of my belly to hold it back. Mary caught my elbow, held me to her. I tried to pull away. She wouldn't let me. The crying kept going, deeper—to the ruin, the oak tree on Storm King Mountain, Bix's sweaty hand in mine. I cried out all the water I had. I had never done that. Not even with Mother or Father or Mano or Angel.

Like dowsing, I smelled rain dried on Mary's clothes, water coming up from her sweat, my tears, pressed my face against her, heard the water in her blood moving in an endless ocean. I paced the tide of me to the tide of her until I felt like after a long sleep. That was the ocean I thought of when I was afraid about Mother, that was the ocean where the *Sally Ride* was waiting, that water through me all the time, through all of us.

I looked up. Mary smiled at me the way Mother smiled when she woke up next to me. When someone loves you, they become your sea.

74
THE ICEHOUSE

When I was done crying, and I was sitting with a glass of water in my hand, I looked around the room in the sun. I never thought we'd be in a room like this, with electric and food and people, with gates and gardens, and the clean manner in which light fell onto a blank Childs filled with what made him safe. For a moment, I wanted to stop there, to sleep and eat and bathe, the fear of the road overwhelming, the shelter of Hancock deceptively real.

"I know what you're thinking," Mary said, businesslike as she bustled to re-up meds for Bix and Keller. "I know you think you could stay here. All this medicine. And Esther and gardens and food. Bix and Keller safe. But this place isn't safe."

"It looks safe."

"It was when it was first built, I guess. Shakers made it. They renounced the world, gardened, invented brooms, and then they made this whole world up here. Utopia. Men and women were equal. Everyone was celibate, they danced to worship. They built these beautiful places, invented selling seeds in catalogues, and adopted orphans, made everything useful. But it didn't last. Utopias fail."

Bix woke up while she talked, Keller sat up. "Childs's family was rich," she went on, "and instead of buying a boat, his father bought Hancock, set up generators, solar. He thought that a village with wood heat would be a good place to wait out The World As It Is, there was a hospital in town, a factory. Then the army put the Camp in Pittsfield, a few miles away. Lots of people died. Fevers, Mosquito Borne, things the antibiotics couldn't stop. Like everywhere: bad water, too much heat, bad crops, no babies. Same story at a hundred places around. Childs's father died. Childs raided the hospital, the army tracked him, and then the Camp imploded, the base fell apart. A lot of the army scattered, went west. Childs got the arsenal, and the medicine, and took in some refugees to work the land. He has a lot of guns, more than I've ever seen in one place, more ammo than anyone around here for fifty miles. We've got to get you out, all of you," Mary said, "fast."

The way Mary explained it, Hancock was worse than the man in the tower. Outside the window, dawn light was dimming, clouds moving in, room shifting into coolness. A shiver of wind went through the building. Without thinking, I walked to the window. The old panes shook. I closed my eyes and felt the air tighten and narrow around my rib cage as the pressure dropped. I breathed into the water that was coming. "Storm," I said.

Mary raised an eyebrow and looked. "Really?"

"I can feel them."

There was a knock on the door. Mary turned, spooked. "Come in."

Childs opened the door, pushed Esther in front of him; over her shoulder was Byron's bag full of additional medicine boxes. Byron carried a water jug in his hand. Behind them stood two men. The first was Warren, from the night before, short, thick-built, dark beard, broken blood vessels on cheeks and nose, gun in one hand, Byron's arm in the other. The other was a tall man, wide in the shoulders and pale, a gun over his shoulder. Childs carried a rifle, rolling into the room like a surge. The last man pulled the door shut with his foot; hairs on my arms stood up.

Childs nodded at Keller. "Breathing, I take it? I told you,

Esther, we don't have the resources for charity anymore." He looked at Mary. "I thought you understood that. More people could show up here at any time. People get messy without rules."

"Scared people make rules that make messes," said Mary.

"I'd suggest you keep from talking right now," Childs said to Mary, "because you aren't from here, and you've made a mess for yourself." Childs nodded to the second man. "Monroe?"

Monroe nodded back, crossed behind Keller's bed, pulled the needle delivering antibiotics and fluids and painkillers straight from Keller's arm, then packed up the bag of medicine and walked to the door. Keller moved like he was going to fight for the medicine, but Warren let go of Byron and took hold of his rifle. "Childs said you can't have that anymore."

Mary caught Monroe, took the medicine out of his hand, turned back to Keller to put the needle back in his arm. Monroe grabbed Mary back, but she hit him, and he fell on the floor hard. She shoved Monroe's face into the ground, put her foot on his back.

"Stop," Childs said, slow and quiet.

Warren flipped his gun to his back and pulled Mary off Monroe. He hit Mary in the face, stomach, ribs, jaw. Mary went down on her knees with blood on her mouth. Bix screamed. Warren was big. Mary hit back but it did nothing. Warren kept hitting. Mary was on her knees. Warren used his foot, kicked her leg out until she curled on her side.

I backed away, shaking. Bix tried to get up, she and Keller poised on the edges of their beds, shaky. Esther screamed, "Stop, stop, stop!" Keller stood up to put himself between Mary and Warren. Esther screamed, "No! Keller!"

Mary covered her head with a hand, she bled, she growled, she kicked to catch Warren's feet. He didn't stop.

Childs pushed Esther forward till she fell on her knees, medicine boxes falling all over the floor, he walked toward Warren and Mary, raising his rifle to his hands. "That's good, Warren."

Warren stood to his full height and picked Mary up by her elbows, pinned her arms behind her back. She was limp, bleeding. Childs pointed his gun at Mary. Her hair was loose, her face slick and red, one eye punched shut. "That was useless, what you did, Mary," Childs said. "There was no goddamned point to that. There's no more medicine here for him."

Monroe got to his feet, went back and finished the job of taking Keller's medicine away.

No one of us moved. "Jared," Mary stuttered, "we have a pact with you. He won't let you."

"Jared won't care. Last time he was here he told me you were causing trouble. And here we have a safe place to keep you." Childs motioned to the door and Warren dragged Mary out.

"Mary!" I screamed.

The door closed, and they were gone.

Bix yelled, "Where are they taking her?!"

Esther looked at Byron. "Icehouse."

He nodded. "Childs is using it as a jail."

Esther moved to pick up boxes. "Idiots didn't even take all of it."

"Mary said we have to leave," I said.

"We have to get out of here," Keller said to Esther while she worked. "We have to get Mary back. We have to get to the farm. We can't stay here."

Esther looked for a long time at Keller, then stood up and walked to the window. It was raining. She was framed from behind by the storm. She looked at the table, scattered boxes of medicine, Keller on the bed, the hole from the needle, moved to get a bandage to cover it up. "Byron, you know what I'm going to say, right?" Byron nodded from where he sat. "It's time." She picked up a box of medicine. "He thinks I won't use this now. He thinks we'll stay. We've talked about this, since you were old enough to know what this place is. You were the first person I ever saw, the only child I ever saw, make it through the Mosquito Borne, even when your parents didn't. Showing up here with Darling out of nowhere."

"Darling saved my life on the road," Byron said.

"He sings, but does he talk?" Bix asked. "That scar?"

"The scar and the speech aren't related," Esther said. "He doesn't talk much, but he sings. Or maybe not talking is related to his throat, just not medically. Darling can't talk about what happened out there, and Byron can't remember. I tried to help him talk when they showed up here. Part of why I stayed, even if Darling never talked again. But I'm finally more afraid of staying than of going." Esther looked at Bix and me, walked to Keller, put a new needle in his arm. "I want *us* to take *you* out of here and get you safe. And Darling. Where's Darling?"

"Probably back out in his shack. He might not come."

"We'll make him come. Tell them," Esther said to Byron. He sat silent. "Either you tell them, or I will." I could see years of caring for Byron in her shoulders.

He drew a breath, about to dive into a deep river. "I have a wagon, in the Round Barn, in a locked room. I've been building it from stolen lumber and metal." Byron paused, looked at Esther. "And I have bows and arrows. I've been making them and hiding them. And some ammo and guns. If we can get them, get Mary out of the icehouse, and get Keller and Bix in the wagon, we can leave Hancock."

"But you have to take us with you where you're going," Esther said. "We don't have a farm to claim."

I thought of the diorama, the pumpkins and the wood-smoke, the hope of a place safer than Amen. Every settlement was a magnet for dusty children's clothes, boxes of hoarded medicine, the man in the tower. But we could make something like Amen. I thought we needed a village, but we really just needed ourselves, the Logbook, a roof and water and walls, a garden and some arrows for deer, an open door for those we could trust, and a closed door for people like Childs. If Father and Mother and Angel and Keller made it once, here in The World As It Is, we could make it again. "If we do have a farm, if it is still standing, it's your farm, too," I said.

The windows shook, the sky lowered, clouds swallowed the hills, thickness came to the air. I could feel the storm starting, one like a category I made in the Water Logbook, "A Storm for Hiding You When You Go Out to Scavenge." Some storms took the things you knew and upended them, placed the car on the roof, the windowpane in the garden, the person in the ocean, the boat on the land. This one wouldn't upend us; it was not going to send a tornado. It was not going to surprise like the hypercane or drown like the ruin. This one would be lightning and heavy cloud, rain hard and dense so that people were hard to see from far away. You could be almost invisible in a storm like this, perfect for taking a wagon from a barn, breaking a woman out of jail, limping the wounded out of the village, disappearing into hills where no one knew your destination.

"We all want that," Keller said. "If we have a farm it's yours too. And Mary's."

On the farm Mother described, we could be down a dev-il's corkscrew of our own, with Mary and Esther to keep us well, with Keller recovering, Bix's leg healing, Byron looking at Bix that way. With the water pump Mother promised, we might live.

"It's starting," I said, pointed out the window. Pricks of rain hit the glass. "But a storm is good cover."

75

LEAVING HANCOCK

The storm built. The wind made dancing bits of dust between the buildings, the trees doubled over, cold seeped in. We waited until the dark was falling.

We stashed all the obvious medicine and food in packs. Bix didn't tell anyone she had the gun in hers. I checked the Logbook again. Maybe I'd add things about the kinds of shelter you could expect on the road. Or maybe that would be another Logbook. If I opened it now, I'd see Mother's careful handwriting, tiny and cramped, picked out with her left hand. The pictures of Mother were there, too. I hadn't let myself look at them since we got on the Hudson. The night after we buried Father, I wanted them, and in the feral house, and at Dan's farm. I wanted Mother all those times. But it was too much to ask her to be with me under the oak tree, or in that tin-roofed barn. I unzipped the pocket on the front of my pack. The baggie was there, timeworn plastic, marred by wet, the surface like fabric, hard to see in the low light. There she was at the taverna in Greece. She was alive with joy, and I closed my eyes to memorize her face, zipped the baggie back up, and put it away in my pack.

"Everything set?" Esther asked.

"Yeah."

"Here." I showed Esther what Father wrote in the notebook that night on the Hudson when we could see the ruin of the nuclear plant. I read out, "'The Pike to Lee, take the exit, walk south of the Pike past the Big Y, at the fourth traffic light is the left turn for Tyringham, take that road, then look for Fernside Road, that's a right turn, down a hill, over a bridge across a wetland, up another ridge, the farm is right on top of the ridge, a white house on the high side of the road, big porch, a big barn on the lower side of the road, to the left.'"

"Tyringham," said Esther, "that's a day's walk from here."

"It is?"

"Yeah, when I came here from Boston, I had this map I read while the caravan moved toward the Camp. I tried to memorize everything. I'd never been to this part of the state. Boston was all I knew really, the coast. I could find my way around there."

"Did you see the ocean when you lived in Boston?" I asked her.

"Sometimes. I loved swimming."

"In the ocean?" I looked out at the rain on the trees and roofs.

"Yeah, it was wonderful."

"I want to go onto the ocean."

"You do?"

"Mother always told me that there were boats out there, research ships. There was one called the *Sally Ride*—"

"I've heard of it," Esther interrupted, packing a bag. She didn't look up.

"You have?" My heart was pounding, and she couldn't see.

"Yeah. It was out of Boston. I read about it online, before." She zipped shut her pack, got out the stashed bag of extra medicines Byron had taken from the basement before Bix's surgery and hidden under a blanket, jammed it in another pack. "And there's this woman, a scientist, Virginia. I met her here. The boats come in every three years, because they have to land somewhere after a while. They come back to a temporary port on the New Sea, way up the Connecticut River. She's got a son, I think, somewhere on a farm. She visits."

I stared at Esther, the storm, the pack forgotten. "That's not real."

"No, seriously." Esther didn't notice me shaking with hope. "I met her here in Brother Sister House. She paid for her stay with some meds from the ship. She had a cut that needed checking. She came through on her way to see her son."

Esther kept working like she hadn't just told me that everything I ever was hoping for was something she'd touched. "You mean it?! You mean it?"

"Why would I lie, Nonie? You'd like her—Virginia. Maybe you'll meet her, maybe her son's farm is near your farm."

My chest was lit up so bright it could have been a lantern, it could have illuminated every settlement from Old City to where we stood. "Virginia," I said. The room still smelled of medicine and dried blood. The hum of the generator was gone, the hum of the storm loud outside.

"Virginia." Esther was smiling, catching my joy. "All we have to do is find your farm—" A cracking sound interrupted her, a sound like every tree in a forest split in half, then raised up in the air and hurled at each other, breaking into splinters, that furled up and were gone. "What was that?" Esther stood, walked to the windows.

"Sounded like a roof coming off," said Bix.

"Probably was," said Byron. "That's good. A broken roof means we have a better chance of getting out without being seen."

Esther looked at Byron. "We should go." He nodded.

Esther left alone, carrying nothing. If Childs saw her, she'd tell him she was helping with the storm. Instead, she'd go to the Round Barn, where the wagon was, get the parts and assemble what she could. "Don't you let Byron take any chances." She looked at Bix in the lantern light. Bix nodded and Esther left and closed the door behind her.

Wind hit us, shook the building like a kitten in the teeth of a tiger. Small flickers of light showed in other buildings, other windows, electric off and on. The rain was as loud as pebbles against the wavy old glass. I stood up and walked to Keller's bed, lay down, curled next to him, rested my head on his chest. Father told me Mother drowned when her kidneys stopped. Keller had water where his air should be. But Mary said the water would sink back into him, down to the roots like after a flash flood.

"You OK, little warrior?"

"I'm OK."

"Next big push," Keller said, "and we'll be there."

"Can you walk?"

"We'll see."

"Nonie," Bix said, "we've got to go." She had a cane to limp out of the building.

Byron disconnected the medicine from Keller. "We'll hook this back up in the wagon." He packed the medicine in a bag and added it to the stuff in his pack.

I found my shoes beneath the bed. A gust shook the window. I stood up. Darling knocked softly on the door, then slid in, drenched, his wool hat back on, his cheeks still bright. He looked excited, or freed, like he was being asked to a party and had decided he would love it.

"You're coming!" Byron said.

Darling held his finger up to his lips, and Byron nodded, then got up and hugged him, Darling smoothing down Byron's curls and kissing the top of his head. He let go and held out his hands so he could help carry the bags Byron prepared.

Bix looked back at me, nervous. "You know what to do?" she asked.

"Esther gave me keys to the icehouse lock. She said she hid them from Childs years ago, kept them in case," I said. "I'm the smallest, they won't see me."

"OK." She looked at me. "Father wouldn't want you to do it."

"Father did everything himself."

Bix nodded, put on her pack. "We go first, since we'll take longer." Darling nodded and took Byron's hand, and Byron took Bix's. They looked roped together like when we were running from the hypercane the last night of Amen. "Right. We'll meet you and Mary at the Round Barn." She hugged me with her free arm, but she let go before I was ready, watched my face fall. She let go of Byron, took her pack off, unzipped the big pocket. I thought she was getting the gun. I didn't want it. But she pulled out Father's cap. It was faded, muddy, the AMNH a dull color, the blood washed away at last.

She handed it to me, and I stood there not moving, looking at the letters, remembering Amen. She took it from my hand and put it on me; it was too big, but she angled it up. "There."

I tucked my hair behind my ears, pushed the bill back until I could see her. She put her pack back on her shoulders, grabbed the cane, went to Keller, balanced him against her; then they walked with Byron and Darling out the door.

76

RUNNING IN THE RAIN

I closed my eyes, tried to keep from shaking, slowed my breath, listened to the water in the air. The room was empty, quieter than I expected, my first moment alone since the ruin, since the canoe slipped from my hands. No one was with me to tell me when to leave, enough time to go unseen to the icehouse in the dark. I slowed my breath, counted the minutes. There was water under everything and in me. Virginia was out in the *Sally Ride* somewhere, as real as Mary or Esther. I could do what was needed. I could do it if I remembered the water. I put my pack on, pulled my hood over Father's cap. Wind hit. I took the lantern and left the room as the walls shivered.

I took the path to the icehouse. Everywhere people ran toward the roof that blew off in the storm. No one noticed me. Men passed with dogs and guns. I was going the opposite way, past tents and shacks and piles of firewood, tractors, rain barrels overflowing, roof remains on the path. The Round Barn was to my right, blurred in a band of rain. The lantern guttered; it was hard to see beyond its circle of light.

The icehouse was ahead, just where Esther showed me on the map she drew in the room, cold, no light, no people in front. Esther said the guards would go to the broken roof, leaving Mary alone in the wet room, the dirt floor turning to mud.

I didn't want the memory of the ruin, Father's blood, Bix's limp, Keller's leap into the water. Father, Mother, if they were with me in the rain, they would tell me that failures happen, and they don't mean you'll never succeed. I couldn't fail Mary. She was suffering for us, throwing herself between us and the man in the tower, taking Esther and Byron and Darling with us. I heard her in my mind: *Nonie, you idiot, can't you tell who to trust?*

The icehouse was a redbrick building, gray roof, a white exclamation point of ornament on the top, two white doors. Mary was inside, the key in the pocket of my jeans hot with my worry. I walked up the ridge of lawn in front of the doors, careful not to run, not to be seen. I took the door on the left. It was locked, slick with rain.

"Mary!" I yelled.

"Nonie? Get out, the guard is coming back."

"There's a roof collapsed. No one's here. Esther had a secret key." A padlock and chains held the door shut. I set down the lantern, let the light show me the lock. I got the key out of my pocket, dropped the key, my hands shaking, it didn't catch, it slipped. Maybe it was the wrong one. I was sweating, feeling the boat slip through my hands again. I closed my eyes, turned it. It caught. The lock came open and I slid the door wide. I picked up the lantern and looked into the dark. Mary was inside, filthy, the side of her head covered in blood, ponytail undone. It smelled of bare floor and night mess. "They sent me because I'm small," I told her. Mary reached out for my hand, both of us wet, we had to hold hard. I felt her fingernails bite my palm, like when Bix held me on the stairs in the hypercane, in the dark of the ruin. I pulled her up. "Everyone is in the Round Barn, there's a wagon, we have Keller, we're leaving."

She nodded, trying to understand. "Keller's OK? Bix?" I nodded. Mary looked over my shoulder into the rain. "Nonie, someone sees us."

I looked behind me. Back where I'd come from, a man

was watching us. He was hard to make out in the dark rain. "Guard?"

"I don't know." Mary was deliberate and slow. "But, run, I'm right behind you."

I ran. I watched him. He shouted something. I could hear him, he was screaming Childs's name into the rain, looking back over his shoulder and waving his arm toward us, trying to get other people to join him. I ran, lantern jumping as I bounced it with my heavy steps on the wet ground, the mud giving way. I could hear Mary just behind me. I looked back again; he was closing the triangle of space between us fast. We made the Round Barn before he did.

The doors at the back were open. We ran into the dark stone circle of the building. Inside, my light splashed up to the wide roof over my head, a spiderweb of beams; farther in there were more lanterns, a wagon, narrow as a coffin-and-a-half, the bed on bicycle wheels. Above the wagon bed stretched a plastic tarp, suspended like the top of a covered wagon; the poles of a stretcher stuck out at the end, Keller's boots. At the back stood Darling. At the head of the wagon, Esther stood with a walking stick in her hand. "Mary!" she called.

"Esther, someone's coming!" Mary yelled.

Esther ran back the way we'd come, stick pointed toward the sound, out into the rain, and I heard her voice raised, a man yelling, a blow, a sound of wet falling.

"Nonie!" Mary yelled, and I turned from watching for Esther. Pumpkin was tied to the wagon's harness. Mary stumbled to her, grabbed the reins, started leading the horse and wagon to the doors. "Keller's in here? And Bix?"

"Yeah," Bix yelled from the back of the wagon as Mary got Pumpkin moving at a trot, Byron and Darling running behind. Esther ran back into the barn. I turned to see her pulling the man who saw us behind her. He was on his back, wet, eyes closed. She held one of his legs in one hand, her walking stick in the other.

"Anyone see?" Mary asked her.

Esther let go of the man's legs and left him lying on the muddy straw. She ran to catch up. We passed through the doors; the rain hit hard, wetting my face under the bill of Father's cap, soaking my hood; the lantern light picked out the drops; wind shook the tarp. Ahead was the blank east wall of the Hancock fence. There was a gate on that side of the fence, no guards, around it fields and an orchard in a blur of dark.

"Byron!" Esther called, pointed forward to the gate. Byron ran to the fence, trying to open the chain lock holding the gate closed. Even in the dimness, I could see him struggle with his key ring. Esther sprinted past Pumpkin, reached the gate and the lock. Byron stepped back. Esther took the keys, fumbled with the wet lock, shook, but she got it open, and the chain slid free to the ground. I looked over my shoulder and could see no one.

77

YOU MAKE THE WAY BY WALKING

The tarp whipped back and forth. Wheels rolled over rutted lanes next to the blacktop road that opened from the gate. Mary and I walked at the front, Darling at the side; Byron and Esther walked behind. The storm moved the forest around us. We made it a mile like that, the wagon shaking, bicycle tires thumping, stuck in mud, Pumpkin balking.

Then there was a voice behind us. "Hey," it called, so far away, "Esther!" The storm carried it, high above the road, up and around us, like wind. Mary stopped the wagon. She took her knife out, held it, soaked with rain, listening.

"Esther!" The voice closer.

Mary handed me Pumpkin's reins, made a *stay here* motion, and walked back to Byron and Esther. The storm was a wall of wind and stinging rain around us. I put the lantern on the ground in front of me, made a room of light in the dark that just barely stretched to all the rest of us, circling the wagon in the dark.

There were distant footsteps in the mud. "Where's Esther?" Childs's voice carried. The guard had gotten his attention and he had followed us. "Where is she?"

Mary held her knife, Esther set her walking stick against the side of the wagon, took a long knife from her left boot. Bix looked out from under the tarp, the gun from the ruin in her hand. Byron walked to the wagon bed, peeled back the tarp and took out a shotgun he had stowed there, opened the chamber, put in two shells he took from his pocket, joined Bix and Esther and Mary at the back of the wagon. He nodded to Darling, who was standing where the trees met the road, so silent he was almost invisible, his hat and hair soaked. Darling nodded back, knife out, and stepped silently into the forest, walking toward Childs on a parallel path. I started to move toward Byron, but he waved me back. *Pumpkin,* he mouthed, miming a spooked horse. I nodded. In the lantern light, Mary looked at Byron and Esther, Bix and then me. *Ready?* she mouthed at us. I saw everyone nod, then did myself; I'd started shaking. She looked at Esther. *OK,* she mouthed, and pointed toward Childs with her chin.

"I'm right here, Childs," Esther yelled.

"Get out of here, Childs," Mary yelled at him. "She's leaving."

"Mary," Childs's voice was still distant, "you know we can't have her leaving, taking everybody along. Taking medicine. There are more people following me. Might as well stop now."

"No one's following, you stupid college boy, not in the middle of this storm. We've got the odds on you. I learned more in basic than your daddy taught you growing up on that fake farm."

Childs's voice was controlled. "You know that basic training didn't do the soldiers at the Camp any good when we had ammo, and they didn't. And it won't do you any good without guns. We buried them all the same, basic or no basic. We're going to make you come back, Mary. You're going to bring those meds back, and the food. And you are going to do it because all the people I care for need it." He sounded logical, like he had people backing him, like we were on the wrong side of a ledger—that's how the man in the tower sounded.

Mary yelled back, "We want to leave with our own. Esther and Byron and Darling want to leave. Keep them and you're no different from the Camp."

"Esther and Byron and Darling owe things to me!" Childs yelled. "You are stepping in where you don't belong, as if there is an army to back you, a government. But there's nothing." Mary looked at me, gestured with her chin to the wagon, telling me to check on Keller. Still holding Pumpkin's reins, I pulled back a corner of the tarp and looked inside. I could see through the wagon to the back where the tarp was also pulled back. Bix held the gun from the ruin and half her body was out the back of the wagon, her bad leg still inside like she hadn't figured out how to move it without pain. Keller sat up in the dark. He nodded and I nodded. *Little warrior*, I could almost hear him say, *you're good*.

In the lantern light I peeked around the side of the wagon to see Darling walking closer to Childs through the forest. Esther walked toward Childs too, slipping into the forest behind Darling, knife out. Bix crawled quietly out of the wagon, wincing, leaned on her cane still holding her gun.

"You've already lost, Childs," Mary said.

The tarp crackled. I couldn't move. The cloth of my jeans, the hoodie, the shirt, all stuck to my skin. Father's cap dripped water from the bill. There was a gunshot. Bix screamed. Mary screamed. Pumpkin shifted, rattling the wagon. Mary stumbled forward and shook. I turned to Pumpkin to settle her, tightening my grip on the reins, standing close to her. "Easy," I said like Mary would. I turned back and Mary lay in the mud. Then, through the rain, I saw Childs, his gun high, walking toward our wagon.

Childs stumbled in the wet, his gun dipped, but he kept walking forward, raised his gun, fired, the bullet missed us, but I heard it hit a tree near my head. Childs raised the gun to shoot again, but there was a shadow behind him. Darling stepped out of the forest to one side, knife in one hand, wrestling the rifle down with the other. He shoved his leg in front of Childs's leg and took his forward momentum and his balance. Childs fell, lay on his face in the mud. From the trees, Esther ran forward to them, her knife shining in the rain, picked Childs's head up from the mud by the hair and slit his throat. It was fast and so quiet.

She let go, and Childs fell back into the mud, making wet choking sounds. Blood and rain soaked the mud under him. Darling looked at Esther and put his knife back in his pocket, threw Childs's rifle into the back of the wagon and turned him over. Childs's eyes were open, the rain washing off the mud; my lantern light just reached to show the slit in his neck still spilling blood. Water ran over Esther's hair, over her skin, pouring down her onto Childs's coat, blood seeping to cover his clothing, his mouth a perfect O.

"He's not moving," Bix said. She put her gun into her back pocket, limping forward on her cane. She hadn't fired a shot. Byron ran to Mary and picked her up where she'd fallen. Her arm oozed blood.

"That asshole winged me," Mary said.

Keller climbed out of the wagon and stood, holding himself against the side in the rain. "Get back under cover," Esther ordered him. "Don't undo the work I did."

"Are you OK?" he asked. "Is Mary OK?"

"I'm shot, you idiot!" Mary said.

"She's OK," Esther said. "Back inside, Keller. We don't have all the antibiotics in Massachusetts."

"Are *you* OK?" he asked Esther again.

"No!" she yelled at him, starting to cry. She walked back to the wagon and sat heavily on the back step, her shoulders shaking. "No! No, I'm not."

78
LEAFCUTTER ANTS

It stopped raining. Esther sat a long time sobbing on the back of the wagon. If it hadn't been her, it would have been one of us. Childs was the man in the tower. The man in the tower hunted you until you didn't make him afraid.

"Think they'll send anyone to catch us?" Bix asked Mary as Esther poked at her wound to get the bullet out.

"I think we cost too much," Mary said.

We should have buried Childs, but we left him. Maybe the bear from the pump house would find him, and Childs would fuel him for winter, turn his skeleton back from a puppet to an animal. Maybe the people from Hancock would find him. Maybe finding him would be relief and permission and they would let us go on. *Utopias fail,* Mary said. Childs tried to make his own, and maybe it was over.

We ate stale fry bread from Mary's pack, Childs's blood thinning out in puddles. We listened for anyone. Esther dug the bullet out of Mary's arm and treated it from supplies in the wagon, bound it and put it in a sling. It was quiet. We needed fire, shelter. I sat on the edge of the wagon bed while I ate and drank.

"Nonie?" Esther was calling. "We've got to walk."

"OK." I looked at Keller.

"I can't walk," he said, "not all the way to the farm."

"Not yet," I said.

He nodded. "Not yet." He took my hand and held it.

Esther called, "Nonie."

I held his hand. I held it for Father and Mano and Angel and all the things I hadn't stopped. And I held it for the thing I helped stop, and what it cost to look at the man in the tower, to know him, to get away. "Not yet," I said. The "yet" was hope, and I gave it. I didn't have anything else to give.

"My turn?"

"What?"

"It is my turn, isn't it?"

I tried to remember the last time we played. Keller in the canoe, the last moments before the storm and the ruin. *Ladybug, ladybug, fly away home.*

"No. It's my turn. But I played while you were sick. You should go, Keller."

"OK. I'll go. Out of turn. I have an animal in mind, and this animal is very plentiful, so many species, so many types." He was quiet for a moment. Took a bite of bread. I waited. "And it is an insect. Did I say that?"

"No."

"It is an insect."

"OK."

"And it makes the most complex communities on earth. It is prosocial. Like us. These animals need each other. And they keep the colony alive, even if they lose parts of the colony. They farm. They support each other. And they make it."

"I don't know." I never got stumped. My brain was slow. "There are a lot of insects that do that."

"Well, they are pretty special," Keller said. "They take leaves and then chew them up and use the undigested material to grow fungus. And then they feed the fungus to their larvae."

"And they are named for that, sort of. Right? Leafcutter ants. *Acromyrmex.*"

I held his hand tight. Of course it was ants. They were

always keeping going, everywhere, even in the Park, even after floods. Not leafcutters, not this far north, but ants, they
always found a way to remake the world they held together.

"I have to go."

Keller nodded.

"I have to go carry a leaf."

Keller smiled. "Nonie, you made a joke!" I blushed, but
he couldn't see it. "You're good," he said, like I'd heard him
in my head.

"You are too." I kissed his hand, fast and awkward, left
him to rest.

"Now *I'm* going to need those drugs," Mary said to Esther
as Esther bandaged her arm.

"Lucky for you I've seen way worse."

We put Mary in the wagon next to Keller and Bix. They
were tight in there. We started walking. Esther and I walked
on either side of Pumpkin. Byron walked at the back with
Darling, who still hadn't said a word. They kept watch. I
could hear Darling singing quietly, couldn't pick out the
words. The dawn came. I blew the lantern out, hung it on
a nail sticking out from the wagon frame. We watched the
light come up. We walked down a long road, past empty
forest. We didn't hear anybody.

Darling started singing again. "'We've hauled some barges
in our day,'" he sang.

Esther laughed, only a wry half smile on her face. "A little
on the nose, Darling!"

I could hear Byron laugh too, but Darling kept singing:
"'And we know every inch of the way.'"

"What if there's nothing there?" I asked Esther.

"At the farm?" she asked. "I don't know. I guess we'll figure it out."

"Father thought maybe Clare, my mother's sister, made it to the farm, got there from Old City. But Father liked stories where things turn out OK. And they don't all turn out OK."

"But what if this one does?" asked Esther.

79
BATHYSPHERE

We stopped the wagon to eat again, and I sat next to Bix on a rock by the side of the road. She was sweating still. She rolled up her pant leg. The bandage was wet. "You OK?" I asked.

"Not yet, but I can walk."

I touched her forehead. "You still have a fever."

"Esther isn't done fixing me."

"Or Keller, or Mary."

"She's got a lot to do," Bix said. "I keep thinking of Mother, what she'd have done if we'd got back to the farm before she died."

"She'd have died anyway, no way to fix her at the farm," I said.

"No, but I kept her from it," said Bix, "from dying there. Me, the way I was about water."

"It wasn't you," I said. For the first time, I knew that was true. It was easy to get stuck. It wasn't only Bix or Keller or Mother or Father or Angel or Mano—it was us that got stuck all together. That was what happened in The World As It Is. "She loved Amen. I think she wanted to die there."

"I think she wanted to die wherever we were," she said. "I wish she was with us."

We never said that about Mother. "Me too."

"But I get to keep you, right?"

I wanted to tell her that keeping me was sure. But I didn't know what would come, sickness, or the Lost, or maybe I'd leave for the boat. "I hope so," I said. I looked over at Bix. "It is my turn next, for the game, isn't it?"

She thought. "I went last."

"So, it's me."

She nodded.

"OK. I have an animal in mind. And that animal is a bird. It shares a name with a kind of bird that was all over Old City. Father used to call them rats with wings. Remember? But Mother said they were rock doves. Anyway, this animal shares the name . . ."

"Pigeons?"

". . . but it always finds a way home."

She smiled. "Homing pigeons?"

"*Columba livia domestica,*" I said.

"They know how to find the way home," she said.

I was quiet for a minute. "Esther told me the *Sally Ride* is real," I said. "And she met a woman from it. A real woman, Virginia, who has a son up here somewhere."

"The boats are real?"

"Sounds like it."

She put an arm around me, and we sat there like that while the clouds moved over us. We got up, put away the food, Bix got back in the wagon, and we started walking again. I was at the front with Esther, Byron at the back. Darling wandered behind and to the side, looking at the forest, still and silent inside himself. The wagon was a schooner behind me, a boat now, a raft, sailing ship, submersible, submarine, my bathysphere at last—a quiet place of safety in a world I couldn't control, but this time not solitary but full of people.

The rain tapered, the wind came in tall gusts, afternoon came. We hauled the wagon over ruts, embankments, past a rotted car. I dragged downed branches out of our way. Byron and I hauled tree trunks from the path. We walked under the Mass Pike, past the rotted Big Y, dark houses, toppled traffic lights. It neared dusk. I saw a sign for Tyringham, then one for Fernside Road. We passed silos, listing and pale blue, down a slope, across a swamp, the hulk of a semi, a pile of rust and weed crashed headlong into the muck. All as Father wrote it down on the Hudson. We crossed a bridge over a stream full of rainwater. No one was behind us. Fernside took us up a ridge into a thick forest. The sound of us echoed off the trees. The road was dirt and rutted with heaves and washouts. We passed houses hunched on the ridge, one burned, one falling in. Keller opened the tarp ends when the rain stopped. We stopped for water. Mary left the wagon bed and held Pumpkin's reins with her good arm. In the hour before sunset came, we made our slow way to the top of the hill. We found a clearing.

"I want to walk the last bit," Keller said.

"Me too," said Bix.

"OK with you, Esther?" Keller asked.

Esther looked them over. "Not the best idea," she said, "but I get it. Bix, use your cane. Keller, lean on Byron. Take it slow. We don't have anything to run from."

There was a cottage on the left side of the road, a peaked barn roof behind it, a high meadow to the right. Presiding over all those buildings, at the top of the meadow, was a farmhouse with a porch, looking like the one Mother called up in our minds, painted white, covered with vines, windows intact, bird nests under the roof. Some of the shingles were gone, showing tar paper and plywood beneath, the paint peeling. But the chimney stood, the front was sound; it wasn't a ruin. The tall lines of the framing were straight-backed— a grand old lady falling asleep at a picnic.

Bix stood still in front of it, balanced on her cane. The creak of the wagon stopped.

"Is this it?" I asked her.

"That's what it looked like in Mother's pictures," she said.

There was no Clare to meet us. It was abandoned. In the bones of the house, I saw the stories Mother told us—the ice cream on the porch, the blueberries, the meadow and the sugar bush, the cottage and the barn swallows and the water pump. There would be things inside, papers, photographs if we needed proof that we belonged to it. The sagging hull we stood before was what was promised. It was neglected. It was tattered. But it was ours.

I scanned around us. Clouds crossed the sun. We were above the valley. Fog blocked the view of the stream and bridge and wetland. Another storm front was coming. I looked at the house. There was movement in the eaves of the porch; a bird flew out of a nest in the shadows, then flew back to settle in before the rain.

I thought I saw a figure by the railing, Mother standing in the gray light, tall, shadowed, her eyes looking to the sloping meadow between the house and road. But I blinked and the porch was empty. There was no Mother. I looked in the direction she'd been looking. There was a slash of black metal in the weeds. It was the pump, the one from Mother's story, safe water, enough to make a new Amen. Relief washed down my throat like cold liquid. Mother was always pouring this future into me, and I didn't see, until I did. She was my first sea, and she left me this water, waiting all along.

It was ours, the water at the farm, but it was no different from any other water, every drop of moisture that fell since there were only protozoa, trilobites, orthocones. It was inside every single human being. When I missed the sea, I could lean my face into another person—with worry or dangerous joy or grieving—and feel their tide. The World As It Is is only a furious tide of people, linked by blood and tears and sweat, a push toward each other we can't stem. Water was over Mother's grave, beside Father's, under the boats, in my blood and the blood of everyone I loved. I felt it all. I felt the weight of all the water in the world.

I turned to Bix. "Let's get inside," I said. "It's going to rain."

80

THE WEIGHT OF ALL THE WATER
IN THE WORLD

It was not enough to leave Amen. It was not enough to go up the Hudson. It was not enough to find Olana and its tower. It was not enough to walk thirty-seven miles to Hancock. *Sometimes what looks like shelter is only menace.* Finding the farm was the least important part of leaving Amen. A building is just a body through which you live a life. What mattered was the people we found and lost, not the places. Leaving Amen only closed one door and opened this other one.

I don't think about the years between then and now so much. It was calm, hard, so quiet. The house leaked with rain, ran through with mice, shivered with papers and photos in tatters, the faces of Mother and Clare as girls and much older faces that held the shadows of their faces. We worked to keep the cold out, clear chimneys, replace doors, scavenge lumber from the barn. We warmed enough rooms for all of us.

Esther healed us until Keller hardly coughed anymore. Then he asked Esther to stop nursing him; he wanted a different way to be seen. Mary took over, checking Keller's lungs and bossing him until he was well. Keller piloted the kitchen woodstove, where it was warm. He cooked food just the way Esther liked it and told her stories about Mano and Angel and insects and Joliet, listened to her stories about the ER in Boston, about residency and surgery. She sat with him, making teas from what she and Mary foraged, and slowly they changed toward each other until you'd see them crouching hip-to-hip in the kitchen, looking into the firebox when the coals needed attention like it held a secret that only they knew.

After the antibiotics courses were done, Mary walked Bix up and down the stairs until her leg worked right. When she was tired, Byron tended Bix like they'd married when they met that night at the Hancock gate, instead of how it happened, a year later with Darling making the ceremony. I hardly ever heard Darling's voice, except when he sang. At the wedding he sang, "'Oh, to grace how great a debtor / Daily I'm constrained to be / Let Thy goodness like a fetter / Bind my wandering heart to Thee.'" He fixed a shack on the edge of the woods near the road into a place where he was alone and included all at once. Byron helped but said it was not nearly enough to thank him for saving his life in the freeze he couldn't remember.

That first winter there was no garden laid and we were hungry, and there were deer in the forest, but also wolves at night. The water always came from the pump, even in the cold, like a miracle. We washed and mended ancient bed linens and remade furniture, and traded for more, found people hidden from Hancock on other farms and made friends until we could get by. The farmhouse poured heat from wobbly doorways. We hoarded ammo for the guns, found flint in the hills for arrows, packed down trails to harvest wild apples on the ridge.

No one came to stop us. Sometimes people came because they knew Esther was here, or Byron, or Mary, and they wanted to be healed. The sick had their own cottage we fixed up, room to store the medicines we took, and keep more when we found them. The next year people came from Hancock and stayed—Byron's friends, Esther's patients— rebuilding outbuildings to live in, fixing the barn and trading for cows and chickens and dogs. Mary started going back to Hancock to trade, so different with Childs dead. One time she came back with Agnes, who she knew from before, and they built a cabin near the house where sometimes you could see them holding hands in the dusk. Agnes helped with the nursing work. The farm looked like Hancock, or a dozen other places that people made. It looked like Amen, a new one where we weren't fossils, it looked like pumpkins and smoke.

I unpacked the Logbook, and I put it in a box near the fireplace on the first floor, where we could keep it dry. I bartered for a new book, one just for me, this one about leaving Amen. Keller got a new book too. At night we sat on the porch and wrote with a lantern between us, listening for the whirr of moths and bats in the dark beyond the steps. Maybe we had run away to the taiga. Maybe we were the kind of people hiding paintings on French farms. In either case, the books we wrote held masterpieces of storms and clouds, katydids and butterflies.

Virginia came back to the hills, years later, to see her son. She went to Hancock and Esther was gone. The people told Virginia that Esther was here, and she stopped in. She met Keller and Esther's son Elijah. She met me. I was seventeen then. We'd been on the farm four years.

I told her I thought about her every day since Hancock, when Esther told me, in a room that smelled of blood, that what I'd longed for was real. She said she'd come back, and maybe I'd be ready to go with her. And now it is that year, and she's in a bedroom upstairs, and I am ready. You cannot always be in Leningrad. You are allowed to hope for something that doesn't just save, something that builds.

Mother gave us the idea of the farm—the forests and the water pump and the blueberry bushes—a place in which to settle like she'd settled us at Amen. She taught us to imagine it so we could make it real. Father gave us the map to get here. He told us that the old farmer's stone walls that lace these woods were all we need to hold in the good things. They seemed powerless, unimposing, until you remembered how they changed the land for good and for ill. We can change the land again with softness, making right what we got so wrong in the years of greed. We don't need a gate that locks, or a tower. We are safe because we invite more people, all of us making a new World As It Is every day.

When we were in Amen, I thought that there was no one stuck like us. But Mother and Father and Keller and Angel and Jess—all of them who lost The World As It Was—kept us alive with hope thrown hard at the darkness. They didn't see where their hope landed us, but here we are. Keller and Esther are out felling trees for winter heat. Bix is inside baking bread with Deirdre, her girl with Byron, the one they named for Mother. I'm sitting with Elijah. In a few days, I'll walk with Virginia back to the ocean, which I haven't seen since we left Amen. I'm finishing this book to leave behind, safer to keep it here than to take it to sea. It's Bix's now, along with Amen's Logbook, my Water Logbook lacing through its pages with all the things I know about water so far.

I'll start a new Logbook on the *Sally Ride,* and a new period, for which I don't yet have a name.

ACKNOWLEDGMENTS

It took me eleven years to write this book. While I was writing most of it, I was a single parent, suffering from chronic illness, and without much money to keep going. There is no way to name or thank everyone who helped me, but these people cannot be thanked enough.

To Dex, who invented Animal in Mind and invited me to play it, and who kept sleeping after I got up to write this in the middle of the night. To Andy, who said when we met, *You're not writing an apocalyptic book, are you?* and then read all the drafts.

To Julia Lord for reading this on the train that follows the banks of the Hudson River and finding it the perfect home. To Elisabeth Dyssegaard, who is that home and gave it its name. To Marcia Markland for the editing and the vision and the words that I needed when I was writing in bed with a broken kneecap. To my residencies at the Millay Colony, Hedgebrook, the Banff Centre, and Ragdale where I wrote other books while this one stayed alive in my chest.

To Amanda, who answered every single call, and Martha, who told me just keep going, and Robin for the story about the bear who was not this book's bear, and Shana for telling me water is a resource and a source, and Molly W., who told me I was writing for a reason, and Jacqui, who told me to start with the storm, and Mairead, who told me that I was a good mother and a kind one, but I had to not be a good mother with the people I made up, and Ari for the use of her parlor for the Zoom meeting that sold this book.

To all the writers and mentors and helpers—Rosie and

Walt and Kelly and Daphne and Robert and Zoe and Scott and Lawrence and Gretchen and the Otters and the Ragedydalians and Tom and Bethany and Karen and the Book Club and Molly D. and Dayna and Amy and Lindsay and Meghan. To Josephine, who knew I needed to read *A Paradise Built in Hell* and was on this ride at the same time. To every one of my students at TLL who kept vigil during the plague, wrote their way out of it, and drew the sea creature of the week on the blackboard when we could finally meet in person.

To Aunt Lois for taking me to AMNH when I wanted to go, and Aunt Jane for every book she ever sent, and Uncle Brian for telling me that one short story was me becoming a writer. To Bill and Eric and Libby, who kept alive a promise to Brian. To Marsha for Andy. To Sherry and Dan for making me a middle child. To Tommy, who called me from a flooded basement in Superstorm Sandy and started this entire thing.

To my father, Charlie, who taught me to shoot and to dress a deer and to love the forests and the water. To my mother, Nancy, who took me to pick blueberries, and who left behind three different drafts of this book, which she'd printed out and read. After she died, I found them on a shelf next to the books that had made her a geologist, and the DVDs of all the movies where the scientists save the day.

ABOUT THE AUTHOR

Jacob Hand

Eiren Caffall is a writer and musician whose
work has appeared in *Guernica,* the *Los Angeles
Review of Books, Al Jazeera,* and *The Rumpus,* and
on three record albums. She is the recipient of a
Whiting Foundation Creative Nonfiction Grant
and a Social Justice News Nexus fellowship at
Northwestern University, among other awards.
The author of a memoir, *The Mourner's Bestiary*
(2024), she lives in Chicago with her family. *All
the Water in the World* is her first novel.